Christine Merrill lives on a farm in Wisconsin, USA, with her husband, two sons and too many pets—all of whom would like her to get off the computer so they can check their e-mail. She has worked by turns in theatre costuming and as a librarian. Writing historical romance combines her love of good stories and fancy dress with her ability to stare out of the window and make stuff up.

Louise Allen loves immersing herself in history. She finds landscapes and places evoke the past powerfully. Venice, Burgundy and the Greek islands are favourite destinations. Louise lives on the Norfolk coast and spends her spare time gardening, researching family history or travelling in search of inspiration. Visit her at louiseallenregency.co.uk, @LouiseRegency and janeaustenslondon.com.

Laura Martin writes historical romances with an adventurous undercurrent. When not writing she spends her time working as a doctor in Cambridgeshire, where she lives with her husband. In her spare moments Laura loves to lose herself in a book, and has been known to read from cover to cover in a single day when the story is particularly gripping. She also loves to travel—especially to visit historical sites and far-flung shores.

SNOWBOUND SURRENDER

Christine Merrill,
Louise Allen
and
Laura Martin

MILLS & BOON

First Published in Great Britain 2019
by Mills & Boon, an imprint of HarperCollins*Publishers*
1 London Bridge Street, London, SE1 9GF

Snowbound Surrender

© 2019 Harlequin Books S.A.

ISBN: 978-0-263-26939-0

Their Mistletoe Reunion © 2019 by Christine Merrill
Snowed in with the Rake © 2019 by Melanie Hilton
Christmas with the Major © 2019 by Laura Martin

MIX
Paper from
responsible sources
FSC® C007454

This book is produced from independently certified FSC™ paper
to ensure responsible forest management.
For more information visit www.harpercollins.co.uk/green.

Printed and bound in Spain
by CPI, Barcelona

CONTENTS

THEIR MISTLETOE REUNION

Christine Merrill

To Chaos. Nice kitty.
Here is a story for you.
Now, please get off the desk and let me work.

Chapter One

$\backsim\!\!\infty\!\!\sim$

After six months, it still felt strange to be home.

It was even stranger to be holding a sword again. During one particularly savage battle Jack Gascoyne had prayed that if God kept him safe till sunset he would never pick up a weapon again.

Had he been in Navarre? Or had it been Valencia? When he tried to remember individual battles, they ran together in a bloodstained blur. It hardly mattered. He had broken the promise quick enough and continued fighting through the carnage of Waterloo.

Now the war was over and the foil he held felt like a toy compared to his cavalry sword, flimsy and useless should he actually need to defend his life.

He should not even be considering such mayhem. He was on Bond Street at Angelo's Academy. His opponent, Frederick Clifton, was no real threat. Other than growing taller, Fred was every bit as soft as he had been fifteen years ago, when they'd still been pretending that sticks were swords. Even this thin blade would slice through him like butter, should Jack decide to apply his skill.

It would serve the fellow right. He'd wounded Jack in a way that was far more painful than a sword slash and the cut had not healed in five years. Damage to the heart did not always scar over with time, as he had been promised. This hurt had stayed fresh and painful, bleeding the love out of him until his soul was cold and dead.

While Jack's spirit had rotted, Fred was still happy, healthy and completely oblivious to the pain he'd inflicted. He thought they could fall easily back into the role of childhood best friends as if nothing had happened between them, before or after the war. 'It is good to have you home again,' Fred said, his expression warm and sincere.

'It is good to be home,' Jack said automatically. It was what everyone wanted to hear from him, but he wondered if it was true. After all he had seen, London at Christmastime had an unreal quality. It was like staring at his old life through a sheet of ice.

'I had hoped to see you sooner, of course.' There was a hint of reproach in his friend's voice, a reminder of duties that had been forgotten. The

Cliftons had considered him family, before he'd gone away. Family was supposed to stay in touch.

But he had one of his own to contend with. 'I apologise. There was so much to do. Visiting my brother…'

Fred nodded and gave a practice lunge to test the balance of his weapon before facing him to make a bow of acknowledgement and a swishing salute of his blade. 'And how is Sir Robert?'

'As disappointed in me as ever,' Jack said, returning the salute. The relationship between him and his elder sibling could not quite be called an estrangement, but it had never been easy.

'No pride for the honour you did your uniform? No relief at your safety?' Fred said, surprised as they raised their swords to fight.

'Nothing obvious,' Jack replied.

'Do not let him trouble you. He was always thus. And you still have friends who love you dearly and are eager to add to your acquaintance.'

'You are speaking of your fiancée,' Jack said.

Fred began the bout with a direct attack that was easily parried. 'I wrote to tell you of the engagement. I received no answer.' There was a hint of petulance in his tone, to remind Jack again where his obligation lay.

'I meant to congratulate you in person.' Parry and riposte. The action of his sword was strong and sure. But it was a weak conversational counter, since he'd given no indication thus far that he knew or cared about Fred's plans to marry.

'Thank you,' Fred replied, obviously distracted since he'd failed to block Jack's blade as it touched his shoulder. 'Miss Forsythe is eager to see you, since I have spoken of you often.'

'I am sure she is a lovely girl.' Jack's jaw clenched. Was Fred really dead to the irony of expecting good wishes from the man whose hopes he had ruined? He followed up his first attack with a second, to the stomach, the force of which was met with a woof of expelled air.

Fred straightened to regain his wind, then dropped back into fencing stance, advancing. 'And it surprises me that you have not enquired about Lucy.'

Just the mention of her name shattered Jack's concentration and allowed Fred to score a touch, directly to the centre of his chest. If he had been so careless in any of the last five years, he would not be alive to be so troubled by the memory of her.

'How is she?' he managed to say, trying to pretend that the answer did not matter to him.

'Much the same as she ever was. If you come home with me for Christmas, you may see for yourself.'

The ice around him cracked and, for a moment, everything was unbearably real. Jack did his best to keep a calm tone and a neutral expression. 'Your sister is still with you?'

Fred laughed. 'Where else would she be but at home?'

'I thought…perhaps she had married by now.' He had done his best to think of nothing but that. There had to be something that put her firmly out of reach and out of mind. It was clear by the rush of blood he felt at the thought of her that time and distance had done nothing to change his feelings.

Her brother laughed again, scoring another touch against an opponent who was suddenly without defences. 'For the moment, at least, she is still unattached. But not for want of trying on my part. I found her several men who would have done nicely and she refused them all. But it seems she is finally about to settle. The local Vicar has been the front runner for her affections for some time.'

'The Vicar.' A man of God was exactly the sort of husband Jack would have expected Fred to choose for Lucy. Someone quiet, proper and altogether wrong for the girl he remembered.

'She has put the fellow off for so long that I was worried she meant to stay on the shelf. But things are coming to a head and I expect we will have good news on that front before Twelfth Night.'

'That is good to know,' Jack replied. 'She was a lovely girl.'

'Still is,' Fred corrected. 'I rather fancy the idea of a double wedding. But I cannot make her decision for her.'

'Not any more,' Jack said, pleased that there was no trace of bitterness in his voice. 'She is of age now, is she not?'

'Two and twenty,' Fred replied. 'Well past time for her to settle down. But she is still the most obstinate creature imaginable and refuses to be rushed.'

When he'd last seen her, she had been nothing of the kind. She'd been as eager and impetuous as he had been, both of them hurrying to arrive simultaneously at some place they'd no right to go. To drive the thought away, Jack renewed his attack with a grunt of exertion and a thrust to the gut that would have ended his friend if it were not for the button on the end of the blade.

Fred gasped in approval and surrendered his weapon. 'Well done. Did you learn that in Portugal?'

'Spain,' Jack said.

'You must teach it to me. In exchange, I will provide you with the finest Christmas dinner to be found in any of the north counties and a stocked cellar as well. Good food and good company. It shall be just as it was in our youth.'

'It sounds delightful,' Jack said, surprised by the sound of his own voice. He'd meant to tell

Fred to go to the devil, if such a thing was suggested. His plans for Christmas Day were far darker and lonelier than anything Fred could imagine. But if there was still hope...

There was not, he reminded himself. Though Lucy was not already married, she had found someone who might make her happy. She would be wed soon enough. He'd not heard a word from her in five years to hint that she wanted to renew what they'd shared or wished to see him again, even over a holiday table. But it seemed he was as big a fool as ever he had been and could not resist one last look at the only woman he would ever love.

Chapter Two

'Jack Gascoyne is home.'

Lucy Clifton's heart thumped in her chest at the sound of the name that had not been spoken aloud in their house for almost five years. Then, as she had with every other element of her life, she gained control of it, smothering it to silence. She answered her brother, Frederick, without looking up. 'He was so long in Belgium after the war that I had begun to wonder if he meant to return at all. Is he well?'

'No,' her brother said, in a dire tone that made it impossible for her to pretend uninterest.

Fred's brief answer did nothing to quell her fears. Was he whole? Was he unhurt? Was he as handsome as she remembered, or would it be easier to resist him, should she see him again? If he had been sickly, or missing a limb, she'd have hoped that her brother might have added this information freely after the negative. Instead, there was something in her brother's silence that made whatever was wrong with him sound even worse than a life-altering injury. 'What is the matter? Was he hurt in battle?'

Fred shook his head. 'He is intact, as far as I can tell.' Then he added cautiously, 'But something is not right about him. When I saw him, it felt as though I was talking to a stranger.'

'Time changes people,' she reminded him, wishing that it had done more to change her own feelings.

'So does war,' her brother added, unsmiling.

It did not really matter what had caused him to forget her. There were any number of reasons that he had not come home to them, the chief one being that he had not wanted to. Just as he'd often done when they were younger, he had walked away from the trouble he'd caused and let others deal with the resulting mess. For a moment, her sympathy was overwhelmed by the anger she felt when she thought of him. Then she forced it below the surface again.

'If he is a changed man, then I suspect that is why we have not seen him before now,' she said, wondering if her brother had any inkling of the true reason he had chosen to stay away. 'He has other, newer friends that understand him better.'

'Perhaps so. But they are neglecting him, or he them, for he is in a sad state. But I am sure a visit here will put him to rights again,' her brother said as if character could be turned like a wheel.

'If he is content, then it is not our business to alter the man,' she said, feeling the first flutter of panic at the thought. 'He might be perfectly happy as he is.' Just as she was. She had worked hard for the equilibrium she'd achieved and would not have it upset by what she was sure her brother was about to suggest.

'Happy?' At this, her brother gave a bitter laugh. 'He is nowhere near that. If you had seen him, you would be much less cavalier about leaving him to his suffering.'

'Perhaps,' she said, with a shrug. It was not as if he'd made an effort to come back to ease the pain in her heart, despite certain promises he'd made in moonlight. Nor had he bothered to soften the blow with a letter of warning. One day he had been there. The next, he had been gone, leaving her frightened and alone. If fate had punished him for his faithlessness, it was something almost like justice.

'Since his family will do nothing, it will be up to us to bring him back to himself,' her brother said, with the same urgency he had used to try to warn her off Jack when he'd first discovered the schoolgirl *tendre* she'd borne for his friend.

'Major Gascoyne is old enough to make his own decisions.' Yet, strangely, she was not. Even though she was well past twenty-one, all the important decisions of her life were still left to her brother. For the most part, she had been obedient to his suggestions. But now, he meant to involve her in something she wanted no part of.

He gave her a pitying look. 'It surprises me to find you so hard-hearted. At one time, you would have been the first to rush to his defence.'

'Perhaps I have changed as much as he has,' she said, feeling her resolve begin to crumble. She wanted that to be true. She had made plans for marriage. For a future. But she could feel them slipping away with each word her brother spoke.

'Well, I suggest you change back, for a fortnight, at least. I have invited him to spend Christmas with us.'

It was what she had been longing to hear for years. But now, when she had finally given up hoping and put childish dreams aside, it was the last thing she'd wanted. She always felt melancholy at Christmastime, perhaps because that was when he had left her. Even the continual attention of the man she meant to marry had not improved her mood. The return of Major John Gascoyne was unlikely to make it better.

Fred ignored her silence and continued. 'I want him to meet Millicent. And of course, you will want him to approve of Mr Thoroughgood before that knot is tied.'

'His opinion is the last one I'd solicit when choosing a husband,' she said. 'He is far too wild to be a good judge of such things.'

Fred gave her a curious look. 'My, but you have changed. There was a time when you thought he hung the moon.'

'And then I grew up,' she said, firmly, smoothing her skirts.

'Be that as it may, Jack belongs here for Christmas. He has never had more than us as family and should not have to spend his holiday alone.'

'True,' she said with a sigh, wishing it wasn't. His parents were dead and his only brother had never been anything but critical of him. If her brother was right and he was truly in need, they were the only ones who could help him.

'I knew you would understand.' Fred released a long, slow breath of his own. 'I owe him Christmas dinner, even if I can do nothing else. He is my best and oldest friend. But we did not part as such. I have always regretted it.'

'And why was that?' she asked, surprised. He had not mentioned a problem before. He had simply come home from London to announce that Jack had bought a commission and was on his way to Portugal. Then he had ceased to mention him at all.

'It was a foolish quarrel.' Fred looked away from her, not quite able to meet her gaze. 'Nothing that you need worry about. But I would not want him to think I intended to continue it, after all this time.'

'How noble of you,' she said without feeling. She and Jack had parted on the best possible terms, or so she'd thought. When last she'd seen him, he'd held her in his arms and promised her a bright future. And then he'd disappeared. If he was miserable, there was a certain satisfaction in knowing that she would not be suffering through the holidays alone. This year, they could both be wretched together.

Her brother was staring at her with his head cocked and his mouth set in a firm, disapproving frown. 'Do not be childish, Lucy. Whatever he did to upset you, you have had a good long time to get over it. You are a grown woman now and should know better than to let an old grudge stand between you. He needs our help and we will provide it.'

'Of course,' she said drily, wondering just what Fred knew about what had occurred right before Jack had gone off to war. It could not have been much or he would not have been so cruel as to make her spend her last days as a single woman with the only man she would ever love, the man who had seduced her and fled.

Chapter Three

'He is here!'

As he rode up the front sweep of Clifton Manor, Jack could hear Frederick Clifton announcing him from inside, even before the servants had fully opened the door. Now his host was beaming in the doorway as if the Prince Regent, himself, was favouring the house with a visit.

Jack had chosen to forgo his carriage and ride alone to Clifton Manor, complaining of a megrim to his manservant and insisting that he needed fresh air after the stifling atmosphere of London. In truth, his headache had started after he'd spoken to Fred and grown stronger as the holidays neared. To ride north on horseback required that he stop frequently to rest his gelding. It gave him an excuse to put off the inevitable arrival at a party that he was a fool to attend. As each mile passed, he prayed that something would occur to prevent the future he feared. Now that he had arrived, he was hesitating as the groom reached for his reins to lead the horse to the stable, still trying to stall.

Perhaps she would not be as lovely as he remembered. Maybe he would discover that the feelings he had for her were nothing but the memory of what might have been. One last look at her might be all he needed to free himself from the past.

Since she'd made no effort to contact him in all this time, it was clear that she had forgotten about him. Or perhaps she hated him for the liberties he had taken on the last night they'd been together. If she was about to marry, she had moved on, just as he'd known she would. But, apparently, he needed to see the truth to believe it.

'Stop dawdling with that horse, Gascoyne, and come inside!' Fred was still standing in the open door, smiling at him as if Christmas had arrived early. So, he did as he was told and went into the house.

For a moment, it was just as he remembered from a dozen Christmases of his youth. When he crossed the threshold, there was lambswool ale waiting for them along with a hearty clap on the back, shouts of welcome from Fred and friendly enquiries as to the difficulty of the journey and the state of the weather.

Everything was normal except Jack, himself.

He did not belong here any more. His presence would be a blight on the season.

Then he heard her.

'Jack.' His name escaped her lips in a breathy rush of joy and relief, sounding too much like it had on the last night they'd spent together. He turned from her brother, searching the room for the source of that single word, making sure that his face was schooled to a socially acceptable level of affection and his posture showed no trace of the urgency he really felt.

'Lucy?' She was standing in the archway to the dining room and the light from its tall windows made a nimbus around her gold hair that blinded him for a moment. Or perhaps it was her smile that had caught the breath in his throat, just as it had when he was a schoolboy. Her face was as perfect as ever it had been, with the same slightly crooked smile that balanced the too-sombre light in her brilliant blue eyes. There was still a smattering of girlish freckles across her upturned nose. As a child, they'd made her look ready for mischief. As a woman, they called attention to her kissable, pink lips. But it was his own imagination that made him wonder at the body hidden beneath a rather drab and serviceable day gown. Despite the high neckline, he could see that time had filled out the gamine angles into soft, huggable curves.

He was across the room in two steps before remembering that she could never be more than the best part of his youth. The man worthy of her hand had disappeared somewhere on the way to Waterloo. Before he could stop himself, he had caught her by the waist, lifting her high into the air and saying again, with even more fondness, 'Lucy.' He spun her once, making her laugh.

For a moment, he imagined letting her slide slowly down his body, until her lips were level with his so he might take the kiss he wanted from her. Then, common sense returned, and he set her back on her feet again and kissed her quickly on the cheek before taking both her hands in his. 'You are lovely as ever.'

She laughed, dropping into a curtsy. 'And you, Major Gascoyne, are just as handsome.' It was just the sort of greeting he had been hoping for, yet it was not. There was no sign in it that she was any more serious than she would have been to another old friend. Nor did it make him think she had felt the loss of him as strongly as he had of her.

'Do not be so formal,' he muttered, suddenly uncomfortable. 'Call me Jack, just as you used to.' He forced a grin to take away the hint of desperation in the request, then added, 'And I believe the term you are searching for to describe me is dashing.'

'Incorrigible, more likely,' she said, pulling a hand free and giving him a playful slap on the arm. 'Women are supposed to be the vain ones, not men.'

There was a moment of silence between them as their casual greeting ran out of words. Perhaps she was sincere in her superficiality. But if he was not careful, he would take her by the hand and lead her away, to a place where he could unburden his heart of things that could not be said in front of her overprotective brother.

As if he noticed the awkwardness, Fred interrupted it. 'Speaking of women, there is one here that you have not met.'

'Your fiancée,' Jack supplied, turning away from Lucy to look for her. The other woman had been standing next to Fred all along and he had swept past her as if she had not existed.

'Major Gascoyne, may I present Miss Millicent Forsythe,' Fred announced, nudging her forward to accept the introduction.

Jack stepped forward as well, to take her hand and bow over it. She was a pretty enough girl, he supposed, with plump curves, dark eyes and shiny brown hair. 'Miss Forsythe,' he said, kissing her hand. 'How nice to see that Fred has provided me with a such a delightful Christmas present.' He steeled his nerve and looked back at Lucy with an expression that betrayed none of his true feelings. 'Lucy and I played together as children. She is like a sister to me.' He looked back to the other woman. 'I hope, in time, you will come to view me like a brother as well.'

Finally, he felt some sign of the past between them for he heard a soft intake of breath behind him, a hissing of air between clenched teeth. But when he turned back to Lucy, she was smiling, just as she had been. 'Surely these introductions do not have to be made in a draughty entrance hall. Come into the house proper, Jack. There is a storm brewing outside and I will not have you catch your death on our doorstep.'

He glanced outside, where the slate-grey sky had begun spitting snowflakes. 'You are probably right. And it appears you have other guests arriving.'

'You are the first of many,' Fred announced. 'The Manor will be full to the rooftop by the time they are all here. We are having a proper house party to celebrate your homecoming.'

Jack had no desire to be anyone's honoured guest. But it was probably for the best that this house was to be crowded. Jack and Lucy had been together for only a few minutes, but the two of them had already begun to feel the strain of each other's uninterrupted company. Then Jack realised that the next man through the door was to be the local Vicar.

Since Jack had no right to designs in her direction, Mr Thoroughgood could not really be considered a rival for Lucy's affection. All the same, he felt a slow burning jealousy at the man's pale good looks and perfect manners. There was something a little pompous in the way he went directly to Lucy, favouring her with a deep and respectful bow and enquiring after her health. Then he offered any assistance she might require in the settling of the guests, reminding her that he was ever at her service. His confident smile and quiet voice were exactly the traits that would win her brother's approval when the offer finally came. Mr Thoroughgood would be the perfect husband.

For most young ladies, at least.

Jack's insides clenched. He wished he were back on the battlefield. There he could strike out against this interloper, removing him from the field with a single blow. This was not the man for Lucy. Not for his Lucy. She needed someone with spirit, someone who could make her laugh, hard and often. Someone who could make her happy.

The Vicar was not that man. But then, neither was he. Jack was the last man on earth to give a woman a joyful future. So he turned away from her, just as he had once before, and went to find his room.

Chapter Four

Once all the guests had arrived, the crowd adjourned to the parlour, where a buffet of sweets awaited to refresh them after their journeys. Lucy had arranged for an enormous silver bowl to be filled with Regent's punch and set trays of mulled wine and eggnog beside it. Next to those were heaps of mince pies, thickly sliced cakes and enough nuts and oranges to satisfy even the greediest child.

She watched the happy people around her with numb satisfaction, wishing that she could enjoy it even a tenth as much as they did. She pretended to smile in response to William Thoroughgood's prattling, nodding in time to it without paying much attention. But though she should be ignoring him, her eyes followed Jack Gascoyne around the room, observing as he made polite conversation with the other guests.

She could still feel the flush of anger in her

face from Jack's greetings for her, though she had assured William that her colouring was caused by the heat of the fire. She was a sister now, was she? He had chosen to forget the best night of her life and act as if she was simply a childhood friend. She had held that night in her heart and mind like a diamond to be treasured. It had helped her get through the lonely years he'd been gone and kept the hope alive that he might still return to her.

But it had meant nothing to him. The diamond had been glass all along.

There was no point in revealing it to him or showing him the hurt he had caused her. She could not announce in front of anyone else what the problem was, since such an indiscretion should never have happened at all. The truth would ruin her.

So she waited. Guests came and went and she greeted them, saw to their needs and had servants show them to their rooms.

The hours passed, the afternoon ended and the room was nearly empty, except for Millicent Forsythe, standing in a corner, looking rather lost as the last group of friends abandoned her to dress for dinner.

Before Fred could claim her again, Lucy went to her and held out her hands. 'You must be tired, Miss Forsythe. Do not be afraid to treat our home as your own. No matter what happens, you will always be welcome here, just as Jack is.' She had meant to give a warm greeting to her future sister, but the result had sounded dire, as if she was expecting a disaster.

Now Millicent was staring at her, obviously puzzled, and looking far too miserable for a woman who was weeks away from her wedding. 'Nothing has happened,' she said firmly. 'Nothing at all.'

'Of course not,' Lucy responded, feeling like a fool for infecting the girl with her own dark mood. 'Your room is at the end of the hall on the first floor. My brother is in the entrance hall. I am sure he will help you find your way, should you ask him.'

Millicent gave her a nervous smile. 'He should not even know the location of my room. We are not yet married.' Then she gave a single, apprehensive glance in the direction of her fiancé.

Lucy knew from experience that it was possible to get into a surprising amount of trouble without ever leaving the ground floor. 'I am sure he can guess it,' Lucy replied. 'He has lived here his whole life. But if he gets lost, he can knock on doors until he finds your maid.'

'But if I go, you shall be alone with Major Gascoyne,' the girl said, blinking. 'Do you wish me to find someone to chaperon you?'

Lucy gritted her teeth and pressed her palms flat against her bombazine skirt. 'Chaperons are not necessary. I do not flatter myself to think his mind would turn in that direction over me.' She looked across the room to where Jack stood, looking out of the window at the snow which was battering the windowpanes. 'As he said before, apparently, Major Gascoyne is like a brother to me.' Before Millicent could question her further, she gave the girl a gentle shove in the direction of Fred.

When her brother saw his beloved, his face lit up with a smile brighter than a ballroom chandelier. The sight was all it took to make Miss Forsythe evaporate like hoarfrost, leaving Lucy alone with Jack.

As she looked over at him, the years seemed to drop away, revealing the boy she had fallen in love with. His shoulders were broader, perhaps, his legs muscled from riding and his features had lost their boyish softness. But other than a thin scar on his chin, he was physically unmarked by the war. His eyes were the same clear grey, though more sombre than they used to be, and his chestnut-brown hair was shorter and cut in the style of a man who did not have time to bother with fashion.

'Let us drop the pretence,' Jack said, interrupting her thoughts. 'Miss Forsythe was correct. We should not be alone together.' He had obviously been eavesdropping.

'I do not see why not,' she replied. 'You have not bothered to speak to me since that hypocritical greeting when you arrived.'

He crossed the room and glanced down the hall to make sure that Fred and Millicent had gone upstairs before wheeling on her with a stern frown. 'You know perfectly well how risky this is. Have a care for your reputation.'

'I suppose I should mind my honour, since you never did,' she said, then spoiled it by pushing past him to close the parlour door, leaving them shut in together. As there had been the last time they were together, there was a kissing bough hanging in the doorway. That year, it had been an elegant arrangement of ivy, mistletoe, apples and ribbons, that she had made with the express purpose of trapping Jack Gascoyne in a kiss.

It had grown less involved with each year he had been gone and she had come to dread the preparation of it, not wanting to think about kissing him or anyone else. This year, despite the fact that her house was full of company, there was but a single red ribbon holding a sprig of mistletoe, the berries of which could be numbered on her fingers.

He turned slowly to face her and waited to see if she would speak again, giving no indication that he had noticed her anger. Then, at last, he said, almost to himself, 'I should not have come here. But I could not refuse your brother's invitation without a reason.'

'Without a reason?' She resisted the temptation to shriek like the mad old maid her brother was afraid she had become. 'What happened between us before you went away is reason enough for you to avoid this house.'

'Some would say it was reason to come back,' he corrected.

'If you had returned earlier, perhaps I would believe you,' she snapped. 'But to appear after six months in England, only to call me a sister?'

He shrugged. 'You made no effort to contact me, in all the time I was gone.'

'Because you dishonoured me,' she replied.

By the way he started at the words, she could almost believe that he did not realise what he had done. Then his composure returned. 'You seemed to enjoy it well enough at the time.'

'Only because you tricked me,' she said, blushing. 'All I wanted from you was a kiss.'

And she had got one. But after? It was a lie to blame him for what they had done together. She could not quite remember how what had begun as an innocent kiss under the mistletoe had ended with him sprawled over her on the floor as she clung to him, begging for more. He had sworn that he would never leave her, if only she would give him the most precious of gifts. And she had said yes, without a moment's hesitation.

'What happened between us was not intentional, I assure you,' he said with a wolfish grin. 'I was as surprised as you by the way it ended.'

'Which part?' she asked with a sceptical grimace. 'When you seduced me? Or when you abandoned me?'

'Is that what you thought?' he asked. Now he seemed honestly shocked by her interpretation of events.

'You took my maidenhead and assured me that no harm would come of it. Then you left and I never saw or heard from you again until this night.'

For a moment, his face had no expression at all. Then his brows knit in honest confusion. 'Your brother did not explain to you?'

'He told me that you joined the army,' she said, her voice breaking with the memory. She had not wanted to believe that he could be so cruel as to do so without as much as a goodbye. But as time had passed with no word from him, she had been forced to admit that it was true. 'I waited for three weeks, terrified that I might be carrying a child whose father would not claim it.'

Now he looked as if he had been slapped. Had he not given a single thought to the consequences of his departure? Then his hands reached out to comfort her, only to drop as she stepped clear of them. 'You have nothing to be concerned about,' she said, though the fact should have been obvious by now. 'You have no hidden bastards in this country, at least.' Then she added, 'That I know of. I have no idea how many other girls you might have left in a similar manner.'

'I did not mean to leave you,' he said. 'I went to your brother as soon as we had parted. After what we had done, I thought a speedy marriage might be necessary.'

'You told him?' she said, mortified.

'I would not be alive if I had. He would not have bothered with a duel. He would have shot me before I could finish my offer. And I would have most heartily deserved it.'

'You offered for me?' Now she was the one who was shocked.

He nodded. 'I gave him no indication of what had happened. I simply told him that I had loved you since we were children and asked for your hand.'

'And he refused you,' she said, as suddenly everything became clear. 'It is so nice to know, after all this time, that you intended to do your duty by me.'

'It was not duty,' he insisted. 'It was…' Then he stopped as if he could not quite manage to say the word 'love' a second time. It was just as well. They both knew it was far too late for such an admission.

'Your reason for offering does not matter,' she said brusquely. 'Fred said nothing of meeting with you.' But now, at least, she knew the subject of the argument that her brother had just recently admitted to and his desire to do right by Jack if the war had damaged his spirit.

'He told me that you were too young and I was too irresponsible to take care of you,' Jack replied.

'I'd have run away with you, had you asked,' she reminded him. An elopement would have proved her brother right. As time had passed, she had realised that neither of them had been ready for marriage. It was probably for the best he had left her. But that did not change how she'd felt, at the time.

'Fred said I was too wild,' he muttered, like the sullen boy he had been. 'He did not trust me with you.'

'It was a bit late for him to come to such a conclusion,' she said with a laugh. 'We had known each other all our lives and he had made no effort to keep me safe from you. In fact, he always thought your outrageous behaviour to be excellent fun.'

'Not always,' Jack said. 'Apparently, such things are not nearly so amusing in a brother-in-law as they are in a friend.' He scuffed the toe of his boot on the rug and she saw the other side of him, the handsome, young imp who had stolen her heart. Without meaning to, she put her hand out to touch his sleeve, then dropped it away again as she remembered the risk of getting too close to him.

'But why did you leave me without explanation?' she whispered.

'You did not know that, either?' He looked up at her sharply, surprised.

She shook her head.

'I left him a letter to give to you. When I did not get an answer...' His voice fell away just as her hand had earlier.

'What did you say?'

'That, if we did not marry, I could no longer trust myself in your presence.' He thought for a moment. 'Perhaps not the right words to leave in a missive that was probably read the moment I left the room. But I made no mention of what had gone before.' He cleared his throat. 'I made it very clear that I did not trust myself with you outside of the sanctity of marriage and that I meant to return, when you were older, and I had made my fortune, or at least after I could assure Fred that I had settled sufficiently to be worthy of you.'

She let out the breath she had been holding in a slow sigh.

'I asked you to write to me, if you needed me,' he said with a significant raise of an eyebrow. 'And even if you did not, I begged you to tell me that you were willing to wait for me.'

'I was angry that you'd left without word,' she said.

'So, of course, you did not write,' he said with understanding, but no emotion at all.

'But I did wait,' she reminded him.

'And I did not,' he said gruffly. 'I gave up hoping.' The look he was giving her now said that the past was the past and that anything between them was finished.

But it didn't have to be. If he wanted her, she was still free, as was he. For the first time in ages, hope fluttered in her breast and she imagined a future quite different from the orderly marriage and life of service that awaited her as a vicar's wife.

It might hurt William's pride, should she decide against him. But his wooing thus far had smacked of expediency, not ardour. His heart would be undamaged if she called an end to their courting. And hers would breathe a sigh of relief.

But the man in front of her seemed to have nothing more to say on the subject of love, either. Apparently, she would have to prod him to life. 'These stories of the past are all very enlightening,' she said. 'But it is the present we must contend with. And the future,' she added with significance.

'Indeed,' he agreed. 'Your brother says you are near to making a match with Mr Thoroughgood.'

'So it would appear,' she agreed.

'I spoke with him briefly. He is a most serious and learned fellow...'

'I will relay your compliments to him,' she said, praying that there was more to the sentence.

'But I do not think he is right for you.'

She knew that as well. But she had waited for Jack until her options were limited, hoping for love. When Waterloo had come and gone with no sign of his homecoming, she had settled.

But now he was home. She smiled, realising that they still stood in the doorway, under the mistletoe. 'Do you have someone in mind that would suit me better?'

Perhaps she was being too obvious in her questions. But she wanted some hint that he had come to make things right between them and he was playing far too coy.

She was not expecting the answer she received. 'I know no one who will suit. But I know you well enough to think that you need a man with spirit and a sense of humour, and someone who will appreciate those qualities in you. Thoroughgood is wrong on all counts.'

'What?' It was all she could manage, for the

answer he had given rendered her near to incoherence.

He gave her a firm and somewhat puzzled smile, as if he felt he had been perfectly clear before and should not have to repeat himself. 'I would not offer advice on the matter, if your choice seemed more appropriate. But I have known you so long that I cannot help but be concerned for your future happiness. I fear you would make an abominable vicar's wife and would make yourself miserable by trying.'

She shook her head, amazed. 'You return after all this time and have nothing more to say than that?'

'If you were expecting something more—' his brow furrowed '—then I must remind you that it has been five years,' he said. 'Things have changed.'

'"Love is not love which alters when it alteration finds."' She touched her cheek, wondering if she was really so different from the girl he had once wanted. 'If they are so easily forgotten, then the feelings you claimed for me were not as deep as you claimed.' It made her feel all the bigger fool for succumbing to him then.

'It is not you,' he said, hurriedly. 'You are every bit as lovely as you were on the day I left and just as hard to resist. It is I who have changed.'

'Of course you have,' she laughed. 'You are

a war hero now. If I am to believe what I have heard, you are quite well off and no longer dependent on an allowance from your brother to cover your bills.'

'I have changed for the worse,' he argued. 'Ignore the nonsense about my being an officer and a gentleman. One cannot be a good soldier and remain untouched by the brutality of the profession.' He turned away again, staring into the fire, and his hand gripped the mantel until his fingers went white.

'But that is over. You are home now,' she reminded him.

He smiled sadly. 'Would that a change of location was all it took to return to the man I was.'

'Time will help,' she said.

He shook his head. 'It will not change what I have already done. And the man who could behave in such a way is not a man worthy of your affection. Now, if you will excuse me, I must wash for dinner.' And he left the room, walking beneath the kissing bow without even looking up.

Chapter Five

Dinner at the Clifton table was much the way he remembered it from childhood, when the house had been his refuge against the capricious affections of his own family. He had spent most summers and Christmases at the neighbouring estate belonging to his grandfather, Sir Henry Gascoyne, but since the family seldom bothered to come along, it was more exile than holiday.

But once the Cliftons took note of the boy living largely unsupervised next door, his loneliness ended. He became an honorary member of their family, playmate of the children and doted on by parents and servants alike. Now, apparently, Fred had notified the cook that Master Gascoyne had come home, for a fricassee of chicken and mushrooms had been set on his end of the table and he helped himself to a liberal portion. The recipe was too simple for a holiday meal, but since the night he had mentioned it was his favourite, no Clifton meal was complete without it.

Tonight, this gesture of welcome was warm, but undeserved. He was too unsettled to enjoy any of the delicious foods on the table. He had broken his promise to Lucy, who had been foolishly loyal and waited for him. Though he'd thought that there would be nothing worse in his life than battle, greeting his lover this afternoon had been the hardest thing he'd ever done. It was also the cruellest.

He had not realised that she would look even more beautiful than she had when he'd left her. She'd felt right when he had kissed her and even better when he'd put his hands on her waist. It was like finding a lost part of his soul. For a moment, he had forgotten his plan to remain aloof from her. He'd wanted to be her last kiss as he had been her first.

Then he'd turned from her, called her sister and pretended it meant nothing. She had been angry when she'd confronted him later. But there had been a dangerous undercurrent beneath it. She had been searching for a reason to forgive him. She'd acted as if it should be easy to cast off his sins and come back to her, to be what they had been to each other.

A return to Lucy was impossible. She was too pure, too good. If she learned of the things he had done in the name of King and country, she would flinch from him in disgust. He would not taint the memories of the past by trying to rekindle something that could never again be as sweet as he'd remembered it.

After dinner, he mingled with the other visitors, feeling the same out-of-place sensation he'd had in London these last few months. On one side of the room, a group of guests were playing charades. On the other, he could hear another crowd gathered around the pianoforte singing 'Ding Dong Merrily on High'. Neither occupation interested him, nor did the Buffy-Gruffy game or playing Hunt the Slipper with Miss Forsythe and the other young ladies.

Everything was by turns too loud or too quiet. The laughter seemed forced and inappropriate. He wanted to shout at them that there was no reason to celebrate when good men had died while they'd stayed safe at home.

But death and dying was the lot of a soldier. He'd known it when he had gone to war. Yet he had not understood how wrong it would feel to have survived. It seemed he would spend the rest of his life starting at loud noises and shadows and waking in the middle of the night unable to sleep because of the battle he was convinced must wait him in the morning.

To steady his nerves, he decided to share the activity that Fred had chosen: honour guard to the punchbowl. He stayed on one end of the table, while his friend manned the ladle, both of them imbibing liberally.

He'd drunk far too much since Waterloo, trying to numb his mind to peacefulness. But it was strange to see someone who was supposed to be celebrating his engagement dipping so deep and it made Jack wonder if there could be something wrong between the pair. But the days where he could ask personal questions of Fred were long gone, so he held out his glass to be refilled and they sat in silence.

Nearby, a group of children were taking turns at the snapdragon bowl, pulling raisins from the burning brandy and shrieking as they singed their fingers. The younger of the two girls was leaning too far forward, her curls bouncing just out of reach of the flames. At any moment, there was likely to be an accident that would spoil the evening.

Without waiting for permission, Jack rose from his chair and crossed behind the girl, pulling her back out of danger. Then he explained patiently of the risk she had been in and showed her that proximity was not the key to the game by rolling up his shirt cuff and snatching a fruit himself.

He returned to the table to find Fred smiling fondly as he poured himself another cup. 'My friend, you are truly a changed man. Remember the Christmas you leaned too far over the bowl and burnt off your eyebrows?'

'I burned my cheek as well,' he admitted. 'There is still a patch that my valet swears cannot grow a whisker.'

Fred laughed heartily at the memory. Jack had no right to be annoyed by the fact, for he had laughed as well on the day it had happened, far too drunk to feel the pain.

'If you had not had the damnedest luck, it would have been far worse. You walked away from accidents that maimed other men. Remember the time you rolled my curricle on the road to Basingstoke?'

'It was the horses who were lucky,' Jack said, wincing at the memory. 'You threatened to trounce me to make up for the loss of them, but they escaped without so much as a bruised flank.'

'I'd have hit you for destroying the carriage,' Fred said. 'But I was too busy popping your shoulder back into place.'

'Then I brought up my accounts all over your best coat,' Jack concluded, his guilt turning to dread as he looked back on what a reckless cad he had been when Fred had refused to hear his offer. The stories told so far were hardly the worst of what he had done.

Fred grew more sombre. 'When you said that you would change your character and make your fortune, I had little hopes that we would see you again. A man's luck can only go so far and you had used up more lives than a dozen cats.'

'It turned out I had a talent for staying alive,' he replied.

'And you have come back with the money as well,' Fred said with an approving nod. 'The pickings on the battlefield must have been good, for I understand you have purchased a fine house in Grosvenor Square.'

'When I left, I had hardly enough money to keep myself alive,' Jack added. With grandfather and parents dead, he'd had to beg his brother for the money to buy a commission, but had paid it back threefold after just a year.

'When I heard that you had returned and were as yet unmarried…' There was a long pause as his old friend tried to collect his thoughts. 'I worried that we might have a similar argument to the one that I feared had ended our friendship.' He reached out and touched Jack's shoulder in a gesture of apology for words that had not even been said. 'I cannot tell you how it delights me to be proven wrong. Since you have been here, I have seen the improvements in your character. In fact, compared to the layabout you used to be, you are almost too serious.'

Jack tipped back his glass and drained it to prove that some of his bad habits had not completely disappeared. 'If that was meant to be a compliment, it is not a very good one.'

Fred shrugged, embarrassed. 'It is just that I am both pleased and concerned. If there is anything that you need to ease your homecoming, you have but to ask.'

'This visit was enough,' Jack said, wishing that this awkward conversation could end. But in truth, being in this place with old friends had made him feel a little more human.

'And, should you wish to ask me about Lucy's future?' Fred said, watching closely for his reaction. 'Know that my answer now would be quite different than it was the last time.'

He favoured Fred with a blank look and silence.

'You were always quite fond of her,' Fred added, pausing as if hoping Jack would comment. 'And, at least until we hear something out of Thoroughgood, she is still free.'

'And old enough to make decisions without your permission,' Jack added.

'True,' Fred replied. 'But that does not stop my interest in what becomes of her.'

'Then do not try to push her on to me, as an alternative to the Vicar,' Jack said, abruptly.

'I did not think you would find it a hardship,' Fred replied, indignant.

'I would not,' he snapped. 'But she should not

be tied to the sort of man who had planned to celebrate Christmas by putting a ball through his brain.'

'You would not...' Fred said, shocked.

'Left to my own devices, it was a distinct possibility.' Jack sighed. 'And that is why I do not think myself a fit husband for your sister.'

He set his punch cup aside, no longer thirsty. When he looked up, he was staring into the eyes of Lucy Clifton. She was several yards away from him, too far to speak without shouting over the din of the other, laughing guests. But words had never been necessary to understand each other. That, at least, had not changed with time.

He shrugged back at her, still unsure what it was that she saw in him that held her interest, other than the ghost of his former self.

She gave a sigh of disappointment at the doubtful look he had given her. Then, with a flash of her blue eyes, she glanced above her.

Mistletoe.

The kissing bough was not as impressive as the ones he remembered from the Clifton Hall of his youth. But the barest scrap of leaves and berries would serve the purpose if he dared to steal a kiss. Lucy was willing, waiting, radiant in the candlelight, her eyes sparkling in invitation, her cheeks glowing red from the effects of the punch and carols.

And despite what he had just told her brother, he was tempted. There was no harm in a quick buss between old friends. It was the height of foolhardiness. But then, she had always brought out his desire to throw caution to the wind.

But that was before. He had come here to say goodbye to her and to assure himself that she would be all right without him. He was not here to rekindle a romance that should not have happened in the first place.

He gave his head a small, firm shake, refusing her offer.

Her eyes flashed again, this time in annoyance. Then she looked past him to catch the attention of the man she planned to marry, giving him the same come-hither look.

Mr Thoroughgood stepped forward to take her hand, just as he might at the altar. Then, with a patronising smile, he pulled her out from under the kissing bough and murmured something that raised a blush of embarrassment on her cheek.

Jack struggled to read the man's lips and understood but a single word.

Paganism.

And his Lucy, who had been the bravest, most forthright girl he'd ever known, allowed him to lead her from the room.

Jack turned away, back to the punchbowl.

Chapter Six

The next morning, Lucy found her brother in his study, going through the month's accounts. But she could tell by the way he flinched as she opened the door that, in truth, he had been hiding from her. 'We need to speak,' she said, and a guilty flush was added to his cringe.

'I assume this is about you and Gascoyne,' he said, squaring his shoulders and preparing for the worst.

'Among other things,' she agreed. 'He told me what happened before he left for Portugal. You meddled in my life. You told me nothing of his offer.'

'I did it for your own good,' he said with an apologetic smile.

'Still, you had no right.'

'On the contrary. Once Father died, I had not just the right but the obligation to see that you made a good match.'

'That does not mean you should not have consulted me as to my wishes,' she reminded him.

'I knew what you would have said,' he replied, shaking his head. 'You followed Jack around like a puppy, from the moment you were out of leading strings.'

'I adored him,' she agreed.

'And in return, he got you into no end of trouble,' Fred replied. 'Boosting you over fences to steal apples from his grandfather's orchards.'

'It was hardly stealing since they practically belonged to him,' she replied.

'Riding astride on the stallion.'

'Side saddles are pointless things,' she replied. 'You would know it if you ever tried riding on one.'

'Except the horse threw you,' her brother reminded her.

'He threw you as well and you did not think anything of it.'

'He broke your arm.'

'An unfortunate landing,' she agreed. 'But it healed as good as new.'

'And that Christmas,' he added, 'Jack gave you a full cup of punch, not to mention port and cigars.'

'Only one puff,' she said. 'I did not like tobacco. But the port was excellent. I do not understand why women are not allowed to drink it.'

He ignored her perfectly reasonable statement. 'Until he bought that commission, Jack Gascoyne led you into every scrape he could contrive, and you went willingly all the way.'

'True,' Lucy agreed with a smile.

'I know you were infatuated with him. But at seventeen, you were far too old to be his partner in crime.'

'But not too young to be his wife,' she reminded him.

'You might have been old enough to marry, but even at twenty-one, he was too young to be your husband. He had more debts than money and lived at the whim of a family that was constantly threatening to cut him off from what little they gave him. He could not have supported you. It was for the best that he went to war, for you had reached an age where he could no longer be trusted to behave like a gentleman around you. He admitted that himself.'

Perhaps there was something in her expression that gave away the truth, for now he was staring at her as if he suspected what had happened. So, she hurried to return to the attack. 'He wrote me a letter to that effect. He promised to return. I never received it.'

Now Fred looked guilty again.

'I went on for five years, heartbroken because I thought he'd left without saying goodbye.'

'I had no idea that you still thought of him at all,' Fred replied.

'Because you did not want to know,' she said. 'You never asked me what future I wanted for myself. You have been too busy trying to match me with the likes of William Thoroughgood to see if I was happy or sad.'

'The Vicar is a fine, upstanding man,' her brother replied. 'That is why I suggested he pay court to you.'

'He is so upstanding that he is as stiff as a plank,' she snapped. 'Yesterday, he forbade me from standing under the kissing bough in my own home because mistletoe is a pagan plant that will jeopardise my immortal soul.'

'What were you doing standing under it?' Fred said, missing the point.

'I can tell you what I was *not* doing,' she said. 'And that was waiting for the Vicar. And don't you dare dictate to me over mistletoe. Our guests have been giving and collecting kisses all day and you have not said a word against it.'

'They are not my sister,' he said, as illogical as ever.

'And your sister is no longer twelve,' she said. 'But if I was, I would still be standing under the kissing bough and hoping to be noticed. It is harmless fun, Fred. I have no intention of banishing it to the servants' quarters as Mr Thoroughgood suggested.'

'That does seem rather drastic,' Fred agreed at last.

'It is indicative of the future I will have if I marry him,' she said.

'You are of age, Lucy. Your future is your own,' he said. 'I just thought…'

'That after years of pulling pranks and roving about the countryside with you and your friends, I would turn into a retiring flower when it was time to marry and become a parson's wife.'

'I did not think it would hurt to present the option,' he said with a shrug.

'If Thoroughgood is the best you can do, then please, do not think, any more,' she said. 'I will be nice to him while he is here, for your sake and to spare his feelings. But that is all.'

Fred sighed dramatically. 'I suppose you have your heart set on Gascoyne again.'

'There has never been another man for me,' she replied.

'Then you are likely to be disappointed,' he said. 'When I encouraged him to renew his suit of you…'

'You did not,' she said, wincing in embarrassment.

Fred held up his hands in surrender. 'Just to

tell him that there would be no resistance from me this time.'

'If he wanted me, your opinion would not matter,' she said, glum.

'It is not that he does not want you,' her brother said, gently. 'He is in a worse way than I imagined. Last night, he was talking rot about ending his life.'

In all the time he had been in mortal danger, she'd thought she was used to the idea that any day could bring news of his death. Since he'd returned, she had found small relief in knowing that, even if he was not with her, he was at least safe. She could not abide the idea that, now he was so close, she might lose him again in a way far more permanent than simple rejection.

She would not allow it. 'He might have felt thus last night,' she said, firmly. 'Tonight might be another matter entirely.'

That night was Christmas Eve and Jack was surprised to find that he was dressing for dinner with eager anticipation. Perhaps his mood was helped by a decent night's rest. Or perhaps it was the snow that had fallen, steady and deep, since the moment he'd arrived. When he looked outside, the world was covered in a virginal white blanket, untouched by humankind.

Or perhaps it was simply the prospect of see-

ing Lucy again. Even though he could not have
her, his dark mood was not quite as black as it had
been, knowing that she was close. It had been so
long since he had looked forward with anything
but dread, that the feeling of joyful expectation
was as rare as a unicorn.

Would there be roast beef or goose? Or perhaps a turkey? Or all the above? Would the Clifton pudding be as good as he remembered? Would
Fred finally open the ancient port that his father
insisted on saving for a special occasion?

There was no question that Lucy would be
hostess. But was it wrong to wonder what she
might wear? The anticipation of seeing her again
was rather like playing the electrifying machine
that had been kept in his grandfather's salon.
Someone turned the crank and everyone else
nervously joined hands and held their breaths,
waiting for the jolt to travel through the party.
Common sense said to let go. But some stronger urge demanded that one hang on and enjoy
the shock.

Tonight, it was a shock to see her in her mother's place, in a gown of ice-blue silk, with the
family jewels at her throat. There was nothing
unusual about her attire. In style and expense she
looked none too different from the women he had
ted in London while trying to forget her.

But he had not found himself intrigued by the way the candlelight settled in the hollows of their shoulders, nor were his eyes drawn to the shadow between their breasts that disappeared into the bodice of their gowns. Sitting across from Lucy, he had to struggle not to stare at her like a starving man in front of a feast.

Though he had loved her no less, he'd spent much of the last five years thinking of Lucy Clifton as a child, pretty but naïve, and in need of sheltering. But the woman at the table tonight was controlled, intelligent and beautiful. Worst of all, she intrigued him in a way that he hadn't expected. He wanted to sit with her and have her tell him everything he had missed while he had been gone and how she had become even more wonderful than he remembered.

'I swear, this dinner was the best we have had,' said Fred, interrupting his thoughts. 'Well done, Lucy. Well done.' As the last of the pudding was taken away, her brother clapped his hands, beaming down the table at his sister.

Lucy blushed prettily in response. 'I hardly deserve credit for it. The menu is the same every year and Cook and the kitchen maids did all the work.'

'All hail Cook, then,' he said with another grin, raising his glass in the direction of the kitchen. 'Perhaps it is simply the company we keep this

year and that we are eating without the threat
from France, thanks to our friend, the fearless
Major Gascoyne.' He applauded again, this time
directing his approval to Jack.

Jack's feeling of contentment evaporated at this
hyperbole. 'Really, Fred. It is not as if I brought
down Napoleon single-handed.'

'Since Wellington is not here to receive it, you
must accept the gratitude of the nation,' Fred said
with a shrug. 'A toast to Major Gascoyne.'

'Here, here!'

Now the whole table was raising their glasses
to him and he had to fight the desire to run.

'Now you are embarrassing Jack instead of
me,' Lucy said, drawing the attention away from
him as if she had sensed his discomfort.

'I cannot help it,' Fred replied. 'I am simply
glad to see that he has returned safely.' Then he
looked to Jack. 'It is good to have you home, old
friend.'

'And good to see you, as well.' Jack was surprised to find that it was not quite a lie. He had
cursed the fellow often enough, while in Portugal,
for without Fred's impetus he'd have never gone to
war. But now that he was home, he realised how
much he had longed for his friendship.

He took a hurried sip of his wine to fight a
wave of sentimentality. Perhaps it was rich food,
the smell of the yule log burning and the fresh

greens brought into the house at the darkest time of the year that made one prone to such open displays of emotion. His throat closed as if in a prelude to tears. This, all of it, was what he had missed when he was away on the Peninsula, the homey familiarity of it.

After dinner, the parlour games did not seem as grating as they had on the previous evening. Against his better judgement, he bobbed for an apple, chasing the fruit around the basin in futility before submerging his head to trap it on the bottom. He came to the surface again, sputtering from this baptism, hair and neckcloth soaked, feeling younger than he'd felt in ages.

Someone was handing him a flannel to dry himself and he took it without looking, taking a bite from the apple before wiping his face and sweeping his hair out of his eyes.

'It is cheating to go to the bottom,' Lucy said in a soft voice, linking her arm in his to pull him away from the others. 'You are supposed to chase it about on the surface.'

'Really?' he said, unable to help his grin.

'It is called bobbing for apples, not diving,' she reminded him. When he turned to look, she was hiding her own smile behind her hand.

'I prefer to think of it as fortune favouring the

bold,' he said. 'Sometimes it requires an extraordinary effort to take the prize.'

'Like going away to war in an attempt to win my hand?'

That was not what he had meant at all. He had wanted to spar playfully with her, as they used to do. Now the present was interfering again and spoiling his mood.

'Or cheating to win a child's game,' he said. 'Do not make your brother's mistake and turn me into some sort of paragon, Lucy. Believe me, I am no one's hero.' He turned to leave her, walking down the hall.

'You were my hero, once,' she said, following him.

'People change,' he said, trying to regain the reserve he had been using to keep her away.

'And sometimes they change back,' she agreed. 'Tonight, you are taking part in the games that you scorned yesterday.' Before he could correct her, she added, 'And you are cheating, just as you used to.'

'It is a wonder you put up with me, since both you and your brother have been quick to tell me what an ass I was,' he replied.

'Your tendency to reckless impulse was what made you fun,' she said with a shrug. 'You have obviously outgrown your worst habits, or you would not have survived the war.'

'That shows how little you understand, about war and about me,' he said, running a clawed hand through his hair.

'Then explain it to me,' she said, her voice soft and coaxing. It made him want to open for her, like a book, to see if she would erase the worst of what was written there or slam it shut and look away in disgust.

'I did not live through these last years by learning restraint,' he admitted. 'I have indulged the worst impulses. I rode through the countryside, killing with impunity.'

She was still smiling at him, as if she found his darkest admissions amusing. 'Were you a bandit?'

'I might as well have been,' he said. 'Before their blood had dried, I looted the enemy. My new house is built on money stolen from the dead at Vitoria.'

'I am given to believe that the practice is common on battlefields,' she said.

'I murdered and I stole,' he repeated, shaking his head in disgust.

'At the orders of Wellington,' she reminded him. 'They made him a duke for it.'

'That does not make it right,' he insisted. 'I have done things that render me unworthy of the company of any decent young lady. You deserve better.'

'When you left, you were confident of your

worth,' she reminded him. 'But now that all of England would honour you for your service, you have doubts.'

'Because I was a better man, before the war,' he argued.

At this, she laughed. 'When you left me, you were not a man. You were a boy. In that, I suppose my brother was right. It is probably for the best that we had not married. If I had run off with you after one impetuous night, I suspect you would have made me very unhappy.'

He looked around to be sure she had not been heard, then pulled her down the hall and into the parlour. Then he shut the door against eavesdroppers. 'Be careful what you say. Anyone might hear.'

'Once again, you are proving that you are more careful of my honour than we were before. Back then, you drank too much. You gambled. Your pockets were always to let. You fought with your family when they tried to correct your character. You took risks and encouraged me to do the same. You took my honour in this very room without a thought as to what might happen after or who might interrupt us.'

'If I was so repellent, you should not have allowed me within ten feet of you,' he said, indignant.

'As I said before, I loved you,' she said and he watched her expression soften.

'Back then, you were all I could think about,' he said, with an equally fond smile.

'And now?' She gave him an encouraging smile in return.

'I want to protect you,' he said. 'And that means I should stay away from you.'

'One thing has not changed,' she said, looking at him carefully, as if she could read his soul by looking into his eyes. 'You are as stubborn as ever. You seem to think that hardship has done you ill. You are more serious than you were. And more cautious as well. But I see nothing unworthy about you, if that is what you fear. You served your country well and have earned any peace you wish to have.' Then she sighed. 'But I am disappointed that you did not wish to have it with me.'

Now he felt more ashamed than ever. 'I told myself that you had found happiness in my absence. I was afraid to seek the truth, lest what we had done…what I had done to you had ruined your chances in some way.'

'If I had died in the street because of you, I am sure my brother would have informed you of the fact,' she said, smiling.

'That is nothing to joke about. Suppose there had been a child? I was halfway to Lisbon before

I considered the possibility. Only then did I realise what a fool I had been for leaving you.'

'You were foolish. So was I for not putting a stop to what we were doing and saving us both the risk. But I do not regret it, do you?'

'No,' he said without hesitation. 'I cannot imagine my life without that night in it. It has been the one touchstone by which I measure all happiness, all goodness.'

'If there had been a child, I would have written you,' she said. 'And demanded that you return. Do not think that my pride would have been greater than common sense. If there was any mistake made, it was a long time ago and I have forgiven myself for it and you as well. And as for the rest?' She shrugged. 'Perhaps you cannot go back to the way you were. But that does not mean you are obligated to continue down a path that you do not like.'

Her logic was clear and hard to refute. And though he had meant to avoid her and preserve his sanity, his heart felt lighter for having talked with her. 'Very well, my dear Lucy. For you, I shall be a better man, just as I always intended.'

'Then let us celebrate your new resolve,' she said, looking up and past him.

They were still standing in the doorway of the parlour, beneath the kissing bough, in the same spot they had been when she had changed his life.

He shook his head and made to back away.

'Just one kiss, Jack. There will be no harm in it.'

She had said something similar, that faraway night, and he had been just as entranced then as he was now. 'Just one,' he repeated, stepping close to her and lowering his mouth to hers.

She tasted of apples. Or perhaps it was him. Her lips were sweet and fresh, and they made him feel young, awake and alive, just as he had when plunging his head into the apple bucket.

Her arms twined about his neck, clinging to him as if she needed his support. How she would laugh if she knew that she was the strong one, breathing new life into him as she opened her mouth in surrender. Though he knew he should, he could not manage to refuse her offer. He deepened the kiss and gave her what she wanted.

With each thrust and parry of their tongues, he felt his fears for the future lessen. He put his hands around her waist, steadying her and himself and wishing this innocent moment could never end. But just as he had the last time they kissed, he felt dangerous stirrings in his body and the desire to end the night in passion.

Gently, he set her aside, making her moan and reach for him again.

'You said one kiss,' he reminded her.

Her grin was as impish as ever. 'I lied.'

'If you thought that this would change anything… If you thought it would change me? You were wrong,' he said, silently praying for the strength that he had not had when he was younger.

'I do not want to change you,' she said. 'I like you just as you are. I only want to change your mind.' Then she rose up on tiptoe, kissed him on the chin and plucked two berries from the kissing bough, whistling as she opened the door, walked into the hall and left him alone.

Chapter Seven

Lucy woke on Christmas morning feeling a strange combination of hope and dread. It had been a surprise to learn that Jack viewed his time in the cavalry through such a dark lens, but perhaps it was inevitable. The boy she remembered would have run off to war filled to the brim with dreams of glory and adventure. Disillusionment was unavoidable.

She had seen enough veterans missing arms and legs and eyes begging in the streets of London to realise that his life could not have been as easy as he'd assumed it would be. He should have known that he would return scarred in some way.

Perhaps that was what upset him. The Jack she remembered from childhood would have declared a scar to be dashing and an eyepatch piratical. Instead, he had been spared serious injury, but he had likely lost friends and comrades and seen good men, mangled beyond repair.

Though he had returned unmarked, he was as damaged as any of them. That did not mean that, given enough time and love, he could not heal.

But she could not give him the help he needed when everyone, including Mr Thoroughgood, assumed she was about to become a vicar's wife. What had she been thinking to give an ear to his courting? The sort of woman he needed should be even-tempered and obedient, with a gentle touch for the invalid and a good hand for stirring up a calves'-foot jelly or nourishing broth.

She could not make either of those to save her life, nor was she particularly patient. In fact, she was so defiant that, after being lectured on the subject, she had proclaimed to her maid that she would let the mistletoe rot in the door frame before yielding to the pressure to remove it.

She could not exactly put the Vicar out of the house on Christmas Day, especially since the servants were still clearing the roads of snow. But that would not prevent her from some small act of rebellion. To this end, she dressed with care in her newest and most colourful day dress.

It was not a particularly outlandish costume, but William had disapproved of it when last she'd worn it, calling it too risqué, simply because it was turkey red. She could think of no better way to tell him, without words, that she no longer approved of him, or his advice. Today, it made her feel as Christmassy as the sprig of holly on the mantel.

When she passed the morning-room door, it seemed that not everyone shared her festive mood. Miss Forsythe was sitting alone in an out-of-the-way corner, weeping into her sleeve. Lucy bit her lip as she debated the etiquette of the situation. As hostess, it was probably her duty to quash the poor girl's desire for privacy. If she could not cheer her, then perhaps she might convince her to cry in her room, where she would not annoy others.

She entered the room and sat next to Millicent, pulling a fresh handkerchief from her pocket. 'I am sorry,' Lucy said, offering her the linen, 'but I could not help noticing that you are in distress. Is there anything I can do?'

'No,' the other girl replied. The word was drawn out like the howl of a wounded puppy. 'I am fine. Thank you,' she added, swallowing the next sob by sealing her lips tight against it and letting it escape in a whine.

Lucy gave her what she hoped was an encouraging smile. 'Since none of my other guests is crying on Christmas Day, I cannot help but think you are exaggerating your good spirits.' She paused. 'Is it something Fred has done?'

'Yes,' Miss Forsythe said, then swallowed and announced hurriedly, 'No. Everything is fine.'

'If he is making you so unhappy, I am sure my brother will release you from your engagement,' Lucy said, silently cursing him for whatever he had done to make the poor girl so miserable.

'Where did you get the idea that I would wish for such a thing?' Millicent responded in a shrill voice. 'Does he no longer want me? Has he said something?'

This level of alarm was surprising, for Lucy could not imagine what Fred might have said that would frighten her so. 'Nothing, other than that he dotes on you. I simply noticed that your courtship was short and his offer very sudden. If you wish to postpone the wedding…'

'No!' Now Millicent looked positively frantic, hovering on the edge of a fresh flood of tears. Then she wailed, 'Your brother must… We will marry as soon as the banns are finished, just as we planned,' she said at last, between the sobs.

'That is good,' Lucy said, still unsure whether it was or not. She had never seen anyone so miserable over the prospect of getting exactly what she claimed she wanted. And she and Fred did seem happy when they were together. She was quite sure that she'd almost caught them kissing the night before last. When she had walked into the parlour, they had been nowhere near the kissing bow, but so dishevelled and red-faced in their casual postures that they had to have been hiding something.

Which did nothing to explain why Millicent was sniffling now. Lucy sat down beside her and reached out to take her hand. 'No matter what has been said or done thus far, do not feel constrained to marry in a direction where your heart does not lie.'

'My heart,' Millicent said, as if wondering what part that organ played in choosing a spouse.

'If there is anything I can do to ease your distress... A talk with my brother, perhaps...'

'I am fine,' the other girl insisted. 'Everything is fine. And to change the plans might create a scandal.'

Lucy bit back a retort. If she continued as she was, crying in public, Miss Forsythe would experience the embarrassment she now feared.

There was a commotion in the hall, as the door to the main salon had opened and guests were flooding out of it and coming in their direction. Millicent gave a hurried swipe at her face, trying to sweep away the tearstains as Lucy hid the soggy handkerchiefs behind a cushion. By the time Fred opened the door, things looked close to normal.

'We missed you at Morning Prayer,' he said, with a tight smile and a raised eyebrow towards his betrothed.

Lucy stared back at him in reproach before saying, 'Then the Lord will get two complines from us later.'

Miss Forsythe simply looked guilty.

Before Fred could ask about her, Lucy announced, 'Millicent was keeping me company', which elicited an eager nod from the cowardly girl.

'Well, I hope the pair of you will be finished with your conversation by afternoon. Mr Thoroughgood has suggested that we take an outing to the ice pond for some skating.'

'Surely the weather will keep us indoors,' Miss Forsythe agreed in a soft voice. 'And I am not too steady on skates,' she added. 'I would not want to risk a fall.'

Lucy started. She could think of at least one reason, other than natural timidity, that would make a girl concerned about the possibility of a fall. It would also leave one prone to irrational tears and a fear of the future and a wedding too slow in coming.

But Fred was grinning at her, obviously unaware of the reason for her distress. 'Since the coachman has already affixed the runners to the carriage and broken a trail to the village, there should be no trouble reaching the pond at the bottom of the garden. And as for skating? I am sure you will not have problems with these.' He produced a pair of skates from behind his back. 'They are fine Dutch blades that will strap right to your shoes.'

'You can persuade a gentleman to pull you about in the sledge should you get tired,' Lucy supplied, wondering how soon it would take for her new sister to claim fatigue.

'That would be very nice,' Millicent said. The last of the tears had disappeared and she was looking at Fred with a gaze that would melt ice.

'Are you sure it is not too warm?' Jack said from behind him, glancing out the window and gauging the temperature with his hand by the warmth of the sun on the window glass. He looked to Fred with a serious expression. 'Yesterday's snow is already beginning to melt and the ice may not be thick enough to support us.'

'It has not been warm for long,' her brother insisted.

'I am sure if Fredrick says it is all right...' Millicent added.

'If Frederick is sure,' Jack said, letting friendly mockery creep into his voice. 'Then how can I refuse?'

'Skating sounds like a very proper way to pass the afternoon,' the Vicar supplied, pushing past them and entering the room to stare at Lucy's dress in disapproval. 'You will have to change before, of course. But it will be good exercise for the young, with none of the risks of some Christmastime activities.'

He meant the kissing bough, she supposed. 'This dress will be warm enough,' Lucy replied in a tone as cold as the mill pond. 'I have heard it is even possible to dance on ice, if a partner is skilled enough. Perhaps Major Gascoyne can teach us to waltz. It was all the rage in Brussels.'

Despite himself, Jack grinned. Then he seemed to remember that there would be no more waltzing in their future, with or without ice.

'Perhaps, if the ice is thick enough,' Jack said again, with doubt.

'I will have the servants test it before we go out,' Fred assured him, surprised. 'And I never thought to hear you worry about such things. Back in the day, you were always the first on the pond and the last to leave.'

'People change,' Jack said, looking at the sun shining on the snow.

That afternoon, they went to the pond as planned, where the servants had marked out a large circle of ice deemed safe for skating. Then they had sharpened and polished the skates and arranged benches on the shore with blankets and hot drinks for any of the guests who tired of the fun. The little sledge that Millicent had wanted had been freshly painted since last winter and was a brilliant red and gold, the ribbons pressed and hung with silver bells that jingled when the gentlemen took turns pushing the ladies about on the ice.

Despite Jack's cautions not to do anything foolish, the children formed lines and played crack the whip, sending each other hurtling off towards the bank when they could no longer hold on and laughing each time they fell.

Lucy envied them. If she had been alone, she would have raced across the pond, until the wind blew the pins from her hair and turned the tip of her nose numb. It would be sweet freedom to go so fast, perhaps with the sort of man who would hold her and cheer her on rather than cautioning her to be a sedate and proper lady.

There was to be nothing so exciting for her. After the interlude in the parlour, Jack seemed intent on ignoring her, leaving her in Mr Thoroughgood's competent and non-waltzing arms.

In fact, everything about the Vicar's behaviour out of doors was as hidebound as it was inside the house. He made sure that he was the one to help her on with her skates and, as he did so, his eyes kept an unwavering focus on her feet so as not to risk glimpsing her ankles. Then he slipped her hand into the crook of his arm, wedging it tightly so there was no chance of escape. 'Do not worry, my dear. There will be no risk of falling while I am here.'

'Of course not, Mr Thoroughgood,' she said, half-wishing that they would take a tumble, just to prove him wrong.

But even if he had been unstable, he was averse to moving at a speed faster than he might have managed if he had been picking his way across the ice in his boots.

As they inched forward, he shot a disapproving glance towards Jack, who had warmed to the idea of skating now that they were out on the ice. He was pushing the sled with all his might. His skate blades dug deep into the ice as he gained speed, making two young ladies shriek with laughter as he gave a final push and released the sledge to spin wildly across the pond.

It was inappropriate to feel jealousy. But she could not help a little envy. Her own partner was moving so slowly that she had given up trying to skate at all for fear of outdistancing him in a single glide. Instead, she had to let him tow her along like an inanimate object.

But she could not remain silent much longer. They seemed to be getting uncomfortably close to the edge of the area that had been swept clear by the footmen.

When she pointed out this fact to him, the Vicar tutted in disapproval. 'My, but you are argumentative today. You must learn to trust my judgement in things large and small. And I say we should move further away from the crowd, Miss Clifton. We do not want to risk being knocked down.'

'Are you sure it is safe?' she said, more worried about safety than fighting for autonomy. 'The servants have tested this portion of the ice. But I do not know...'

'Do not trouble your head, Miss Clifton,' the Vicar said in a firm tone. 'We are in far more danger skating too close to those young boys and their sharp blades than we will be on fresh, clean ice that God himself has produced for us.'

She was more than a little annoyed. Jack might have been a bounder, but at least he had not treated her as if she was a foolish woman, not even when they were young. Later today, when she had managed to disentangle herself from Mr Thoroughgood's grasp, she would untie any further bonds that the Vicar had on her and go her own way. It would be better to have a future full of loneliness than to spend the rest of her life in resentment. She could not stand another cautious admonition and, if Jack remained insistent that he would not have her, she'd just as soon have no one at all.

Suddenly, there was a loud crack, followed by a moment of terrifying silence as the world dropped away beneath her. Before she could fully understand what was happening, she had sunk below the ice, into the water. Perhaps it was from the cold, or perhaps the shock of being thrown into the situation that would probably end her life, but time slowed and each moment had clarity and distinction, to be considered in turn as it passed.

She still had lungs full of air. It was quite possibly all the air she could ever have. Thank the Lord she had been too startled to gasp, or even to cry out for help. Had she done that, her life might be over already.

She was sinking, fast but not far. She had been swimming in this lake for most of her life. Even after fighting through the weeds, the bottom was barely ten feet from the surface. That was still almost five feet above her head. A few good kicks and…

She had never had to fight against her skirts to swim. The metal blades that made it so easy to glide on the ice were as heavy as lead now that she was trying to kick free of them. But she had no choice other than to try for the surface so she scissored her legs furiously until she felt slow, upwards movement.

Unlike her summer swims, the water hurt wherever it touched her skin. It was cold and sharp as knives. She had to bite her lip to stop her teeth from chattering and releasing her precious breath. One hand was weighed down by a wet mitten, the bare skin of the other burned. She could imagine the Vicar holding an empty muff, still in shock that she was gone.

And her eyes. Dear God, it hurt to open them. And there was no point in doing it, for what had seemed clear as diamonds from the top blocked all light, here below.

She managed a last kick and felt her hands bang against what ought to be open water. Rather than breaking in waves, it was a solid wall blocking her escape. She groped desperately, searching for the hole that she had fallen through. Instead, it felt like the ice had let her pass, then frozen solid again to trap her.

She pounded on it once, in anger, then felt it slipping away as she began to sink back towards the bottom. Her throat and lungs burned now. But her hands, which should be sore from beating on the ice, felt nothing at all.

The panic that had been in her mind just a moment ago was blunted by the cold as well. What was the point in fighting, really? Another second or two and she would forget why she had bothered in the first place. This was her world now, and it was growing warmer by the second. All she had to do was take a breath and go to sleep. She could decide what to do next when she woke.

And then, light. Movement. Cold. And some-one shouting, 'Breathe, Lucy. Just breathe for me.'

She did, gasping, coughing and retching. Then the shuddering began as feeling returned. Her teeth were chattering so hard that she could not speak.

'I have her. It's all right. I have her. Blankets. We have to get her warm.' Her rescuer's voice was unsteady as well, shaking from the cold of the same water that had almost drowned her.

She was being carried, but her eyes were too blurred to tell by whom. Her lashes were stuck shut, probably frozen, for the light reached through them like the bars of a cage. And then, everything was dark as something was thrown over her head and she was rubbed vigorously until everything hurt.

'Ow.'

She felt the person carrying her laugh. 'Gently. You are hurting her.' It was Jack. But he did not sound amused. He wasn't laughing at all. He was trembling, just as she was.

'What about you?' Her brother was talking.

'Now that she is safe, I will be fine.'

'There is a coal heater in the sleigh. And blan-kets.'

'We must let her breathe as well.' A hand swept the rug that had been covering her away from her face and she gasped in another cold breath, instantly regretting it for it burned her throat, making her cough.

'It will be all right.' The arms about her tightened.

She wanted to argue that she was not sure it would. She could feel Jack staggering as he carried her, either from her weight or exhaustion, she was not sure. But then she was being lifted into the carriage and Jack fell in after her, sprawling across the seat as Fred jumped up to arrange the blankets around them.

'I must see to the rest of our guests. The ice is not safe.'

'Hopefully, the rest of them have the sense not to stray out of bounds,' Jack said, with another shudder. 'But get them off the water. I will see to it that she is taken care of and send the carriage back for the others.'

The coach started forward with a lurch and a jingle of harness bells, and they were on their way back to the house. Her shivering was not precisely lessened, but Lucy had begun to feel warmth on her legs from the little heater on the floor and Jack seemed to be exerting manly control over his own chills. He slid from the seat, crouching on the floor of the box, trying to undo her skates before letting out an oath. 'My fingers are still too useless to undo the knots. Damn, but that water was cold.' He patted at his wet shirt front as if searching for a pocket.

'What happened to your coat?' she said, confused.

'I stripped out of it before coming to get you. Your brother was drying your hair with it earlier.' He reached to the seat beside her where it had been abandoned and pulled a penknife from the watch pocket. 'God knows what happened to the waistcoat. It is probably still on the piece of ice we hauled out of the way to get to you.'

'I am sorry to have caused so much trouble,' she whispered.

'Do not be foolish,' he said gruffly and slashed though the bindings of her skates. 'You were not the one to choose the path you took. Nor do I blame the Vicar too very much. The chunk that broke free and tipped you in was a good six inches thick. It could have happened to any of us.'

'It was most brave of you to go after me,' she said softly, shuddering again.

He looked up at her with an expression that warmed her in a way that a coal fire did not. 'I was never so frightened in my life as when I realised what had happened to you. If I had not got to you in time…'

She might have died. And he might have done the same in his rush to save her. For a moment, she imagined the pair of them, locked beneath the ice, inches apart, but unable to touch. 'Let us not think of that,' she said. 'Come back under the blanket and get warm.' They were alive. They were together and, no matter what he thought was best for them, he had risked his life to come to her when she needed him most.

He still hesitated, so she patted the carriage seat again and lifted the corner of the blanket with a weak, trembling hand. Then she said with the sternest voice she could manage, 'Do not be an idiot, Major Gascoyne. Sit.'

He took another unsteady breath and looked up at her with a surprisingly nervous expression. He had reason to be cautious, she supposed. Judging by his treatment of her on the lake, he wanted her to believe that he would rather snuggle under a blanket with anyone else but her. Or perhaps he was just trying to prevent further lapses like the one they'd experienced in the parlour.

She managed an exasperated huff, before shivering again. 'Come, now. I am soaking wet, but not so repellent that you must sit on the floor to avoid me. We are both cold, we will both feel warmer if we sit together and I swear I will tell no one at the house what we have done.'

'You are not repellent,' he said sullenly, steadying himself on the seat and climbing up beside her again, then rearranging the blanket over them.

'Even drowned like a rat, you are the most beautiful thing I have ever seen.'

She laughed and relaxed into him, burrowing under his arm when he did not offer to put it around her. 'You are a liar and I love you for it.'

It was too honest and she felt him stiffen, ready to pull away again.

'A little, at least,' she said, trying to sound light, flirtatious and harmless. But she had never been particularly good at playing the coquette and suspected that she was even worse now that she was cold and miserable. 'And I do feel ever so much better with you sitting here.'

He shivered again, still too proud to admit that he was freezing as well. Then he surrendered and held her tighter, using both arms, and pressed his legs against her skirts, tangling his feet with hers. 'It cannot matter,' he said firmly, to himself. 'It is not dishonourable if I am too cold to be a danger to you.'

'The Vicar was far more of a danger to me than you could ever be,' she said. 'He was the one who insisted that we skate past the area that had been tested.'

He made another dismissive noise, settling in even closer to her, and she felt the first glow of real warmth. 'Do not worry about him. He skated to safety the minute the ice cracked.'

'And left me to my fate,' she said, sitting bolt upright.

'Do not be too hard on the poor fellow. Not everyone is good in an emergency.'

'True,' she agreed, relaxing back against him. 'But in this case, I am glad that you were there. I should be dead otherwise.'

He let out another shudder and his arms closed on her for a moment before relaxing again. 'As I told you before, do not try to make a hero of me.'

'Well, I thank you all the same,' she said, looking up at his perfect profile. Then she kissed him on the chin. Surely a small reward for her rescuer should not be deemed inappropriate.

He stiffened. A tremor went through him that had nothing to do with the cold and he surrendered, kissing her with all the passion he had shown her so many years ago.

Then he had been clumsy and eager, all elbows and energy. After all the times she'd relived that night in her mind, she had come to the conclusion that he'd had little more experience in love than she. But virginal awkwardness was another thing that had changed since he'd gone away. There was mastery in the way he held her and an exhausted confidence in the kiss he gave her, as if he knew just what it would take to rouse her body and send hot blood rushing from toes to fingertips and several delightful places between the two. Her nipples had been rock hard from the cold, but now they tingled as life returned and, with it, the desire to be touched.

He pulled away long enough to whisper, 'How I have missed this. I dreamed of it, you know. What it might be like to come home to you as if nothing had happened so we might begin again.'

'It is yours,' she said. 'I am yours. Come home to me, Jack Gascoyne. I have been waiting for you.'

For a moment, she felt him surrender, to the idea and to her. Then he was gone again, cold and hard as the ice had been and pushing her away from him. As she reached for him to draw him close again, he grabbed her wrists and held them, not in a tender way, but like manacles to restrain her. 'Do not tempt me further, Lucy. I am too tired to fight you.'

'Then why fight?' she said with a sob. 'Is it because you mean to destroy yourself? If that is what you think to do, then you might as well have left me to drown.'

'Do not say that,' he whispered back.

'I will say what I like,' she said, the anger she had felt that morning returning. 'I thought we might still be together, as we used to be. But apparently, I was wrong. I was ready to reject William Thoroughgood for telling me what to think and what to do and how to dress. But you are worse than he is. You think you can tell me what to feel. You want me to turn my love for you on and off again like some sort of machine.'

'Lucy.' The word was one-part warning and one-part agonised prayer. 'No more.'

Perhaps it was because she was cold. Or perhaps it was how near she had come to never speaking again. But now that she had started, she could not seem to stop. 'You did not know how I hurt the last time you left me. It was why I could forgive you. When I saw you again, it was as if a wound inside me had suddenly closed and I could live again. But by the Lord, if you leave me now, I do not care if you go to heaven, hell or London, you can take with you the knowledge that I will die a little every day from missing you, just as I did the last time.'

Before he could answer her, the carriage had slowed to a stop at the front door and a footman was ready to help them out. Jack reached to help her, but this time she was the one to push him away, stumbling out of the carriage and into the arms of the servants before he could offer to carry her.

He hopped down after her, trying to take her arm, and she pulled away. 'I am quite capable of walking into my own house.' But even as she said it, her teeth began to chatter and when she tried to stand her legs felt weak. She relaxed against the nearest footman, letting him and his mate drag her towards the threshold.

'Miss Clifton has fallen into the lake,' Jack shouted a warning past her to the butler. 'Summon her maid. Heat some blankets. Warm her slowly, mind. No hot baths.' The doors opened and she was swept into the house, borne up the steps to her room and into the warm towels that her maid held out for her. The girl hurried to undo the wet fastenings of her gown and from behind her in the doorway, she heard Jack's voice, ragged with distress. 'Miss Clifton?'

He sought her instruction. He had jumped into a frozen lake to save her. She did not doubt that now he would do anything she asked.

Anything except love her.

She wanted him to hold her as he had, forcing him to give up his warmth and his tenderness, making her feel that she was the most precious thing on earth to him. But what would be the point of it, if he was gone in the morning?

'Lucy?' It was little more than a whisper.

But even if she could keep him here, how long would it be before he left again? 'Thank you for your assistance, Major Gascoyne. I will be fine now,' she lied.

He turned and left her.

Chapter Eight

Miss Clifton could not come down to dinner.

Her brother assured them that it was only a precaution. She was chilled, but otherwise well. But she should not stress herself with presiding over the table. A tray had been sent to her room with shank jelly and saloop, so she might build her strength. If all went well, she would be seen at breakfast tomorrow.

'I visited with her when I returned to the house,' Fred assured them all. 'She is in exceptionally good spirits, considering what she has gone through.' All the same, he discouraged others from visiting and flatly refused to allow the repentant Mr Thoroughgood to come anywhere near her ever again.

Jack, however, was viewed as the hero of the day. He was pressed with an extra glass of claret before dinner and sides of liver and lights and calves'-head pie, which Cook assured him would strengthen both body and mind should he be feeling any adverse effects of his swim. Even Miss Forsythe had temporarily forgotten her beloved and was looking at him as if he had abilities far above those of normal men.

None of it meant anything to him. He had been Lucy's hero when they had entered the carriage. Then he had ruined it all. Now she was hiding in her room, refusing to see him, or anyone else.

He doubted she was ill. He remembered her as a girl of uncommon strength and stamina, climbing the highest trees, beating him in foot races and shaking off the direst childhood illnesses in record time. He had assumed that such vitality would keep her safe into adulthood.

It was why she had survived beneath the ice without panicking. And she had seemed well enough in the carriage. *More than fine*, his body reminded him, thinking of the kiss. That had been a mistake, as had the one in the parlour.

He had given her false hope and himself as well. She had called to the very heart of him, acting as if it was possible to turn back time and be young and innocent again. While he was kissing her, he was ready to believe it could happen. Then bitter sanity had returned and he had pushed her away.

But this time, he had made her angry enough to strike back at him. He'd had no idea that words could hurt so much. Perhaps it was because he had never truly believed that she would forsake him. She had waited for his return, just as he'd hoped. She had forgiven him, though he had not asked for it. Even his rival was so clearly wrong for her that Jack had not taken him seriously.

It did not matter that he was sure she'd be better without him. He had always imagined that whatever happened would be his decision, not hers. Instead, she had sent him away after making him feel the hurt she had felt at his absence, adding it to his own pain like a pile of bricks laid on his aching heart.

But what was he to do about it? If, against his own better judgement, he declared himself and offered for her, even she knew that he would be no better than marrying Thoroughgood. She would end up with a man who was far less than she deserved.

It hurt to be with her, but it hurt even more to be without her. And though he had imagined that there might be peace in death, what if he felt *her* loss of *him*, even on the other side of the veil?

The delectable dinner had no flavour for him. Wine held no attraction. The idea of gaiety and parlour games was an abomination, if she was not there to share in them. He retired early, claiming fatigue, though he felt more agitated than tired.

Once in his room, he paced nervously, unable to sleep, but too tired to stay awake.

At last, after hours of fruitless activity and even more fruitless thought, he fell exhausted into his cold and empty bed.

Lucy started awake from a deep sleep. Despite her maid's fears that there would be nightmares about the accident, she had been far too tired to conjure demons that would plague her slumber. It had been a blessing, really, to go several hours free of thoughts of Jack. He had been the primary player in her dreams, both good and bad, for as long as she could remember. But now, when he should be lying beside her in flesh and blood, she had finally managed to banish him.

Then she realised something was wrong. Why was she awake at all? She forced herself to lie perfectly still, watching, listening. The shadows distilled into form as her eyes became accustomed to the dark. There was someone in the room with her.

It was a man, she was sure, for the silhouette was far too tall to be a maid. In her own home she had nothing to fear, for a robber could never have made it so far into the house without a servant noticing. That left only two choices for the identity of the dark silhouette at the end of the bed and she doubted her brother would behave so strangely.

'Jack,' she said softly, sure of his identity even though she could not see his face.

She was relieved to see his head incline a fraction in a nod.

'What are you doing here?'

'I need to see...your feet.'

The statement was so unexpected that she pulled herself up to a sitting position, fumbling for the candle at her bedside. 'What the bloody hell are you talking about?'

'Do not use such language,' he said, striding to her bedside table to grab the taper and light it off a twist from the fire.

'You taught me to swear when I was a little girl. Given the day I've had, you can hardly blame me for cursing when I am frightened awake by a man in my room.'

'I am used to soldiers' language, but that does not mean I like to hear it from you.'

'And I told you before that I am tired of people ordering me about. If I wanted someone to scold me over language, I would seek out William Thoroughgood,' she said.

He winced at the comparison to the Vicar. 'I am sorry if I sound overly critical of you. And sorry that I frightened you as well. And sorry for everything else,' he added. He was holding the light aloft now, staring down at the lump under the coverlet that indicated her feet. Then he gave her another significant look and added, 'If you please.'

She was more curious than annoyed at the way he was behaving. She drew up her knees and inched her legs out from under the blankets, smoothing her nightgown back over her calves and showing him what he wanted.

'Pink.' He let out a sigh of relief and put the candle in the holder on the bedside table. Then he sat on the edge of the mattress, turning his face from her so she could not see his expression.

'What colour did you expect them to be?' Before she put them back under the covers, she looked at them as well. She wiggled them experimentally, but found nothing unusual about them.

'I was worried when you did not come down for supper.'

'Because my brother is an old woman and would not allow me to leave my room,' she said, then added, 'And I did not want to see you. I am perfectly fine, but he insists that I rest.'

'After I retired, I had a dream,' he said, then stopped.

'That is hardly a sufficient explanation.'

'It was not about the sort of thing that one should discuss with a young lady, especially not at bedtime.'

'You are being prim with me again,' she snapped. 'Do not bother. When you left me, I was not some naïve schoolgirl.'

'Because of my behaviour,' he added.

She sighed. 'The icy water did not kill me. But I swear you are boring me to death with this continual self-pity. And do not think to take credit for the fact that I chafe against the unfair restraints put upon young women. I refuse to be ashamed of the fact, or of my behaviour before or since you left.'

He sucked his breath in through clenched teeth, as if trying to decide what to tell her.

So she added, 'You must remember how hard it was to shock me when I was little, but you and Fred tried often enough. You once put frog spawn in my wash basin.'

'And a bat in your wardrobe,' he added.

'The poor thing was terrified,' she reminded him. 'But I was not. I have hardly grown to be more easily shocked in your absence. What were you dreaming about?'

He swallowed nervously. 'I remember seeing Frenchmen who had survived the invasion of Russia and the damage done to them by the weather. It does not take long for the cold to burn extremities beyond the power of healing. And when that is the case…'

She laughed. 'You were dreaming that my toes

had fallen off?' She wiggled them again, amused, and poked at the side of his leg with her bare foot.

'It sounds ridiculous when you say it thus,' he said gruffly, then caught her feet in one of his large hands and gave them a squeeze.

'I suppose it is nice to know that you care,' she said, staring down at her feet.

'You know I never stopped doing so.' There was real tenderness in his voice and her resolve wavered before she remembered the truth.

'If you care so much, you would not be encouraging me to marry another,' she said, growing angry with him again.

'It is wrong that a woman as special as you are should be alone,' he said, carefully. 'But you should be able to choose whomever you want and not the sort of bloodless fool your brother would pick for you.'

'Then I choose you.' She had been unable to stop the words, even though she knew they would hurt them both.

He shook his head. 'I will never marry,' he said with the firm tone of a man used to giving orders. 'I am a second son. I need no heir. Therefore, I do not need a wife.'

'You do not need?' she said with a bitter laugh. 'That has always been the problem with you, Jack. You think of your needs before others'.'

'How dare you?' If it had been anyone other

than the man she had loved her whole life, she might have been intimidated by the fury she saw in his face. Instead, it encouraged her to see him so moved. 'After all I have done, all I have sacrificed for your safety and the safety of this country, how dare you call me selfish?'

'Fred told me what you intended,' she said gently. 'I know you are in pain, but think of the pain you will cause me should you end your life. If you leave me, I shall always believe that you did it to avoid the marriage you owed me before you left.'

'Then I had no money and a bad reputation. What kind of life could I have offered? And now...' He paused, on the verge of confession.

'Now, you are here, on my bed. If you were any other man, the scandal of your presence in my room would be enough to wring an offer out of you. What is stopping you?' she said, unable to contain her feelings any longer. 'Love me or leave. But either way, you owe me more truth than you are giving me.'

He sighed. 'The passage of time will not mitigate the things I have done, nor will it change the way I feel about myself,' he said. 'I hate what I was, I hate who I have become. My love now would be like a canker on a rose, a corruption of all we had.'

She sighed. 'This is why I miss the old Jack

Gascoyne. He was trouble. But he was not such a bad fellow, really. He acted impulsively, then felt bad for it. And by the next day, he had forgotten what he had done and was ready to sin again. But you, Major Gascoyne, are far too hard on yourself. You have done great things. But you set the tolerance for your mistakes so high that no ordinary man could meet it.'

'But I must have failed, somehow,' he replied and his eyes grew distant. 'If not, why does God punish me? Or perhaps it is the devil, sent each night to torment me.'

'Punishment?' she said, surprised. 'Of what nature?'

'The dream that brought me here and my concern for your safety?' He took a breath as if afraid to speak. 'It was not unusual.'

'You often dream of me?' she said, smiling.

'Too much,' he admitted. 'I dream of losing you. When I close my eyes, I have seen you die in a hundred different ways. After today, I will see you dying of the cold, or I will be forced to watch you drown beneath the ice while I am unable to help. Usually, you are among the dead on the battlefield. A victim in a sacked village.'

'Nightmares?' she said, surprised.

'And in each of them, I cannot help you. Your blood is on my hands.' He ran a hand over his face, as if wiping away a caul. 'Sometimes I am not even asleep and I see things, in my mind's eye, that I cannot stand to look at. I would rather die now than live to an old age with these visions.'

'Have you had many such dreams since coming here?' she asked.

'This was the first,' he admitted, cautiously.

'So they have been better, now that you have come back to me,' she said, willing to take credit for any improvement.

'For the moment, perhaps,' he said, not convinced.

'That is proof that you should stay with me,' she said, patting the bed at her side.

'They will come back,' he said.

'And what if they do?' she asked.

'Then you will see what a joke the brave Major Gascoyne really is.' He laughed bitterly. 'During the day, I can be foul-tempered and distant. But nights are worse. Sometimes I cry in my sleep. In the morning, the pillow is wet with tears. Sometimes, I simply scream myself awake.'

'Do you always sleep alone?' she asked.

'That is not a question that a gentleman should answer,' he said, even more embarrassed by this than his earlier admissions.

'What happened in the past does not matter,' she said. 'After tonight, you will never be alone again. I love you, Jack Gascoyne, and I have done so long before I knew what it meant to love a man.'

'But I told you...'

'I do not care,' she said, reaching for him. 'If you cry, I will cry with you. If you wake in fear, I will be there to comfort you. It is what I wish from you and what I will give you in return.'

He made a noise, deep in his throat, that was somewhere between a sigh and a sob and leaned forward to embrace her. But his cheek was dry when it touched hers and his lips were warm and soft.

As she had in the parlour, she opened her mouth to him, eager for his kiss. But tonight, they were barely dressed and far from discovery, and there would be no more nonsense about single chaste kisses. She knew what she wanted from him and the heartache it would cause should he refuse her.

Before he could resume arguing, she wrapped her arms around him and pulled him down on top of her.

'You do not have to do this,' he reminded her. 'It is not wise.'

'But that does not keep it from being right. If you love me,' she added, 'stay with me.'

'I love you,' he said, taking her hands and pulling them to his lips, kissing each knuckle in turn. 'I always have. When I was on the Peninsula, the thought of you, and the need to keep you safe, was all that delivered me from despair. I kept on because of you.'

'I was praying for your safe return,' she whispered back. 'And my prayers were answered.'

He kissed her then, his mouth hungry on hers, drinking deep, then felling her again with gentle touches of his tongue on hers. He released her hands, then traced the curves of her body and she felt her nipples grow hard against his chest. But she groaned in frustration at the layers of linen that kept them from touching properly.

He laughed in response and rolled off her, so they could undress. It took only a moment to wriggle out of their nightclothes. Then she pushed him down again, back to the incredible feel of skin against skin. And for the first time in what felt like years, Lucy knew she was truly smiling. It was not the polite upturn of the lips that served her in social situations, but a grin of childlike joy that she had not felt since they were young and together, as they were meant to be. 'Happy Christmas, Jack Gascoyne,' she said, unable to resist rubbing her body against the erection she felt beneath her.

He groaned and stilled her hips with both hands, then eased his thumbs forward, between her legs until they met at her centre. 'Happy Christmas, indeed,' he replied, brushing gently against her until she gasped. One finger pressed firmly on the bud of her pleasure while another traced the opening to her body.

'Stop,' she said, breathless.

His eyes went wide with shock and his hand stilled, waiting for her next words.

'Not until you have promised me that we will still be like this next Christmas and all the holidays to come,' she said. 'If you love me again, swear that bad dreams and other women and all the meddlesome brothers in England will not part us.'

'I swear,' he said. 'For always.'

In response to his promise, she did something that she'd had no knowledge or nerve to do the last time and reached down to take him in her hand and guide him into her body. Then she clutched his hip as he slid into her, an inch at a time, in a slow claiming that she did not want to resist. The pleasure seemed to grow by the instant and her body tightened in response to the feeling, which was familiar yet wondrously new.

'Do not let me hurt you,' he said softly against the side of her head. 'I seem to remember, the last time...'

She touched a finger to his lips. 'The last time was the first time...'

'For both of us,' he said with a soft laugh.

'We were young,' she said, smiling.

'You were. It is different for men. The other boys used to tease me for my shyness with women. But I was waiting. There was never anyone for me but you.'

Before she could wonder how long he had waited after, he was moving in her, slowly, then faster, gliding in and out of her body. She relaxed and accepted him, half-surprised that what she had said was not a lie. The second time was very different from the first.

The pleasure she remembered was there, but the pain and awkwardness were gone. At first, he touched her body with a gentle reverence, as though he could not believe she was real. But with each stroke, he grew more sure and firm.

Her body responded with a flood of pleasure at this possession, wet and trembling as his hands cupped her bottom, holding her steady against his thrusts.

'Touch yourself,' he urged. 'Wherever it feels best.'

'I shouldn't,' she gasped, then laughed, remembering how many times Jack Gascoyne had convinced her to do something she knew she should not and how often she had enjoyed it.

'Touch yourself,' he urged again.

She gave her breasts an experimental squeeze, shocked at how good it felt before settling one hand between her legs, near to the place where they were joined. The rub of her own fingers accentuated the movements of his body, taking her to a pleasure she had never known.

The last time he had loved her was good, yet strangely unsatisfying. But this? This was amazing.

Suddenly, her body tightened in spasm around him and she cried out, gasping as he spent into her and collapsed with a sigh of satisfaction, cradling her against his body and letting the last of the tension fade out of their bodies.

They lay there together for a few moments as one, then he pushed away from her, hovering over her for a moment before rolling away.

She reached for him, suddenly afraid to lose him again. 'Where are you going?'

He picked up his nightshirt and threw it over his head. 'Back to my room to find my breeches. Then I mean to saddle a horse and take you to Scotland. We must do what we should have done years ago. We must elope.'

'The storm,' she reminded him.

'If it was fine enough to skate today, we will find a way to manage the roads.'

'My brother...'

'Has his own woman,' Jack said with a laugh that sounded as it had, before he'd left her. Then he grew serious. 'I will write him a letter of apology and slip it under his door.' Then, naked and magnificent, he climbed out of her bed and went to the little writing desk she kept by the window.

'Now?' she said with a laugh.

'I am decided. I love you and, for the second time, I have behaved like a man with no honour.' He looked back at her, his expression stern.

'I did not object, either time,' she reminded him.

'Then do not object when I say that you must come away with me this very night. I will explain to your brother and pack a change of linen. You do the same and we will go.'

He was serious. For a moment, her heart stopped dead, unable to imagine what lay in store for them. There would be scandal. Her brother would be livid, for though he seemed to be encouraging this union, he would not have it begin this way. She might never be welcome in this house again.

But even as she listed the reasons why she must object, she could not feel anything but happiness. She went to him, hugging him as he sat at the desk trimming a pen.

'There, now,' he said, in a poor attempt at a scold. 'No more of that.' Then he looked up at her and grinned. 'Not tonight, at least, or I will forget why we must leave. Perhaps when we get to an inn on the road north.' He looked away from her again, dipping the pen in ink and scrawling a few hurried lines on her writing paper before blotting and folding the note.

Then he shook free of her embrace and scooped his dressing gown up from the floor, shrugging into it. This time, when he looked back at her, his face was radiant. '*Au revoir*, my dear. I will wait in the stables for you.'

As he threw a saddle over his horse, Jack tried not to think about the woman he had left in the house, and the chance that she might have changed her mind. A part of him was still afraid to believe that he deserved her love, but he did his best to ignore it. She had not waited five years for him only to reject him when a happy future was within their grasp.

But with each moment that passed his fears grew. What if someone saw her leaving her room? Suppose she had realised the risk to her reputation or felt her obligation to her guests and decided that she could not leave.

Suppose her brother realised what was happening and tried to put a stop to it? He seemed more charitably disposed to Jack than he had when they were younger. But that was before he had decided to elope with Fred's sister. The one thing that the two men could agree on was that Lucy deserved the best husband she could find. And though Jack was reasonably sure that the man was not Mr Thoroughgood, he still doubted that it could be him.

A proper gentleman would have waited until after Christmas to have the banns read, before a carefully planned marriage ceremony and a lovely breakfast. At the very least, he would have taken the time to get a special licence. But Jack had seduced her, not once, but twice. He did not dare wait any longer to make her his wife.

His fears evaporated when he heard soft steps on the gravel of the path and she appeared in the doorway of the stables. At the sight of him, she rushed forward into his arms with a suddenness that spooked the horse.

He caught her and held her still for a moment before putting a finger to his lips, cautioning her to silence. He needn't have bothered. Now that she was close to it, she stared up at his mount with a cross between wonder and trepidation.

To calm her fears, he brought the beast under control again with a single tug of the bridle and brought him down into a bow of welcome for his new mistress. After giving her a quick kiss, he helped her up on to the saddle where she could sit astride, handing her the reins as he tied the bundle of clothes she carried with her to the cantle. Then he mounted behind her, enjoying the feel of her settled between his legs, his arms around her waist.

He felt her shiver and almost drop the straps as he nudged his horse forward into a walk with his thighs. 'One cannot always fight and steer the bridle,' he said. 'Mercury knows by the feel of my legs what I want him to do.' To demonstrate, he turned them left and right again before bringing their pace to a trot. Then he opened his greatcoat and wrapped it around her, holding her body to his to drive her fear or chill away.

She turned her head to murmur up at him. 'I thought there would be a carriage.'

He laughed.

'I have never ridden like this before.'

'You are completely safe,' he assured her. 'The snow has been packed to the road by other riders and I am a cavalryman, after all. I am more than capable of riding in the light of a full moon with you in my arms.' To prove it, he wrapped his arms more tightly around her and brought Mercury to a full gallop with a push of his heels.

Lucy squealed in delight and leaned back against him, snuggling into his arms, and suddenly he was struck by the rightness of it. Finally, after all this time she was where she belonged and the part of him that had been missing since he'd returned to England was restored to him, making him whole again. And the horse seemed to fly down the northern road, as light as his heart.

* * *

It was nearly dawn and she was dozing against him when he decided that it was time to stop. He guided the horse into the coaching yard of an inn and hopped to the ground, steadying her as she slid after him. Then he called for a room for Major and Mrs Gascoyne.

The innkeeper lifted an eyebrow at this, for he knew well that this was the route to Gretna Green and had seen more than a few ringless ladies calling themselves Missus. But he also saw the coin that Jack tossed to the stable boy and his courtesy was more than sincere enough to satisfy them.

Jack smiled when he looked down at the woman beside him and felt no trace of the innkeeper's doubt. She might not be his wife this morning, but she was staring at him with all the love he could have wished for from a lifetime partner.

'A single room?' the innkeeper enquired with a touch of sarcasm.

'That is all we need,' Jack said, not bothering to look at him.

'That is good, I suppose. With the weather as dodgy as it has been, it is all we have left. And we would not have that if the Cliftons were not leaving just now.'

The romantic fog cleared in an instant and both their heads snapped to look at the man, and then to the doorway of the inn where another couple was preparing to leave.

Millicent and Fred stood together, arms linked, the lady clinging to the gentleman as if her very life depended on his touch. Jack smiled. Apparently, Fred had not been home to receive the letter of apology he had sent. They must have left before Jack had gone to Lucy's room and had likely been doing the same things in this inn that he had done with his beloved.

He had only to look at Millicent's face to know it was true, for at the sight of them, her expression turned from bliss to tears of mortification.

Before he could reassure her that there would be no harsh judgement, Fred announced, 'I can explain.'

Jack folded his arms and tried to pretend sternness. 'The only thing I want to know is how you managed to get here before us. I saw you at dinner last night and here you are, well-rested and ready to start a journey. Did you sprout wings and fly here?'

'Then you are not here to bring us back?' Millicent said in a timid voice.

'We would never be so cruel,' Lucy replied. 'It is clear that you are very much in love and the wedding date is not even set.'

'Mama said we should wait until spring,' the girl said and a tear trickled down her cheek.

'That is three months away,' Lucy said, giving the girl a knowing look. She added a warning squeeze to Jack's arm that hinted at the reason for their sudden haste, as if silently willing him to ask no further questions.

'We discussed the matter yesterday afternoon,' Fred said, giving his fiancée a fond smile. 'And we decided that there was another perfectly good solution. Since the roads had been cleared, I had the carriage harnessed right after the meal,' Fred admitted. 'And we changed horses.'

'We rode double,' Jack admitted.

'I left a note to be delivered to you at breakfast,' Fred said to Lucy.

'I was not there,' Lucy admitted, staring at her brother and daring him to comment on her behaviour.

'I left a note for you as well,' Jack said. 'I slipped it under your door.

'That means we have left a house full of guests to fend for themselves,' Fred said with a wince.

'That is far more improper than a double elopement,' Lucy agreed. 'But there is little we can do about it now.'

'Unless we turn back,' Jack said, with a sigh of resignation.

The expressions that met his very sensible suggestion were horror, disbelief and irritation.

'Now, of all times, you wish to be sensible,'

Fred said after a *humph* of disgust. 'You are running off with my sister, just as I always knew you would. The only question in my mind of late has been why it was taking you so long.'

'She very nearly married that stick in the mud, Mr Thoroughgood,' Millicent added in a surprising show of courage.

'But now you wish to turn back,' Lucy concluded.

'I do not *wish* to turn back,' he said, releasing her to hold up his hands in surrender.

Her brother looked at him for a long moment, then responded. 'I think it is too late for proper London marriages for any of us. We will send a groom back to explain to the servants, promising to make it up to them for ruining their Boxing Day,' Fred said. 'And to my soon-to-be mother-in-law, who will have to be hostess. Then, since we are both resolved to go to the same place, it would make more sense to share the carriage rather than travelling separately. Go in, refresh yourselves. Then let us go to Scotland and see if we can waken a blacksmith.'

The suggestion suited Jack fine. Now that he had proof that Lucy would not suffer her family's disapproval for the elopement, a weight had been lifted from his conscience. He had known that the decision to marry was the right one. Though his mind had fought it, his heart had never doubted.

But the meeting of mind and spirit had been a long time in coming.

As they climbed up into the carriage, he turned to offer his love to Lucy. But instead of words, a yawn escaped him, making her smile. There was a bone-deep tiredness creeping over him, from the long ride and the relief at being home at last, in Lucy's arms. He meant to tell her so. But as she snuggled against him under a carriage blanket, he closed his eyes and fell into a deep, contented and blissfully dreamless sleep.

* * * * *

SNOWED IN
WITH THE RAKE

Louise Allen

Chapter One

~~~~~~~~~~~~~~~~~~~~~~~~

*December 23rd, 1819—the Chiltern Hills,
Hertfordshire*

'Ouch!' Julia Chancellor sucked her thumb and
frowned at the additional bead of red now deco-
rating the holly wreath. 'That carriage door slam-
ming out there made me jump, Fred. Who could
be foolish enough to try driving anywhere in this
weather, let alone up here? The Falconer ladies
must have a very determined guest and one who
has overshot their house, at that.'

Fred—fat, fluffy and ginger—merely glowered from his post on the bottom step of the stairs.
He did not approve of snow, even a light dusting, and snow a foot or more deep he considered
a personal affront. He thumped down on to the
hall floor and stalked off towards the kitchen,

tail erect except for a right-angled kink at the end. *'Mrreow.'*

'It is snowing out at the back as well, you know, you daft cat. Oh, bother this wreath.' Julia fiddled a length of twine through the back at the cost of two more punctures and held up the result in triumph. 'There, just this to fix and I'll make tea. Not that anyone is going to be passing to see it in this weather.'

She reached for the door handle at the same moment as the knocker rattled out a sharp staccato and she juggled the prickly wreath and a pair of scissors as she opened the door, expecting to find a lost and shivering coach driver needing directions.

Standing on the top step was a tall, handsome, dark-haired man. His hat was a thing of beauty, his boots gleamed. In between the two was nothing except naked man. Rather a lot of naked man. He flung his arms wide, presumably just in case she missed any of what was on display. 'Surprise!'

A gasp filled her lungs with freezing air, her eyes streamed, but not before she dragged her appalled gaze up from muscular, hairy, goose-bumped male skin to the man's face. *'You.'*

Her straight-armed shove caught him squarely on the chest with the holly wreath, and Giles Darrowby, Viscount Missenden, fell backwards into the snow with a yelp of pain.

Julia slammed the door and leaned against it defensively. *That man.* She had not seen him for almost two years. She had never seen him before without his clothing—*thank heavens*—but that was unmistakably the man who had abandoned her in the middle of a scandal that had ruined her, wrecked her come-out and sent her into exile in deepest rural Hertfordshire. That deceptively innocent, charming smile was burned into her memory. *Let him try to smile through frostbite.*

He was audible through the thickness of a door designed to stand up to the worst the weather could throw at it, although fortunately she could not make out exactly what he was saying.

Surprise? I'll give him surprise, she thought grimly, her fingers fastening around the key that jutted from the lock.

Then the sharp, thin draught through the lock gave her pause. If the Viscount stayed out there he would die, clothes or no clothes, and, loathe him as she might, she was not going to have a man's death on her conscience.

Julia went into the front parlour, pulled the knitted throw from the back of the sofa and opened the front door again. She had not been hallucinating and the small glass of sherry she had sipped while she was stirring cake mixture had not gone to her head. Even in the evening gloom she could see that the considerable length of Viscount Missenden was sprawled in the snow, already receiving a light dusting of flakes that lay decoratively on his hairy chest and muscular thighs and…everywhere.

He had tossed aside the wreath and, when the light from the hall flooded across him, he moved his hat rapidly to groin level.

Somewhat too late, Julia thought grimly. *I am never going to get that image out of my mind now.*

'Get out of the snow, put this round you and come in before you die in my front garden and ruin the view.' She turned, adding over her shoulder as she hooked the blanket over the handle, 'And hang the wreath on the front door as you come, my lord.'

Giles hauled himself to his feet, slapped his hat back on his head, furled the blanket around himself like a toga and picked up the confounded wreath. *This is the last time I listen to one of Woodley's schemes*, he thought, as he found the string loop with numbed fingers and managed to fix it over the hook above the knocker.

'We can't abandon Felix, poor devil, not to that ghastly woman,' Woodley had said. 'The man is too amiable, he'll never have the resolution to extricate himself. We need shock tactics and I've got just the plan.'

And they had all agreed and cut for it and Giles

had drawn the two of diamonds. Not that he'd protested, it had seemed sensible enough at the time, with the benefit of a good dinner and several bottles of palatable claret inside them. What could possibly go wrong?

Nothing, it seemed, he brooded as he pushed at the door and stumbled into the warmth of a neat little hallway. Nothing except a blizzard and incompetent map-reading and the inescapable fact that he had just exposed himself like some pervert to an innocent female who had absolutely nothing to do with any of this. The fact that it was freezing cold was a slight mercy, but even so, she must have had a far better view of his accoutrements than any decent woman would want.

With an effort he got his boots off—no point in aggravating matters by treading melting snow down the hallway.

'Ouch!' He hopped on one stockinged foot, clutching at the blanket.

'Mind the holly, Lord Missenden,' the decent woman called from somewhere at the end of the hall. 'There may be leaves on the floor.'

'Thank you so much,' he muttered darkly, hobbling forward, hitching the blanket, which seemed more inadequate by the minute, closer around him. Then, as he opened the door on to a kitchen, it struck him. 'How do you know who I am?'

The woman—*lady*, she was clearly a lady from

her speech and the plain but elegant gown she was wearing—looked round from dragging a screen about a tub set in front of the range. She banged it into position and glared at him. Brown hair, just on the blond side of mouse, straight nose with freckles, determined chin, grey eyes and a mouth that, just at that moment, resembled a rat trap.

'Because I have a very clear recollection of the man who ruined me, my lord. Even when he is blue with cold and covered with goose bumps. There is hot water in the copper through there along with buckets and a scoop. Soap and towels are there.' She pointed at a chair next to the tub. 'Where are your clothes?'

'In a carriage disappearing down the hill,' he said grimly.

'I will find you something to wear.'

Giles stared at the kitchen door as it shut behind her. *Ruined? Her? Me?* He had never seen the woman in his life, he'd swear to it. Besides, he did not go about ruining ladies, or any females come to that. Perhaps he had wandered into the clutches of the local eccentric, some spinster who was convinced that every man she came across was making dubious advances to her. *But she knows my name.*

He shivered—and not entirely because of the cold. Either he was snowed in with a madwoman or he had done something appalling he had absolutely no recollection of.

From one corner of the kitchen came a low, menacing rumble of a growl and a vast ginger cat prowled out.

'Nice pussy,' Giles ventured, edging towards the scullery. He had a healthy respect for a cat's armoury of claws and this one appeared to be in a particularly bad mood.

It sat down and sneered at him as he scooped water into the pair of buckets and carried them through, not deigning to move, so he had to manoeuvre around it.

When he had the tub half-filled and the temperature adjusted to just short of boiling with cold water from a brass jug, it turned around and watched while he lowered himself in cautiously, moaning with mingled pleasure and pain as his extremities defrosted.

'Does everyone in this house loathe me?' he enquired after the narrow amber gaze became uncomfortable. Or was there no one else here? Now he thought about it, he would have expected to be handed over to a footman or the cook, not to have the mistress of the house lugging screens and bathtubs about.

The man who ruined me...

Even a gentlewoman in disgrace would have a servant, surely?

The kitchen door opened behind him and the cat made an ambiguous noise as it went to investigate. 'Sir Thomas Kilver has just equipped his entire household with new livery and he gave me the old garments to see what can be salvaged for the poor. My name, should you not recall it, is Julia Chancellor,' she said.

Giles kept a wary eye on the reflections in the brass jug but, mercifully, Miss Chancellor was staying behind the screen and not advancing to flagellate him with more holly or whatever her delusions were suggesting to her.

'I have taken the braid off most of the coats and there are some of the shirts the sewing circle have been making as well. I brought them home to finish the hemming. I imagine something in all of this will fit you. I will put the clothes on the table.'

'Thank you.'

'My pleasure,' she said, her tone unmistakably sarcastic.

'Do you not have a footman, Miss Chancellor?'

'I have a maid and she is at the cottage to the east of this one helping the Misses Jepson, whose own maidservant is about to give birth at any moment. Come along, Fred, I am sure we can trust His Lordship not to run off with the spoons.' The door shut again with a sharp click.

That is a very angry woman.

Giles got out of the tub, towelled himself dry,

then padded over to investigate the clothes she had piled up. It was easy enough to find a shirt to fit him: the sewing circle was obviously intending to outfit sturdy labourers and most of the coarse linen garments would have been big enough. He pulled on his own stockings, then went through the pile of livery suits. Sir Thomas, whoever he was, had half-a-dozen well-built footmen by the look of it and after some experiment he found some breeches that were not too loose at the waist and a coat that did not pinch on the shoulders.

As Miss Chancellor had said, the elaborate braid work had been removed from the coats and the buttons, which must once have been crested silver, had been replaced with horn. Giles dug through the pile in the hope of a neckcloth, but could only find some spotted Belcher handkerchiefs. The resulting ensemble was bizarre enough—Hoby's boots, a coachman's neckcloth and formal dark blue tailcoat and knee breeches—but at least he was warm and, more importantly, decent.

It was much easier to think with his clothes on, he realised. Especially with an ill-disposed female in the next room. Giles frowned at his reflection in the battered mirror propped up on the dresser and raked his fingers through his hair, which had, of course, become a tangled mass. Abject apologies and explanations were in order and after that she might have calmed down enough to realise that they had never met before in their lives. Which still did not explain how she knew his name.

Julia stopped pacing the hearthrug in the parlour and sat down when there was a tap on the door. It would not do to allow him to see how agitated she felt. 'Come in!'

She had expected him to seem less disturbing when he was clothed, but Giles Darrowby merely looked large, dark, imposing and apologetic. At least he had managed that.

'Miss Chancellor. I am aware that I owe you an explanation.' He stood just inside the door, resembling nothing more than someone courageously facing a firing squad.

Julia refused to be charmed by manly fortitude. 'Do come in and close the door and sit by the fire, Lord Missenden. You will be even more of a nuisance if you succumb to pneumonia.'

'Ma'am.' He came in, took the chair she indicated, settled his long limbs and sat back. At least he was no longer looming. 'We became lost. We were looking for Beech House.'

'That is in Lower Bourne, the village at the foot of the scarp. You are in Upper Bourne, which is merely a hamlet on a terrace above it, and this is Beech View Cottage. It was a miracle your coach managed to navigate the hill. Unless, of course, they have ended up in a snowdrift.'

'I had three companions in addition to the driver and groom. They should be able to dig themselves out,' he said confidently. 'We'd been blundering about in the snow and then we saw the nameplate on your gate.' His mouth twisted in a rueful grimace. 'It was half-covered in snow and all we could read was *Beech*. Miss Chancellor, you appear to believe you know me and I have no recollection of having ever met you before.'

'Tell me first what you were doing in the snow stark naked.'

'It seemed like a good idea at the time.' The ruefulness was attractive. The wretched man had charm. 'You are acquainted with Sir Felix Wheaton?'

'We have not met, but I know he has taken Beech House for a house party for the festive season. His own country home some miles away has a problem with the roof, I understand.' She shrugged. 'That is the gossip in the village at any rate.'

'Felix is the best of fellows. Kind, honest, do anything for anyone, chivalrous to a fault—and like putty in the hands of a scheming female. A certain Mrs Fanshawe who has a daughter to marry off has decided that Felix is just the man for a son-in-law. That is to say, he is wealthy, well connected and far too gentlemanly to evade her tactics. He doesn't like the girl, who promises to be every bit as ruthless and grasping as her mother, but he cannot seem to evade her and Mrs F. has manoeuvred him into inviting them to spend Christmas with him in front of witnesses.

'We've been doing our best to put her off—hints about Felix's completely fictitious naughty past, suggestions that he gambles, keeps an opera dancer and so on, but none of that weighs against a baronetcy, an elderly bachelor uncle who is a viscount and a healthy amount invested in Funds. So we decided something drastic was called for. I drew the short straw as the first salvo in the campaign. The plan was for me to arrive on the doorstep, as you saw, pretending that I thought it was the kind of house party where such behaviour was expected and that Felix had wagered I wouldn't do it. The next two would turn up slightly the worse for drink with the baggage and finally Woodley was to arrive with an E.O. wheel and turn the whole place into a veritable gaming den.'

'E.O.?'

Poor Sir Felix.

'Even-Odd. It's a betting game with a spinning wheel. Popular in the hells, but not something to be played in a gentleman's house. By the time we'd finished with him Felix would appear to be a hopeless rake on the verge of gambling away all his wealth.'

'But who else had he invited?' What a ruthless set of men Sir Felix's friends appeared to be. But she had to admit, the plan could have worked. 'You cannot have meant to scandalise an entire group of innocent guests, surely?'

'He was so taken aback and in such a panic when Mrs F. bullied him into holding a house party that we promised we'd see to the rest of the guests. Woodley's sister will be there with her husband and she's game for any rig. The sister of one of the others, Jimmy Truscott, is also staying and, if things got too bad, she was going to fling herself into Felix's arms in a strategic manner. Her mama's with her, chaperoning another two girls, one of whom Felix was dangling after before La Fanshawe got him in her sights, so we have hopes of that as well.' He spread his hands as though offering her the blueprint of their plan. 'We have to do the best we can for him, poor fellow.'

Was it true? Could she trust him that far? But the story was too ridiculous not to be the truth, Julia thought. Too ridiculous and too dangerous in this weather. 'What will your friends do now?'

'Arrive all at once and do the best they can, I suppose. Assuming they've reached the village safely and have discovered where they are,

I imagine they'll soon work out what has happened. But how on earth are you going to manage, cut off like this with no servants?'

'Here on Spinsters' Row we assume that we will be snowed in at least once every year and we prepare for it.' His eyebrows rose at the name, but she ignored that. 'This is particularly bad weather, but between the five cottages we have wood for at least two weeks and plenty of food even if we do run out of milk.' She smiled sweetly at Lord Missenden and saw his eyes narrow warily. 'Once it stops snowing people will begin to dig out the paths and you will be safe then, my lord. In the meantime you are trapped in the midst of a coven of single ladies with one about to give birth next door. You will be at the mercy of my cooking and in the same house as Fred, who would like to shred whatever parts of your anatomy he can reach.'

'You do not like me, Miss Chancellor,' Giles Darrowby observed. He was quite still except for the gentle drumming of his fingers on the arm of the comfortable old chair.

Any moment now Fred will pounce.

She leaned down, picked up the catnip mouse and tossed it into a far corner. The cat stalked off after it.

'I have no very good impression of your character, that is true. I applaud your concern for your friend, but otherwise you appear to be a rakehell, a care-for-nothing and heedless of the honour of young women who cross your path.'

That did get through the negligent air of self-confidence. Lord Missenden's mouth tightened into a hard line and the sensual curve of his lower lip, at which she realised she had been staring, became something else entirely.

'The honour of any woman must be the concern of every gentleman, myself included. You appear to be labouring under the impression— or perhaps delusion—that we have met before. I can assure you, it is not the case.'

'Indeed? I suppose you are going to tell me that you have no idea who Miss Sara Belton is and have no knowledge of her elopement with Lord Cranton?'

'Sara? Of course I know who she is. Cranton is a friend of mine. Her father was planning to marry her off to a man his own age, even though he knew she and Cranton were in love. If you have taken against me because I helped them elope, then you'll get no apology from me.'

'No?' Julia found she was on her feet, trembling slightly with the tightly controlled anger that was threatening to escape. 'I am not permitted to hold a grudge for the fact that you abandoned me to take the blame for the entire enterprise? You were part of a conspiracy to have me blamed for making the arrangements, hiring the carriage they escaped in, smuggling her out of the ball to the inn—and then when you abandoned the coach you were driving as a decoy you simply left me there to face the music. And ruin. Call me unreasonable, but I think I am entitled to some gesture of regret from you.'

Chapter Two

$\sim\!\!\sim\!\!\sim\!\!\sim$

Giles Darrowby stared at her, then got slowly to his feet. 'You were in that coach? You? I looked in quickly to check, but I thought it was the maid.'

'I got a very good look at you. You had your hat off and you were grinning.'

'Because I thought it was all going to plan,' he protested. 'Sara's friends who organised every-thing for her told us that it would be made to look as though the maid was duped and then tied up when she realised what was going on.'

'By Sara's friends I assume you mean Miss Gascoigne and Miss Hailsham?' He nodded. 'They entangled me in this because I naively thought they were my friends. They secured Miss Belton's undying gratitude without having to in-criminate themselves in any way, made sure the maid, who might have given them away, was not involved and no doubt amused themselves vastly at my expense. I paid the price for believing overtures of friendship that proved to be quite false. Do sit down, Lord Missenden. You *loom*.'

'I'm sorry.' He sat down abruptly. 'Sorry for looming, sorry for not realising what was happening. But why would Sara—?'

'I do not think she knew anything about it. I hope not, because I liked her and, although I did not know her very well, she was always kind to me when I was just out and very…awkward.'

A hopeless wallflower.

'I was glad to help her. Was she…? Did they get away safely?'

'You did not know? Yes, they pretended to make for Gretna, then cut across country and were married just across the border north of Berwick. Cranton has Scottish estates so they stayed there until her parents had calmed down and accepted the match.'

'I was gone from London by then.' Her aunt, who had been reluctantly sponsoring her orphaned niece's come-out, had packed her off to the country in disgrace, more worried that she might be blamed for Julia's actions than she was about the effect on her niece's future. Julia had made no protest, glad to escape. She had hated her come-out. Still grieving for her parents, she'd been thrust into the crowded, artificial, frenetic social whirl, so different from her quiet country childhood, and her aunt had made little allowance for inexperience.

Lord Missenden was still frowning. 'But why would Miss Gascoigne and Miss Hailsham do that to you? They must have known what the consequences would be for you.'

'I had upset Miss Gascoigne,' Julia said tightly. 'I hadn't realised. And I do not want to talk about it.' It was bad enough to have been made a fool of, to have mistaken cynical, sophisticated spite for friendship. It was just as humiliating to discover that Lord Tarling—tall, blond, handsome—was only flirting with her so intensely in order to make Miss Gascoigne jealous.

'Miss Chancellor.' Giles Darrowby leaned forward, his elbows on his knees, his hands open as though in supplication. 'Please believe me when I tell you on my honour that I had no idea of what was happening. Cranton was my friend, we organised his end of things and trusted Sara when she said her friends would manage her own escape.'

'I am sure she knew nothing about it,' Julia said, forcing herself to be fair although it felt as though she was chewing gravel to force the words out. He was a gentleman, she had to take his word. 'And I accept that you would not have left me there if you had realised who I was.'

'But I should have checked,' he said, clearly picking up on her inner feelings.

'Yes. Besides anything else, you should have checked that the maid really was all right. It seems, Lord Missenden, that you'll do almost anything for your friends, but the rest of us can take our chances.'

'Harsh, Miss Chancellor.'

'If the cap fits, my lord. I do not propose to say anything more about it. We are trapped here and I have no wish to spend several days in a state of war with you.'

'An armed truce, ma'am?' The charming smile seemed somewhat twisted now.

'Unarmed. I have no desire to ruin my Christmas any more than it already is. However you arrived here, you are my guest now.'

'Thank you,' he said gravely. 'But Christmas? That is two days away. Surely by tomorrow I can be out of here?'

'We are not in London. Nor are we in some great country house with an army of servants. I told you—we are in a cottage perched on the top of the Chiltern scarp facing west into all the weather that comes at us across the Vale of Aylesbury and the old men swear this is going to be a dreadful winter. It would be a miracle if your friends managed to get their coach to the bottom of the hill in one piece, but even if they had to abandon the vehicle they should have been able to get down to the village with the horses—and there they'll be trapped, too. For you to venture out now would be suicidal. It is still snowing and I cannot even see the front gate.'

'Hell,' he muttered, without apology, long fingers beating a rapid tattoo on the faded chintz.

Fred, slinking round the side, reached up one paw and took a swipe at the moving digits. Lord Missenden pulled his hand away just in time and Fred swore as his claw snagged in the worn weave of the armchair.

'Fool cat. Did you not hear your mistress? An unarmed truce. Hold still.' He swept up the growling, wriggling cat in one hand and disentangled the claw with the other. 'Ouch. Ungrateful beast.' Fred stalked off affronted, sat down and began to ostentatiously wash all traces of contaminating human touch from his fur.

Lord Missenden went over to the window and drew back the heavy red velvet curtains. The light in the room illuminated only thick, swirling snow in the blackness. He stood, one hand on the edge of each curtain, staring out as though he could intimidate the weather into a thaw.

A thaw would be welcome, Julia thought, looking at the long-limbed figure, the broad shoulders, the thick hair and remembering what lay beneath those incongruous clothes. *A thaw bringing with it a nice steady trickle of ice water. If I have to be trapped with a man, why does it have to be this one? And why, oh, why does he have to be quite so attractive?*

Physically attractive, that was. Morally he seemed to be something of a loose screw, although his wickedness sounded more light-hearted than malevolent and he did appear to be a loyal friend. But society gentlemen had been a mystery to her when she was doing the Season and she had no real hope of understanding this one now.

He drew the curtains together again with an abruptness that made the rings rattle. 'There are those who would say that a gentleman should take himself off and attempt to reach the village,' he remarked. 'Or a house closer than that.'

'You would not make it to the end of the Row tonight, it would be suicide.'

Lord Missenden put one hand on the curtain again, as though some miracle might have stopped the snow in the past minute, then lowered it. 'You are doubtless right, Miss Chancellor. I will sleep on the settle in the kitchen.'

The kitchen was warm and she doubtless kept the range in all night so it would save fuel and, most importantly, it was probably as far as it was possible to get from Miss Chancellor's bedchamber without bedding down in the log store.

'Why on earth would you do that when there is a perfectly good spare bedchamber upstairs?' she enquired, her dark brows levelling as she frowned at him.

What does she look like when she smiles? Perhaps she never does.

'Because I assume that is close to your own bedchamber.'

His reluctant hostess bent to throw a small log on the fire. As it flared up he saw the freckles across her nose, the impatient pursing of her lips, and felt a sudden, highly inappropriate, flare of attraction.

'If you are going to attempt to ravish me, Lord Missenden, I imagine that a flight of stairs is hardly going to stop you.'

Had the woman no maidenly sensibility? Apparently not, only an abundance of tart common sense.

How very refreshing.

'I have no intention of doing anything of the kind. Your opinion of me is bad, but I assure you I draw the line at ravishment. Very well, I admit that a proper bed would be very welcome, but you will lock your chamber door, of course. I would not want your rest disturbed by any uneasiness.' Goodness, he sounded pompous enough to be his own grandfather.

Miss Chancellor's smile was a faint twitch of

amusement that showed she thought so, too. 'I can assure you I will not be the slightest bit uneasy. I sleep with a pistol beside the bed, you see.'

'Loaded?'

'It is not much use if it is not and, yes, I am perfectly capable of using it.'

'In the *bedchamber*?'

'I think that inviting a potential ravisher to step outside and wait while I fetch it might defeat the object, don't you?' Then, as though they had been discussing nothing more shocking than the weather, she remarked, 'Time for supper, I think. Are you hungry, Lord Missenden?'

His mind—and his body—were so fixed on this exchange—flirtation?—that it took him a moment to translate the question into plain, nonsuggestive English.

She means for food, you idiot.

'Hungry? Yes, very, now I come to think of it. Luncheon was an inferior stew at an inn just past Hemel Hempstead. But you cannot have planned for an unexpected guest. Is there enough food?'

'After two weeks you might begin to find it monotonous, but we will not starve, I promise you,' she said as she stood up.

Giles followed her out of the room and along the chilly hallway to the kitchen. 'Is there anything I can do to help? I cannot cook, I should warn you.'

'Bring wood in and coals for the range, the parlour and both bedchambers upstairs, if you please. Through there.' Miss Chancellor pointed to the back door and then rolled up her sleeves, apparently with no qualms about giving orders to a viscount as though he was the footman.

She looked as though she knew what she was doing, which was puzzling. He would have wagered several guineas that any young lady of his acquaintance would have been completely lost if left alone in a kitchen and required to produce a hot dinner for two. What had her aunt been thinking of? To send her off to this remote hamlet while the fuss over Sara's elopement had died down was one thing, but to leave her here to live as though she was an impoverished middle-aged maiden lady was inexplicable. The thought that perhaps he had contributed to her disgrace and exile was an unpleasant jolt to his conscience. There was nothing he could do about that now, he told himself, but there were tasks to be done and they were all he could do at the moment to make amends.

It was icy outside, but the lean-to shielding the back door provided some protection and the fuel was stacked under cover to one side. Giles risked sticking his head outside. The woods behind, and the hedges that must mark the boundary of the properties, had made a sheltered space like a corridor running in either direction with snow only eighteen inches deep by the house, rising deeper the further away he looked. There was a light flickering to the right that marked the nearest cottage, or perhaps a star, but in the other direction he could see nothing but swirling snow.

Giles filled the log baskets in each room, lugged in coal, laid fires in the bedchambers and finally came back into the kitchen, ears burning with cold, eyes streaming from the contrast between inside and out.

He pumped water into the stone sink and washed the sawdust and coal smudges off his hands with water that only turned his fingers bluer. 'Your well has not frozen, fortunately.'

'Spring water,' Miss Chancellor explained, glancing up from rolling out pastry to drape over a filled pie dish. 'It will be larder pie for supper. I reviewed the pantry and this has all the odds and ends—leeks, cheese, bacon and almost the last of the milk.' She trimmed the edge, cut a cross in the centre so the beak of a stoneware blackbird poked out to vent the steam and brushed beaten egg across the top.

'How does a lady learn to cook?' Giles asked, watching as she opened the top oven door, slid in the pie and shifted a metal plate. The smell of baking apples drifted out, making his mouth water.

'I enjoy it. Dorothy, my maid, showed me and I buy cookery books as well.' She gestured to the shelves above the dresser. 'And compared to London the food is so good here—the milk has not been watered, the flour has not been mixed with chalk and there are fresh vegetables and eggs in plenty.'

'You seem happy.' Giles pulled out a chair and sat down at the kitchen table.

'And you sound surprised that I should be.' She paused, her lower lip caught between her teeth, gaze unfocused in thought. 'No cream, not enough milk... I know, I'll make a brandy sauce to go with the apples.'

'You left London in the middle of the Season, you have spent two years in apparent exile—why wouldn't you want to go back?'

'I was not happy, I did not enjoy it. I... It was hard to find my feet. The people I thought were my friends were no such thing. Here I have real friends, a community, things I can do—useful things. What is there to go back for?'

'The theatre, the shops, the balls—'

'There are shops in the market towns. I do not miss balls. I buy books by post from London.'

He thought perhaps she protested rather too much, but he said nothing, enjoying watching her slim fingers moving skilfully amongst the tools and ingredients, imagining them exploring his body…

He crossed his legs and told his errant imagination to behave as Miss Chancellor lifted a bottle from a shelf, sniffed it and poured a good measure into a pan, then pushed a sugarloaf and some snips towards Giles. 'Can you break some off, please?'

'What about a husband?' He began to hack pieces of sugar off and dropped them into the mortar that Miss Chancellor had brought from the dresser.

'Why would I want one of those?' She found the pestle and began to grind up the sugar lumps, peered in, clearly decided there was enough, tipped the results into the saucepan and began to stir.

'Er… All the usual reasons?'

'A desire to give up my independence? A wish to put my fate into the hands of a man?'

'Children? Protection? Romance?'

'Children? The parish is full of little ones who need help and education. Protection? I have my pistols. Romance… I wonder what you mean by that, Lord Missenden? And, no, do not attempt an explanation because I assume it is a euphemism.'

'You are a cynic,' Giles observed as the smell of hot brandy wafted across the kitchen.

'A realist. Women—or ladies, at least—are expected to ignore reality. I prefer to face it. I value honesty.' She hesitated. 'I do not find parties and crowds agreeable. Perhaps I am shy, but I prefer to find real friends, slowly.'

She said it lightly, with a smile, but there was a shadow that seemed to cross her face like a summer cloud darkening a sunlit meadow for a few seconds.

Giles suppressed the instinctive wince. He was one of the people who had sent her into exile, even though it had been through carelessness, not malice. If he had stopped to check, to wonder, then he might have protected her from the uproar. Women she thought were her friends had used her, he had neglected to protect her, her relatives had pushed her off to the country to prevent embarrassment. *Their* embarrassment.

Was she as shy as she said? Julia Chancellor seemed straightforward—assertive, even. But then they were hardly in a crowd and she'd had her anger with him to carry her past any initial awkwardness.

He had scraped through enough scandalous incidents to know that the memory of the *ton* was short. Along came another 'outrage' and society's short-lived attention swooped off to feast on that. Provided one did not upset a leader of fashion then it was possible to recover from almost anything.

It was harder for young ladies, of course. Any suggestion of sexual impropriety, of a loss of virtue, and they were marked for life—or until parental influence or money could buy them a husband. But there had never been any suggestion of that kind of thing in this case and he would wager a guinea to a groat that if Julia Chancellor had left London for a week or so, then returned and kept her head down, it would all have blown over.

While he brooded she took the pan from the heat and went into the scullery, returning with a bowl of carrots.

'Your parents,' Giles began.

'They died when I was seventeen, of influenza.' From the very lack of expression in her voice as she began to scrape the carrots at the sink, he guessed that had caused her a great deal of pain. 'I went to live with my only close relative, Aunt Hermione, but with a year of mourning I did not come out until I was almost nineteen and I knew virtually no one.' She tossed a carrot into a bowl. 'I was your typical wallflower, I must confess.'

'A wallflower?' She was well bred, intelligent and, to his eyes at least, an attractive woman. Had *all* the men failed to notice her?

He must have sounded sceptical because she chuckled. 'You find that hard to believe? I was both shy and inclined to say what I thought when I did speak. Not the most desirable combination, as was made very clear to me whenever I made an error.'

Another carrot followed the first and bounced off the rim of the pot into the air. Giles caught it and got up to drop it into the water. 'Your aunt seems to have reacted very strongly,' he remarked, puzzled. He leaned one hip against the dresser and stood by to catch more flying vegetables.

'I suspect it was a relief to get rid of me, to have an excuse to say that she had done her duty, but that I was not fit for society. I was an expense, I was awkward and she had two daughters of her own to bring out.'

Giles tried to imagine his own mother behaving like that towards an orphaned female relative and failed. But it did explain the prolonged exile: How could she go back with no respectable lady to sponsor her? 'How did you come by this charming cottage?' he asked.

'The late Lord Carnhurst, who has a house about five miles away, found himself with a superabundance of female dependents about thirty years ago and built this row of cottages to house them. According to local gossip he felt five miles was an adequate distance to be safe from female nagging. It became known as Spinsters' Row as a result, but as the ladies passed away his son sold them and they all went to either widows or spinsters of moderate means. My second cousin Prunella owns this one, but she is living with her invalid younger sister in Bath, so she let me have it.'

A carrot splashed into the pot, splattering Giles with water. The force with which that had landed said rather more about Miss Chancellor's feelings than her bright tone did, he thought. 'Shall I chop these?' he offered. It seemed the safest thing to say.

Chapter Three

Really, for a heedless rakehell Lord Missenden was proving to be an exemplary house guest, Julia decided when he took himself off to his bedchamber with the sheets she had been airing in front of the range. He had maintained a flow of unexceptional light conversation throughout supper, he had dealt with the fires, brought in more wood and wiped the dishes she washed, although she would have been amazed if he had ever been called on to do such a thing before.

Should she have offered to make up his bed? No, she concluded, that was too intimate a service and they appeared to have established a very pleasant, safe-feeling neutral manner between them.

He appeared to have forgotten the shocking nature of his arrival and she managed not to think about it for quite a few minutes at a time. With one last check on the fires Julia filled an ewer with hot water from the copper and followed him upstairs, snuffing candles as she went.

The staircase rose from the back of the hall to the rear of the wide first-floor landing which divided the house in two. At the front the landing ended in a window with a view out over the Vale and on either side at the front were the two main bedchambers with the maid's room, a linen store and box room at the back.

Light shone from under the left-hand door and she could hear the flap of sheets and the pad of feet as Lord Missenden wrestled with bed-making. A muffled curse made her smile as she opened her own door. With the door closed the only sound was the soft sough of the wind in the chimney and the crackle of the settling fire.

Julia set the ewer on the washstand, drew the curtains on the snowy darkness and banked up the fire before she glanced at the door again. Should she lock it? She was alone in the house with a stranger, so that was the prudent thing to do. She began to turn the key, then stopped. If she locked herself in, then she was thinking that Giles Darrowby was a danger and she had absolutely no proof that he was anything but a gentleman.

'I am not some nervous peahen,' she said aloud. 'And if he does try anything then I shall shoot him.' She had not been exaggerating about the loaded pistol in the bedside drawer. Burglars were a real threat—chance-met noblemen who did the washing up and chopped carrots seemed far less of one. She left the door unlocked.

Rational decisions did not necessarily make for peaceful slumbers, she found after half an hour of pummelling her pillow. An attractive young man in the house, let alone one who had displayed his impressive anatomy in its entirety, did not make for tranquil thoughts.

What would all that hairy skin feel like? How hard were those muscles beneath it? She had seen nude male statues in museums and in engravings, of course, but they had all been smooth white marble and equipped with modestly placed fig leaves. It was difficult to imagine a fig leaf that would have ensured Lord Missenden's modesty, she thought with an inward flutter that was more than mere curiosity.

Julia hauled the quilt up over her ears and admitted to herself that what she was feeling was a quite disgraceful desire to put her hands on the man and have him put his on her.

Which is what you get for living the life of an old maid when you are not yet twenty-three, she scolded herself. *It is a natural feeling. You just have to keep it under control. And go to sleep.*

* * *

It was the stillness that roused her, she re-alised after a moment lying blinking into the darkness. She was completely awake. The wind had dropped and the lack of sound was almost a physical sensation. Julia sat up and saw that the fire had burned down to a red glow, casting just enough light for her to get out of bed and light her candle on its hot embers. She banked it up with fresh coals, then parted the curtains. Outside it was dark, her view blocked by the old holly tree that grew outside, but she could see a sprinkling of stars above its jagged crown. It had stopped snowing.

Her toes were cold on the bare boards, but her slippers were by the fire and were warm when she put them on. With her unglamorous quilted robe belted firmly around her waist, she opened the door and padded out on to the landing. What time was it?

The comforting heartbeat of the ancient long-case clock in the hall sounded loud in the still-ness.

Tick, tock...tick. Pause. *Tick, tock...tick.*

She would creep down and make a cup of tea, well sugared to make up for the lack of milk, she decided. Then some instinct made her glance at the long window at the front of the landing and she caught her breath. Outside the snow was dazzling white and bright under the starlight and she could see, far away in the Vale, the twinkle of lights from the scattered farms and hamlets.

There was a battered old ottoman that she used for storing smaller linens standing in front of the window to form a seat and she went to it, all thoughts of tea forgotten as she sat down and gazed out on to a white wonderland.

Giles Darrowby moved so silently that the first warning Julia had that someone was behind her was the feeling of warmth from another body close at her back.

'Magic,' he breathed.

'You can see better here.' Julia moved to make room for him beside her and he moved around the ottoman, furling the counterpane from the bed around him as he sat.

She glanced down, saw he was in stockinged feet and caught a glimpse of the livery breeches. 'Did I wake you?' she asked, almost in a whisper.

'I heard a board creak and thought I had better check in case it was not you or that heavy-footed cat.' His voice was as low as hers, both of them, it seemed, instinctively unwilling to break the silence. 'It looks as though we are suspended in space with stars above and below. Why so many lights? It is past two.'

'In weather like this most cottagers will keep a lantern burning. You never know who might be out there lost in the snow and needing a guiding light, or one of the family might have to go out to tend to animals.' She snuggled down further into her robe, stilling suddenly as her elbow brushed his.

'Here, keep still or you'll let the warmth out.' He shrugged out of the quilt, then wrapped it around both of them.

'Lord Missenden—'

'Giles, I think, under the circumstances.' There was amusement in the low murmur.

'What circumstances?' she asked warily.

'The fact that we are huddled under a quilt at two in the morning watching the stars, Julia. First names are appropriate—the etiquette books are quite clear on the subject.'

'And you would know?'

She felt, rather than heard, his amusement at her sarcasm.

'Of course I do. I am a viscount, after all, a pattern book of correctness. I am not going to bite or anything else undesirable. Lean on me and we can both stay warm.' But when she stayed where she was he made no move to touch her.

'There's the moon,' she said. The merest sickle of silver hung amid the stars. It was the final touch of otherworldly beauty and her resistance melted at the sight. Julia lifted her feet so she was curled up on top of the ottoman, propped against Giles's side, snug under the cocooning quilt.

She felt him shift to accommodate her, tug the cover closer around them both. His arm came around her shoulders, but then he was still again, a warm, strong presence. Her head tipped, came to rest on his upper arm and they sat in silence.

A barn owl drifted past, a great, lethal snow-flake on soundless wings, and Julia felt her eye-lids drooping.

'We are out of time, suspended like angels over the sleeping vale beneath us,' Giles murmured. 'Have you read the poem by James Montgom-ery? He's a Scot, I think. Someone should set it to music. *"Angels from the realms of glory, Wing your flight o'er all the earth; Ye who sang cre-ation's story, Now proclaim Messiah's birth..."'*

'Lovely. You can almost see them, all silver and gold feathers, descending through glory to earth. Imagine being able to fly.' She lost the words in a yawn.

'You can imagine it in your sleep,' Giles said. 'And with warm toes. We have gazed down like the angels too long, you are getting chilled. Up with you, Julia, go to your bed.'

She shrugged off the quilt, put her feet on the floor and, somehow, pushed away from the warmth of his body. 'Goodnight, Giles.'

'Goodnight, Julia. Sweet dreams,' he said as

her slippers tangled in the hem of the cover and she toppled back into his arms.

'Oof!'

He half-stood, caught her as she flailed, and their noses bumped, then their lips, an accidental, sliding, hot fragment of a kiss as fleeting as a shooting star.

It was over in a second as Giles set her on her feet and she fled for the bedchamber.

How awkward is this going to be, I wonder? Giles kept his back to the kitchen door, kept working on riddling the spent ash from the range and building up the fire again as the brisk click of feminine heels came down the stairs, across the hall and hesitated for a heartbeat on the threshold.

He did not have much experience with awkward mornings-after. None, in fact. If a lady invited him to her bed, he made sure to be out of it well before dawn. Not that he had been anywhere near Julia's bed, but she had been under his quilt and in his arms and then there had been that kiss. No, not a kiss, an accidental touch, that was all it was, he reassured himself.

An accident that left him with the tantalising memory of her taste, of the scent of warm female and the prim, sweet fragrance of lavender from her nightgown. An *accident*, so why was he feeling awkward about it this morning? It wasn't as though he had taken advantage of it, had hauled her back into his arms and kissed her until she was too dizzy to think what she was doing— which was what his body had been suggesting with some emphasis.

No, he had let her go, pretended it hadn't happened and had made his way back to his own chilly bed to spend a restless night thinking about icicles, cold porridge and gentlemanly behaviour.

Now the sensation of a critical glare between the shoulder blades had him fighting the urge to turn round and say something defensive. It had been an accident, nobody's fault, but a gentleman would accept the blame if the lady did not see it in that light.

Behaving myself is a thankless task, he grumbled inwardly as he straightened up with the ash pan in his hands.

There were certainly disapproving eyes fixed on him, but they were amber, not grey, and belonged to Fred, whose mood had clearly not improved overnight. Julia was standing just inside the door with a smile on her lips that looked as though it was fixed there by force of will. Her cheeks were decidedly pink.

'Good morning,' she said brightly.

So we are going to pretend that it didn't happen, are we? Fair enough. If she can rise above my arrival on her doorstep in a state of frostbit-

ten indecent exposure, I am sure she is capable of ignoring a clumsy buss on the lips.

Which left him with the unfamiliar problem of what to talk about with a respectable young lady in a situation like this.

Giles 'did' the Season, of course, with all its balls and soirées and masquerades. He attended house parties. He conversed with young ladies, danced with them, squired them about and indulged in very mild flirtation. He rescued wallflowers, dodged matchmaking mamas, kept on the right side of the Patronesses of Almack's and generally behaved like any twenty-six-year-old aristocrat who had no desire to either find himself leg-shackled or to scandalise society. Then he let off steam at the races, in the boxing saloons or at card play in the company of his friends. Of course, that might skate close to the edge of a scandal if they found themselves assisting at an elopement or disentangling a companion from feminine toils.

But how to converse with a lady under these circumstances? Society gossip hardly seemed appropriate. The weather was certainly not going to furnish them with much of a basis for chit-chat and they had exhausted the subject of the village and locality last night at supper. He could pretend that Julia was his sister and behave as though he and Lizzie were snowed up together.

But his younger sister would faint dead away at the thought of being without her maid, her morning chocolate and the shops, so that image was not helpful. *Pretend Julia is a man*, he decided. That was safe. Stick to the practical, don't swear, don't get close enough for the slightest risk of touching.

That worked until he actually looked at Julia. *Pretend. Act. Practical, remember?*

'Good morning. It hasn't started snowing again, I see. So what needs doing?'

'Breakfast first. If you could fill the kettle and set it over the fire, I will make a start. Bacon, egg and sausage with toast and preserves, I think. If you could open the door for Fred, he's got a box of sawdust in the wood store. I'm afraid he'll grumble at you because it is sure to be your fault that the ground is too hard to scratch in.'

That was prosaic and practical enough, Giles thought as he swung the kettle on its hook over the fire and clicked his fingers at the cat. 'Come on, sir.'

To his surprise Fred followed him, muttering under his breath, tail up like a standard. Giles left him to his shock, horror and outrage that the humans hadn't done anything about the snow and stepped out into the clean, cold, gasp-inducing air. Above, the sky was a clear and cloudless blue and a few yards away the edge of the thick beech woodlands that crowned the ridge pressed close, still covered in the golden-brown dead leaves that would not be shed until the spring.

A robin fluttered down and regarded him with an appraising black beady eye.

'I'll see what I can do,' Giles promised. 'Watch out for the cat.'

The frying pan was sizzling as he came back in and Julia was keeping an eye on it while holding bread on a toasting fork to the heat. Giles found butter and plates, cutlery and preserves, then went to pour boiling water into the earthenware teapot. 'Coffee?'

'In the pantry. That's where the sugar is.'

By the time breakfast was on the table it felt as though they had been working together like this for weeks, not just an hour. As Giles reached across to take the weight of the frying pan his hands closed over Julia's and they landed it safely on the table, then separated, he to heap the toast on to a plate, she to pour her tea, his coffee. So much for not touching, he thought, and smiled ruefully to himself. Was he such a cockscomb that he thought this practical woman would be undone just by the touch of his hand?

'What amuses you?' Julia asked as she untied her apron and sat down.

'The fact that I can help in the kitchen without creating havoc.' That was true as well.

The look she gave him was a mixture of teasing and approval. 'I may not have you making pastry yet, though.'

More relaxed now, Giles tackled the food with appreciation, washing down the savoury saltiness with half the coffee. 'I promised your robin I'd take him something.'

Julia nodded. 'He knows I'll come with scraps and water,' she said as she got up and began to clear the table. 'Keep the bacon rinds and cut them up.'

She was no longer wary of him, Giles noticed as they moved around the kitchen, the cat weaving in and out of their legs as if they were engaged in some elaborate country dance, but she was distracted by something, judging by the flickering glances she kept directing at the back door.

'What is wrong?' he asked bluntly when he came back from breaking the ice on the birds' water and scattering bacon scraps, breadcrumbs and pieces of cheese rind.

'I'm worried about Dorothy, my maid. She is staying at Bluebell Cottage, the last one in the row that way.' Julia gestured towards one wall. 'Miss Jepson and her sister Miss Margaret are both quite elderly and it is their only maid who is expecting a baby. There's Molly, the scullery maid, as well, but she's only twelve and they are training her up.'

'I recall you said the baby was due soon?'

'After Christmas. I just hope…' She bit her lower lip as her voice trailed away.

'Where's the father?'

'Will was a thatcher and he was killed in a fall just a week before they were going to get married. Then Annie discovered she was expecting. The ladies are being very good about it—I suspect they are looking forward to having a baby to fuss over.'

'First babies are often late,' Giles said with an authority he was far from feeling.

'How do you know that?'

'I helped deliver one once. Not a first baby, but it came up in conversation.'

'*You* delivered a baby?' Julia stood, apron half-untied, and gaped at him.

'Didn't have much choice. I was visiting my gamekeeper who had a badly broken leg and his wife went into labour a week early. I sent my groom for the doctor, but it took him an age, leaving me the only adult on their feet in a household of four children under ten. Mrs Wilmore told me what to do, I did my best not to make a complete pig's ear of the business and Wilmore was able to add a bouncing son to his tally. By the time the doctor arrived I was feeling as though I needed his attentions more than the mother did, to be frank.'

He sat down. 'Makes me shake just remembering it.'

'Goodness, I *am* impressed.'

'I didn't have much option, really,' he said ruefully.

'Yes, you did.' Julia placed the apron on one side and began to put on a shabby long-skirted coat. 'Many people would have simply ridden away, women as well as men. *Just the gamekeeper's wife*, they'd have said. *She's fortunate that I sent for the doctor.* They might have felt moved to pay his bill, I suppose, but that's all.'

It felt uncomfortable being praised for something he'd felt he had no choice over. It felt strange to be praised for *anything* worthwhile that he'd done, if he was honest with himself. Viscounts tended to be admired for their title, their wealth, their looks, their style—and the rucks and riots that they kicked up to the amusement of the bored *ton*.

'Where are you going?' he asked in an effort to turn attention away from himself.

'To see how thick the snow is between us and Bluebell Cottage. I don't like to think of them being alone now and Dr Hemmingway will never be able to get here if the baby starts to come before the thaw.' She unhooked a vast sacking apron from behind the door and wrapped it round herself, then pulled out a dresser drawer and began to rummage through a heap of knitted items. 'There's a path right along the back of all of the cottages and it is usually more sheltered.'

'It is deep. You won't get through. Let me come and dig.'

'You will ruin your boots,' she said doubtfully as she pulled on a pair that were exceedingly battered and looked as though they were more suited to one of the village boys than a lady.

'That would be a blow,' Giles agreed. 'But not as bad as the knock my self-esteem would take in your eyes if I abandoned the inhabitants of Bluebell Cottage.'

'And that matters?'

Yes, it does. I liked that warmth in your eyes when I told you about the baby. I like the trust you showed me last night. You wouldn't be so trusting or approving if you knew how much I want to take you in my arms and kiss you until you forget about robins and babies and stranded spinsters...

'Of course. I do not want to find myself out in the snow again with the doors locked against me.'

'You've got no overcoat.'

'I'll get warm soon enough. Are there spare gloves and scarves in that pile?'

Chapter Four

Giles seemed to be amused and surprised by her practicality, Julia thought, puzzled a little by that. After all, he knew she had been a country-dweller for almost two years. He had tried to protest when she had trundled the first barrowload of snow to tip on to the lawn beside the house, but had only shrugged when she had pointed out that the space was too narrow for him to turn it easily himself.

While he filled the next one she took a stiff brush to the cleared section, then sprinkled on cinders from the ash can, in between leaning on the broom and admiring the sight of a tall, fit man using his muscles. Giles might not be used to manual labour, but he clearly did not spend his time lounging about with his feet up either.

Of course, she had seen him without a stitch, but that had been from the front and she had been too surprised and embarrassed to do more than take a fleeting glance. But even dressed, from the back the view was admirable.

And I am a perfectly healthy female and surely I can admire what is in front of me?

Then Giles stuck his spade into the piled snow and straightened up, his hands in the small of his back, groaning as he stretched.

'You are almost at the boundary wall,' Julia called. 'It is only about three feet high.'

'Halfway, then?' Giles asked without turning and attacked the snow in front of him until there was the clang of metal on stone.

'Just about.' She dropped the handles of the empty barrow and wriggled to his side through the trench he had cut. 'There are rough stone steps, careful.'

The shovel hit something hard again and Giles began to scrape snow off the stones that projected from the face of the wall, then cleared the flat top.

'I am having a rest.' Julia climbed up, folded the thick tails of her coat under her and sat down on top of the wall. 'There is smoke coming out of two chimneys in Bluebell Cottage. See?'

Giles stood close and craned. 'So someone is up and about.' A whir of wings made him laugh as the robin landed just a foot away on top of the wall. 'Your friend is back.'

Julia peeled off one glove and dug in her pocket

for the crust of bread she'd put there. 'Keep still, I am trying to get him to eat from my hand.'

The robin watched as she crumbled the bread and slowly extended her fingers towards it. Beside her she could feel Giles, stock-still, the warmth of his breath misting in the cold air to mix with hers.

For a moment she thought the two of them together would frighten it, then the robin hopped forward and on to her fingertips, his claws sharp, his beak sharper as he pecked. It tickled and Julia laughed. The robin took off almost vertically, she jerked instinctively and knocked into Giles.

It was not a hard blow, but he sidestepped and his boots, not made for walking on hard-packed snow, slid under him. With an oath Giles skidded and toppled backwards into the snowbank.

'Are you hurt?' Julia hopped down from the wall.

'Only my dignity.' He stayed where he was, sprawled on his back, arms and legs flung out.

'You have preserved rather more of it than the last time you fell on your back in the snow,' she observed. 'At least you have your clothes on.'

'Unkind,' he said and held up his right hand.

Julia took it, prepared to pull, and was tugged forward to land beside him in the drift. 'Beast!' She flailed, sending snow flying as she struggled to sit up and get leverage to help her stand.

'I owed you that.' Giles was laughing as he

took her arm and flipped her over so she was lying on top of him, nose to nose. 'You are nice and warm and dry now.'

It was disconcerting to feel so much hard muscle under her, to feel the warmth of his breath on her face and to be looking so close into his eyes. She had thought them brown, but they were a dark hazel, she realised, flecked with green and gold.

She could remember the taste of him from last night and that fleeting, accidental kiss, and it was hard not to dip her head the inch it would take to sample his lips again. Julia picked up snow in her right hand, planted the left firmly on his chest and pushed as she dropped the icy whiteness on his face.

He should have let her go, that had been her plan. Instead Giles tipped her over until she was in the snow and he was poised above her.

'I should roll you over and over until you are nothing but a giant snowball,' he threatened.

'You wouldn't dare!'

'It is that or kiss you.'

'Oh.' That knocked the breath out of her.

'And I promised myself that I would do no such thing.'

'You did? Why?' The question was out of her mouth before she could think. It was a miracle that the snow wasn't melting to steam about them, she felt so hot and embarrassed.

'It would hardly be the gentlemanly thing to do, now would it?' he said, his voice mocking, the look in his eyes rather more serious.

'And it is hardly the ladylike thing to wish that you would,' Julia said. Where had those words come from? *Her* lips?

She was still wondering as Giles rolled again, pulling her with him so she lay along his body again, clear of the snow.

'You choose,' he suggested as she stared at the crease his half-smile produced at the corner of his mouth.

We are lying in a snowdrift. Surely nothing too awful can happen in a snowdrift, can it? Men don't seduce women in three feet of snow...

Julia lowered her head and let her lips brush against his.

Just a touch, only a taste, like last night...

The touch lingered as his mouth moved under hers, as his tongue stroked against the swell of her lower lip. She felt herself sink down against his chest, no longer tense, and his arms came round her and they were kissing.

It was extraordinary, so intimate, so intense, so...trusting. Julia had wondered what it would be like. *Wet* and *embarrassing* had come to mind even as she had found herself looking at the mouths of attractive men and wondering. There was certainly moisture involved and heat, but strangely it was not at all embarrassing.

Something cold and wet slithered down her cheek and she realised they must be sinking, or perhaps snow was falling on them, but somehow she couldn't care, lost in the heat of the man who seemed to surround her.

This was magic. She could hear bells ringing…

'Miss Chancellor! Oh, Miss Chancellor, please!'

Clang. The sound of a handbell being shaken violently.

Julia sat up with a jerk, provoking a grunt of discomfort from Giles as she elbowed him in the chest. 'What the—?' He floundered to extract himself from the drift into which they had sunk and sat up beside her.

'It is Dorothy, my maid, the one who went to help at Bluebell Cottage. Something must be wrong.' Julia got to her feet and stumbled to the wall. She could see the top half of Dorothy, auburn hair vivid against the whiteness, one arm waving while the other kept swinging the bell.

'Stop making that noise!' Julia shouted. 'What is wrong?'

'Oh, miss! It's the baby. It's started.'

'Oh, hell,' Julia said, and almost sat down in the snow again as Giles stood beside her. 'We will never get the doctor here, or the village midwife, not in this. How deep is the snow at your end?' she called.

'Couple of feet, miss. I could start to clear it. Can you get through?' Dorothy was eighteen, a tall, strapping county lass used to helping out with the cows and the haymaking. She could certainly make an impact on the path while they dug towards her from their deeper end.

'Yes, we can get to you,' Julia shouted back, hearing the edge of panic in Dorothy's voice. 'Although what I am going to do when I get there...' she added to Giles. 'But of course—you know exactly what is needed. Oh, thank goodness.'

'I helped an experienced mother with her husband there, who also knew just what to expect,' Giles protested, even as he clambered over the wall and began to dig again.

'We have both got common sense, you have some experience, Dorothy's a practical girl, for all her nerves about it. We'll manage,' Julia said firmly, more to convince herself than Giles. 'There really isn't any other option.'

They soon got within ten yards of Dorothy as the level of the snow began to lower in the shelter of taller trees and the cottage.

'Give me the spade and you go and change your clothes,' Julia said. 'You are soaking wet.'

'I'll finish this.' Giles kept hold of the shovel.

'You will be no use if we deliver the baby and you come down with pneumonia.'

'And there I was thinking you were worried about my well-being.' Giles handed her the spade and turned back.

I've offended him, she thought, then caught the ghost of a laugh as he vanished down the path behind her.

What sort of gentleman has a sense of humour about being made to dig snow, about being interrupted in the middle of a kiss and about being dragooned into assisting at a childbed?

One I rather like, Julia concluded as she dragged her sodden glove across her tingling mouth and began to dig again.

It was easier to focus on each foot of snow in front of her, on placing each shovelful well out of the way, on looking up and smiling encouragement at Dorothy than it was to ponder on what exactly she had done, kissing a man she was stranded with. No one could get through this snow down to the village, which meant they would have to spend another night together.

Or no… If they reached Bluebell Cottage, then she could stay there, leave Beech View to Giles. The thought should have been a relief. Of course it was.

No more star-gazing. No more kisses.

'Give me that and you go and get changed as

well,' Giles said from behind her. He made her jump and she dropped the shovel, turned and hurried back along the path, back to the warmth and away from those all-too-perceptive eyes, those tempting lips.

'Good morning!' Giles called when he saw the red-headed young woman stop shovelling to stare at him.

'You gave me a fright, sir! Didn't see you for that big drift on the bank.'

'You must be Dorothy. I am Giles Darrowby, stranded in the storm yesterday.' Her eyes widened and, before she could start speculating about just where he had spent the night, he added, 'I gather we have a baby to deliver.'

'Yes, sir, that we do. But there's no doctor.'

'That's all right, I'm…er…experienced with childbirth.'

'Oh, Dr Darrowby! Heavens be praised, you're a miracle and no mistake. I'll run and tell them, they'll be so relieved.'

'Did you just tell her that you were a doctor?' Julia demanded, arriving back at his side. She had changed into a dry gown, he noticed, seeing the dark blue skirt below her wrapping of shawls and a long scarf. Her blue mittens matched and for some reason that made him smile.

'I implied it. If it stops them panicking and keeps the mother calm, it can only help.'

'I suppose so. But what if there are complications?' She bit her lip and shot him a rueful smile. 'I should not borrow trouble, should I?'

'We probably have enough already,' Giles agreed with a smile. 'If there are complications, they will happen whoever I tell them I am. A dozen more spadefuls and we will be through.'

He thought he heard her sigh and glanced down, the snow balanced on the blade of the shovel. Julia's face was tense, her lower lip caught between her teeth. She looked well kissed and he knew he should feel guilty, but all he was aware of was disappointment at the interruption.

'Frightened?' he asked, hoping that his own anxiety was not showing.

'Terrified,' she admitted. 'But that's not going to help. Come on, Dr Darrowby.'

The Misses Jepson were in the kitchen, one talking soothingly to a scrap of a child who was peeling potatoes at the kitchen table, the other clearly about to go out of the far door with a pile of clean linen in her hands. The elder stood up, a formidably tall woman with a face that, unfortunately, somewhat resembled a horse. *But an amiable horse*, Giles decided as Julia introduced him.

'This is Giles Darrowby, Miss Jepson. He has been stranded by the storm on his way to the village. Mr Darrowby, Miss Jepson and Miss Margaret Jepson.'

Miss Margaret, the younger sister, was shorter, plumper and prettier with blue eyes and thickly waving grey hair, rather out of control in contrast to her sister's tight coiffure. 'We are so thankful to have your expertise, Doctor. Or perhaps I should address you as *Mister*. That is correct with surgeons, is it not? I have never quite understood the etiquette of it. One would not wish to give offence—'

'None taken, ma'am. Mr Darrowby will do excellently.' He cut her off before she could launch into the distinction between doctors, surgeons and apothecaries.

'And you are a man midwife?' Miss Jepson interjected.

'Er...no. That is not my speciality.'

I know more about breeding thoroughbreds and farrowing pigs, but you do not want to hear that.

'But I can assure you all the births I have attended have had happy outcomes for mother and child.'

All one of them.

'I will take you to your patient,' Miss Margaret said. 'We've had a bed set up in the small parlour on this floor. So much more convenient, we thought. Dear Annie, she has been so brave about everything.'

As if on cue there was a sound from the front of the house that sent a cold shock down Giles's gradually thawing spine. The girl at the table dropped her paring knife into the water with a splash.

'You are making a fine job of those potatoes, Molly.' Miss Jepson sat down again next to the child and began to talk about how they might be cooked for supper. Giles took a deep breath and followed Miss Margaret as she hurried out of the kitchen.

He looked down and saw Julia beside him. 'Where are you going?'

'I'm not leaving you to face this alone,' she whispered back and gave his hand a quick squeeze.

Touched, Giles fixed his most confident expression on his face, squared his shoulders and marched into the stuffy little parlour.

It was not as dreadful as Julia's ignorant fears had conjured up. No one told unmarried ladies anything about childbirth, but there were always whispers, murmurings that created imaginings at least as bad as reality, she was sure. Certainly having a baby was painful, messy and exhausting, and at one point, when Annie's grip on her hands felt as though it was crushing the bones, Julia had a fleeting thought that next time she was in church she was going to have a firm word with the Almighty about organising matters better. But after the first few hours she saw Giles relax slightly and when he murmured, 'Everything seems to be going just as it should, just as I remember,' she relaxed, too.

There was satisfaction working together on something as basic, as important, as this and she said so when they were resting by the window and Dorothy was sitting with Annie, talking quietly between contractions.

She wondered if Giles would understand what she meant, but he nodded immediately. 'I agree. It feels so...*essential.*' He smiled and shrugged ruefully. 'And it puts everything else that I think is difficult or important into perspective.' He reached over and took her hand. 'I am glad you are here.'

'But I know even less than you,' Julia protested, keeping her voice down in case the words reached the other two women. 'And if it wasn't for me, you wouldn't be here having to deal with this.'

'You are calm, you are practical and you do a very good job of seeming to believe in me.' He let his head fall back against the cushions and closed his eyes.

'That is because I *do* believe in you,' she said firmly. Her hand was still in his and she could tell he had not fallen asleep. Should she pull it away?

But she did not want to and his thumb was stroking back and forth against her palm as though he was absent-mindedly stroking a cat. It was pleasant, more than pleasant if she was honest, and if it helped Giles relax, would it not be selfish to be missish? The tingle the touch created seemed to travel to the most unexpected place and she shifted uneasily on her chair.

Then Annie gasped and Giles sat up, let go of Julia's hand and sat watching intently.

'Listen!' he said and all three women looked at him. 'Bells. It must be the church bells.'

'It is Christmas Eve, of course,' Julia said, startled to discover that she had completely forgotten about it. She went to the window and opened it, keeping the curtain drawn against the cold. 'The sound is carrying on this still air—I can hear more than one set in the distance as well.'

She closed the window again. 'A Christmas baby, Annie. What a wonderful gift.'

Annie nodded, then gritted her teeth while another contraction passed. 'Wouldn't want to do this in a stable,' she muttered, making them all laugh.

'I know, love, straw everywhere,' Dorothy agreed comfortably. 'I'll go and make a nice cup of tea, shall I?'

Chapter Five

The clock struck three as Julia closed the parlour door behind her and tiptoed into the kitchen. Miss Jepson was asleep, bolt upright in the Windsor chair by the range. Miss Margaret snored quietly from the depths of a battered old armchair and all that could be seen of little Molly was her tousled hair sticking out of the mound of blankets covering her on the settle.

Dorothy was slumped at the kitchen table, where she had retreated an hour since at Giles's insistence. Her head was on her crossed arms, her plait half-unravelled. Julia shook her lightly by the shoulder and whispered, 'Hush', in her ear as she sat up. 'Can you come?'

When they reached the hall she closed the kitchen door and leaned back against it. 'It's a boy. He's perfect and Annie is fine, although she's exhausted. Have you had enough rest to take over for a while?'

'Oh, thanks be.' Dorothy scrubbed her hands over her eyes and smiled. 'I thought you'd come to say it was still going on.'

'Mr Darrowby is just, um, tidying up.' Giles had pushed her out firmly while he dealt with things, which Julia considered was a quite noble level of heroism. 'I thought you and I could make the bed again and give Annie a wash and then she'll be comfortable enough to sleep, I hope.'

'And I'll sit with her,' Dorothy said. 'But I'll heat up some broth for her first. The two spare bedchambers are all made up if you and Mr Darrowby want to go and rest.'

The thought of lying down was so tempting that Julia swayed where she stood. 'In a while, let's just get everything straight and Annie and the baby settled.'

When she opened the door into the parlour Giles was propped against a bookcase, his face white with exhaustion. He had gathered all the soiled linen into one bundle, covered the various basins they had used and now was simply staring at the baby in its mother's arms as though he had never seen anything like it before.

Julia took his hand and tugged. 'Go upstairs, there's a bedchamber at the back for you. I'll bring you some tea as soon as we have made Annie comfortable.'

'Mmm.' He blinked at her. 'We did a good job, didn't we?'

'Yes,' Julia agreed. 'We did.' It had been terrifying at times when it was hard to pretend that they knew exactly what they were doing, to stay calm and cheerful for Annie's sake. Giles had been a rock, staying throughout while sending Julia and Dorothy off in turns to rest. 'I do not know what we'd have done without you.'

'I couldn't have done it without you,' he said at the same moment and grinned at her, almost too tired to lift both corners of his mouth.

'Bed.' Julia pushed him towards the door. 'Up one flight, there are two rooms at the back.'

He straightened, nodded and went out as Julia turned back to the everyday miracle they had just helped happen.

'What will you call him?' she asked Annie when the young woman was settled with Dorothy curled up in the armchair to stay with her through the rest of the night.

'William for his pa and Giles for Mr Darrowby and Julian for you, miss, if that's all right.'

'That's more than all right.'

Ridiculous. I am not going to start weeping now.

Julia tiptoed out and collected a tray of tea and plum cake from the kitchen and found the older ladies waking. They were jubilant when they heard the good news.

'We'll just peep in at them, bless them, before we go to bed. And we're keeping you from your bed in your own cottage,' Miss Margaret said, patting her arm as she stood aside to let her go upstairs with the tray. 'It is very good of you, dear. An imposition, I know, but we feel so much better knowing you and Mr Darrowby are in the house.'

'It is no trouble at all, Miss Margaret.' Julia balanced the tray carefully on her way down the shadowy landing. 'Goodnight.'

Neither of the sisters had asked about 'Mr Darrowby's' sleeping arrangements the night before, nor where he was going to stay tomorrow night, she noticed. Either they were exceedingly tolerant in their views or they were such an innocent pair of spinsters they simply did not think about such things.

One door stood ajar and she pushed it with the tray, expecting to find Giles sitting beside the fire. Instead he was sprawled face down on the bed, snoring gently. He had taken off his coat early on in the afternoon, but other than that, he was fully clothed down to his boots.

Should she wake him up, persuade him to at least take off his footwear? Perhaps better to leave him, he would wake up enough to make himself comfortable in a while, surely. She left a cup of tea and a slice of cake on the nightstand and tip-toed out to the other spare room.

Someone had left a robe at the foot of the bed, so she undressed except for her shift, put on the robe and went back to set the door ajar. If Dorothy needed help, she could be with her without having to worry about dressing.

There was a grunt and a mutter from the room opposite and she hesitated, half-turned back. What if Giles had fallen off the bed? He had been so tired...

She went across the landing again and looked round the door to find that he had turned over and was lying on his back, his boots now on the pristine white coverlet. Julia went in, took one firmly in both hands and tugged. It slid off easily and Giles did not wake. Emboldened, she pulled off the other and set them to one side of the bed, then shivered. He was going to become chilled, lying on top of the covers like that.

Julia pushed, one hand on his shoulder, the other at his hip and Giles turned to the other side of the bed with a protesting mumble. She rolled up the covers behind him, went to the far side and pushed again. Goodness, a full-grown man was heavy. He was boneless, it seemed, a dead weight, but finally he was over the top bedding on to the bottom sheet. Now all she had to do was pull the covers up over him and he'd be snug for what was left of the night.

Off balance, panting, she had half-straightened up when a hand closed firmly around her wrist and tugged. Julia toppled gracelessly on to the bed and Giles's arm dropped heavily over her waist, pinning her down. He gave a grunt of what sounded like satisfaction, but the next moment he was breathing deeply and evenly again.

She should struggle, wake him up. But he was exhausted and he was fully clothed. What was the harm? No one would come into the room without knocking, surely?

The bed was comfortable and warm and the presence of the man breathing softly beside her was oddly comforting. And unsettling. But Julia knew she was bone-weary, all she had to do was close her eyes…

Twenty minutes later she found sleep was completely eluding her. She couldn't try punching the pillows or turning over, not without wrestling herself free of Giles's arm. She tried breathing deeply, but that didn't help. And counting sheep was futile. The stupid things just milled about in their fold and refused to jump fences or even walk in a countable line.

Julia opened her eyes and stared up into the darkness and tried to let her thoughts settle, drift away from babies, the fears and joys of the night, an unsettling desire to burrow closer to Giles and the worry about what the neighbours might think about her when they discovered he had spent a night in her cottage. But her mind would not rest and it gradually began to dawn on her that this inability to sleep meant something and what that was. She was no longer content to stay here in Spinsters' Row in her cosy exile.

Not that it was exile, she realised bitterly, wondering if exhaustion had been what was necessary to clear her mind. *I had run away. I was shy and awkward and not happy, then people I thought were my friends betrayed me and so I ran. But I am not going to run any more.*

The resolution was clear and plain in her mind. 'I am finished with hiding,' she mumbled to herself as her eyelids finally began to droop.

She found she could relax against the warm body next to hers. Making that decision was what she had needed to finally let go.

Julia woke to the sound of bells and early, rosy light streaming across the foot of the bed and blinked, trying to remember where she was and why.

It is Christmas Day, I helped deliver a baby last night, I kissed a viscount in a snowdrift and I have made a resolution about my life. My goodness.

Then she became aware of the bed dipping towards the middle and the fact that someone was breathing in her ear and that the viscount in question was no longer in a snowdrift, but in bed beside her.

Her startled gasp must have woken him. 'What the— *Julia?* What are you doing in my bed?' Giles sounded surprised, but not upset by the discovery.

Perhaps, she thought, *he is used to waking up with women.*

At least he had remembered her name.

'I pulled your boots off last night and tried to get you under the covers and you pulled me into the bed and trapped me.'

Giles hauled himself up against the pillows, grimaced and pulled off his coat, then dropped it on the floor. 'That's better.' He looked down at her quizzically 'Why didn't you wake me?'

'Because I would have had to ring a handbell in your ear to do that,' Julia retorted. 'You were deeply asleep. I hadn't the heart to wake you and it was all quite respectable, you are fully clothed, after all.' She sat up, too, and managed an insouciant shrug. Perhaps not quite insouciant enough, judging by Giles's expression.

'Your idea of *respectable* is quite different from mine, it seems. What if someone had come in?' he demanded. 'Then where would we be?'

'Miss Jepson and Miss Margaret would never enter someone else's bedchamber and if Dorothy had come in, I would have explained. She is very discreet.'

'Oh, well, in that case, good morning, Julia.' Giles rolled over and took her in his arms.

It was a leisurely kiss, one that took its time to stray from her lips to her cheek, to her ear to her eyes—which had inexplicably closed themselves—and back to her lips via another exploratory nibble at her earlobe.

After a while, by which time Julia thought that she was becoming much less clumsy in kissing Giles back, it did occur to her somewhat hazily that perhaps this was not wise. Or prudent. Or possibly not even decent. No, definitely not decent.

Unfortunately, by that time Giles seemed to have lost his neckerchief—Julia suspected she had something to do with that—and his shirt was untucked from his trousers and her hands had found their way under it.

The skin of his back was warm and smooth and dipped into the line of his spine and he made a most satisfactory growling sound when her fingers traced down, vertebra by vertebra, to the waistband. She wriggled closer and her dressing gown slipped from her shoulders and now she was immersed in the heat and the scent and the feel of the man in her arms. Or was she in his arms? But it was of no matter because his mouth was trailing kisses down the slope of her breast and then his lips found her nipple and sucked through the thin cotton of her chemise and there was a shriek and she realised it was her.

Giles sat bolt upright, hair tousled, shirt hanging loose, eyes dark and wild. 'Oh, hell.'

Oh, hell? Julia kicked at the bedding and scrambled off the bed, furious to discover her legs were like jelly, angry with him, angry with herself. *Oh, hell? That is the first thing he says after kissing me and...and whatever that was?*

'You, sir, are no gentleman.'

It was a good parting line and it would have been even better if her feet had not become tangled in the trailing sash of the dressing gown so that she tripped, fell against the door, jerked it open and banged her way out before realising that she was making enough noise to rouse the entire household.

There was the sound of feet hitting bare floorboards in the room she had just left and Julia fled into her own room and closed the door just in case Giles was rash enough to pursue her.

The bed was close, but she shied away from it instinctively and took refuge on the window seat, where the cold penetrating the glass was enough to banish the last tendrils of sensual fog from her brain.

What was I thinking?

She hadn't been, of course. She had been re-acting.

The little clock that was ticking on the mantel-piece gave a sharp *ting* and she looked at it. 'Oh, no. Quarter past nine.'

She jumped up, shivered her way to the wash-stand, splashed chilly water about as quickly as possible and got dressed in all the layers she had before she brushed her teeth. Was everyone downstairs listening to doors banging and feet thumping from room to room? What if they had heard that shriek of alarm? And of delight, she had to admit.

All the other women in the house were in the kitchen, Julia discovered when she ran down-stairs, not delaying to do more than plait her hair. Some armchairs had been dragged in from the parlour along with a low sofa and Annie was lying there holding the baby. Dorothy seemed to be cooking a belated breakfast and Miss Jepson was sorting through a pile of tiny fluffy blankets. Of Giles there was no sign.

No one looked at her with disapproval or spec-ulation. Perhaps they had heard nothing or as-sumed that Giles was simply a noisy riser.

'Good morning. How is Master William Giles

Julian Smith?' She went and marvelled at the perfection his mother demonstrated—tiny hands, fingers with a vice-like grip on Julia's, blue eyes and a shock of dark hair on his head.

'Breakfast won't be more than ten minutes, now you're up, miss,' Dorothy said. 'We were going to have ours, seeing as how you were so late to bed, and make yours later, but I'll just add some eggs and bacon and another spoon of tea in the pot. Is Mr Darrowby coming down?'

'I have no idea,' Julia said, wondering if she was blushing as much as she feared. 'His bedchamber door was closed when I came past just now. I'll lay the table, shall I?'

She escaped into the scullery, where Molly was counting out cutlery into piles with her tongue stuck out between her teeth to help with the calculation required. When Julia felt less hot and bothered—and managed to stop wondering whether it was the lingering after-effects of Giles's caresses or embarrassment—she found the plates and carried those through to set by the range to warm.

'Good morning, ladies,' Giles said, choosing that moment to arrive when her back was to the door, which made her jump and almost drop the marmalade jar and sugar bowl she was putting on the table. 'I do apologise for sleeping so late.'

There was an immediate chorus of protests. Mr Darrowby deserved to spend the day in bed having his meals brought on a tray after his heroic efforts the day before, Miss Margaret declared. Her sister worried that they had no steak because gentlemen did like their steak and he probably needed it after his exertions. Annie exhorted little William to see who had just come in, which made him howl, and Molly dropped the toast rack.

It at least gave Julia an excuse for looking flustered. When they were finally all seated and Annie provided with a tray, she managed not to look at Giles by dint of concentrating on buttering her toast and cutting into the excellent bacon. Thankfully, with all the chatter from Miss Margaret, there was no need to make conversation.

'You will stay for Christmas dinner, of course,' Miss Jepson pronounced. 'We have a fine goose.' She did not wait for a reply, but turned to say something to her sister.

'I—' What did she want? Julia realised that she had no idea. The longer they stayed at Bluebell Cottage, the sooner Miss Jepson, with the worry about Annie relieved, would realise how very strange it was that Giles had been in Julia's house.

On the other hand, if they went back to Beech View, then she would be alone with Giles and, however much she might trust him, she was not at all certain she trusted herself. Not after the way she had felt in his arms in the bed upstairs. However hazy she still might be about her future, becoming any man's mistress was not among her plans.

Perhaps wealthy, sophisticated ladies might manage discreet liaisons, but she was neither wealthy nor sophisticated, she was well aware. And how did one cope after such a relationship ended, as presumably it must? It was difficult to imagine wanting to experience such intimacy with a man for whom one did not have deep feelings. And of course, how could one feel more than liking and attraction after just two days? To imagine anything deeper was ridiculous.

Chapter Six

'Julia?'

She stared at Giles blankly across the breakfast table.

'You have just dropped your toast into your tea.'

'I— Oh, goodness, so I did. I was momentarily distracted.' As she mopped at the pool of liquid with her napkin she looked more than distracted, she looked positively distressed.

Which is all my fault, Giles thought bitterly as he got up to fetch a cloth from the sink.

For the moment, the other women had all their attention on the baby, who was gurgling and kicking in what was clearly considered to be an endearing manner.

He sat down and handed the cloth across the table to Julia, who took it with a muttered word of thanks and without meeting his eye. Which was not surprising. Now she was wide awake he was amazed she hadn't hurled a teapot at his head. Or perhaps she was trying to behave as normal because she did not want to alert her neighbours to what had just happened. *Almost happened.*

You, sir, are no gentleman.

The words stung and he knew they were justified. He had found himself in bed with a virgin and protesting that he was half-awake was absolutely no excuse. Arguing that she had been willing was even less of one.

Eventually the interminable meal dragged to an end. Giles attempted to help clear the table, was firmly repulsed by Miss Margaret and retreated to the range.

'Miss Chancellor, should I perhaps go along to your cottage and make sure that all is well? The fires will have gone out and the house will become very cold.'

Julia put down the dish she had been returning to the dresser and straightened her back. The effort it took to look at him was palpable and cut as much as her angry reproof had. 'What a thoughtful idea, Mr Darrowby. I will come with you.'

'But you will come back,' Miss Jepson urged. 'You will join us for the rest of the day and dinner?'

'Yes, thank you, I would be delighted,' Julia said with a very creditable smile.

'I do appreciate your offer of hospitality, but I had best make my way down to the village,' Giles said. The sooner he removed himself from Julia's company the happier she would be, he was certain.

'There has been no thaw,' she said. 'It would be a very dangerous thing to attempt.' Her chin tilted up and she met his gaze. 'For absolutely no purpose.'

He could read no encouragement in those grey eyes. Presumably she was attempting to convey the message that if he came too close he might expect to encounter a rolling pin at the very least.

'We can discuss it while we are checking your house,' he said before the ladies picked up the tension that was sending prickles down his spine.

Julia nodded and began to layer on her outdoor clothing.

They walked in silence back as far as the dividing wall. 'May I—?' He hesitated, unsure whether he should physically help her up.

'Yes, of course, thank you.' Julia seemed surprised that he needed to ask and showed no awkwardness when Giles lifted her, his hands around her waist, until she could sit on top of the wall and swing her legs over. She jumped down and waited for him, her head cocked on one side, looking so much like the robin that he almost laughed. 'What is wrong?' she asked.

'This morning. I wanted to come out to apologise, as much as anything.'

'So did I. I should never have said that you were not a gentleman. But honestly, how *could* you?'

'How could I kiss you? And apparently pull you into my bed and take even worse liberties. Saying that I was half-asleep is no excuse, is it?'

Julia, who had begun to walk towards Beech View, stopped so abruptly that he almost cannoned into her.

'That? I cannot blame you for that. I could have protested, only I did not want to wake you, and to be honest, it was lovely to go to sleep like that, so warm.' She turned away, but not before he saw the colour in her cheeks. 'And I enjoy kissing you, it would be hypocritical of me to pretend that I do not.'

'Then why were you so angry with me?'

'How would *you* have liked it if it had been me who had stopped and said, "Oh, hell", might I ask? You could not have sounded more horrified to find me in your bed than if you had rehearsed for a week.'

Giles regarded the back view of the infuriating woman as she stamped off down the path they had cleared towards her own back door. He contemplated either sticking his head in a snowdrift or going back to bang it on the wall and finally strode after her.

'That was because I *was* horrified,' he said as he caught her up. 'You are an innocent, virtuous lady. You know perfectly well what the consequences of my taking that innocence would be.'

'You mean you would have to marry me? But who would know?' Julia had reached the door to the lean-to, unlatched it, went through to the kitchen door and opened it to reveal a swearing, ginger furball that resolved itself into one large, affronted cat. It gave them a withering stare, then stalked off.

'Oh, for goodness sake, Fred, you had food, you had water, you could get outside. Anyone would think that you had been abandoned to starve.' Julia shed gloves and a scarf and went to the range. 'I think this is still alight. Yes, it is, thank goodness.'

'Confound the cat and the range, too. Do you mean you do not want to marry me?' Giles demanded, throwing hat, scarf and gloves on top of hers. Had he gone mad, talking about marriage of all things? He had not really compromised her, even if it had been a near-run thing, and he had absolutely no desire for a wife, not for years. 'Why not?' he demanded, discovering that he was indignant. 'I am perfectly eligible. I'm comfortably off, I've a title and estates—'

'And a well-developed sense of your own value,' Julia retorted, reaching for a poker and riddling ash out of the grate with some force. 'On the plus side of the scales, I will admit that you kiss very nicely and that you were exceedingly good with Annie and the baby last night. Your title and wealth are of no concern to me whatsoever. On the negative side of the balance is the fact that on both the occasions we have met you were engaged in some madcap, and outrageous, scheme with your friends. Forgive me, but even if I were in the market for a husband, which I am not, you do not appear to be much of a bargain for a woman who cares more about a relationship than a title.'

Giles bit his tongue on the various retorts to that which came to mind, turned on his heel and went to get an armload of wood and a bucket of coal.

Kiss very nicely, do I? And so do you, Miss Chancellor, and I would very much like to stop this conversation and resume where we were a few hours ago.

His sense of self-preservation was adequate to stop him seeing what would happen if he followed his inclination, even though Julia had never once rejected his kisses.

He should have been relieved that she had dismissed his offer so easily, of course. The single life held many attractions and why would he choose a lady of such obscurity when he did decide to settle down? Yet the sensation he was feeling now felt uncommonly like disappointment. It was simply hurt feelings, no doubt.

'You do not *want* to marry?' he asked, stacking the logs by the range and trying to ignore the ache under his breastbone. Every single lady wished to marry, surely? 'Why did you do the Season, if that is the case?'

Julia stopped riddling the grate and sat back on her heels, looking at him as though he had just asked a difficult, but intelligent, question and she was having to wrestle with the answer.

'Because everyone assumed I would. That I must, I suppose. And so did I, even though I was painfully shy and frightened about being in London when I hardly knew a soul. We had led such a quiet life you see, my parents and I. There were lots of friends, but no one very grand, no big parties where status and getting things right mattered one bit.

'I told myself that people would be kind and I wanted to make friends and see the sights and go to the theatre and the bookshops and some parties. But all anyone was concerned about was who was related to whom and how attractive one was and which men were the best catch.' She wrinkled her nose. 'I wasn't pretty enough to stand out and

I certainly was not well connected and I think I was terribly gauche. Certainly I was naive.'

Julia stood up and shook her head at him when Giles started to protest that she was exceedingly pretty. 'You really do not have to, you know. I do not want reassurance or flattery. But I have come to realise that I took my aunt's vapours about my so-called ruin as an excuse to escape and I ran away. But now I am older and know what I want, I can manage things to suit myself. I see now that my aunt is not the only person who can organise my life in London, because I have money of my own, enough to employ the services of someone to introduce me about. I have heard there are several ladies of good family who are short of funds and are only too glad to help someone to maintain appearances. In exchange for a consideration, of course.'

She scooped up Fred and began to scratch behind his ears. 'That is so, is it not? I am sure if I asked my cousin in Bath she would be able to recommend someone to me.'

'Yes, it is so,' Giles agreed unwillingly, finding a corner of the kitchen table to lean against while he looked at her. He could think of half-a-dozen youthful widows who were only too happy to supplement their straitened income in that way. But Julia had suffered one bad experience in Lon-

don already, he had no desire to see her fall foul
of the gossip and sharp tongues again.

'I thought so,' she said with a nod of satisfaction. 'I should have done that, gone back and enjoyed the Season on my own terms and not been
such a coward as to seize on an excuse to hide.
After all, if one is not seeking a husband—and
they all seemed such a gamble—then one can do
what one wants. Theatre, libraries, exhibitions,
shops, concerts. The occasional small party, pic-
nics, perhaps. I have no ambition to attend the
grand balls.' Fred began to purr and hung limp in
her grasp like a vast, weighty fur muff. 'I do not
think I would enjoy the high-flown parties at the
very top of the tree. They must be such a strain.'

It had never occurred to Giles that they might
be, but then he had never spared a thought for
the feelings of the young ladies herded like nervous sheep into the arena to be judged on their
looks and their manners, their breeding and their
dowries.

And condemned and pitied if they fall short.

'They can be, I imagine,' he agreed. 'Here,
give me that dratted cat, he must weigh a stone.
Shall I feed him?'

'If you would.' Julia dumped Fred in his lap
and the cat glowered at him. Giles was in no
mood to back down to a feline with delusions of
grandeur. He stuck Fred under one arm and went

to investigate the larder, ignoring the growls and grumbling.

From the kitchen Julia continued to talk as though she was working out a plan from the beginning, rather than explaining her intentions to him.

'If I find that it answers, then I will hire a small house in a respectable district and employ a genteel companion to lend me countenance. I could come back to Spinsters' Row in the height of the summer, or even visit one of the seaside resorts.'

There was a pile of meat scraps in a bowl under a saucer and Giles took them out and dumped them on to Fred's plate, set it down and stacked up some broken timber in the corner while he was crouched down. 'Julia, do you want that small wooden box and that broken cask in here?'

'No, not at all. I was going to use them for kindling. Why?'

'Just an idea.' There had been some tools in the lean-to, tidily hanging on the wall above a bench. He picked up the box and one of the cask ends, a perfect wooden circle. 'May I use your tools?' he asked, retrieving his hat and scarves.

'Yes, of course.'

Julia was standing in the middle of the kitchen, lost in thought, and he wondered if she had even heard him properly.

'Don't you want to marry *anyone*?' he asked, one hand on the latch of the back door.

Perhaps one day I might find a gentleman I like and who likes me and then, with no pressure from anyone else, I could make up my mind about marriage. But I am not going to take advantage of a man I like rather too well, just because he feels he ought to offer for me.

'Oh, I shouldn't think so,' Julia said lightly. 'And certainly not for the sake of it and not because of circumstances.'

Giles made an ambiguous noise and went out into the lean-to with his odd armful of wood.

Some aspects of marriage did seem desirable… Julia glanced at the door and then hastily away. Very desirable and tempting, but dangerous for a single woman. She shivered. It had been a narrow escape that morning: not from Giles but from her own sensual desires.

If she did ever find someone else… She stopped that thought dead in its tracks. If she found *someone*, the theoretical gentleman would not be an aristocrat, of course. That was aiming too high and, in any case, if there were any unattached ones around of the right age there was something wrong with them, no doubt. She looked again at the door. Or even if there was not, they would be rackety, high-living lords putting off matrimony until a suitably well-bred, well-dowered lady came along and the passage of time and the need for an heir forced them to do their duty.

Like Giles. Lords are all very well for kissing, what you need, my girl, is a nice rural dean or perhaps a country doctor...

Julia checked through the house, performed a few housekeeping tasks, trying very hard not to think about Giles Darrowby and what might have been if she had succumbed to temptation and accepted his very dutiful, and doubtless most unwilling, proposal. She liked him, she found him intelligent and amusing and good company. He had been wonderful with Annie and the baby, patient with Miss Jepson and Miss Margaret and their anxieties. And he stirred something deep and wonderful inside her that she wished had remained undisturbed.

But, she told herself as she came back downstairs with her hands full of handkerchiefs that she had edged with lace and lavender bags that she had filled in the summer, *I will not settle for anything other than a love match like Mama and Papa, and I do not care if that makes me hopelessly unworldly and provincial. How awful to be married to a man who felt trapped into it.*

'What's wrong? Are you cold? You shivered,' Giles said as she entered the kitchen.

'You made me jump! What are you doing?'

Giles was sitting on the rug in front of the range, rasping at something with a file. 'Making a cradle for the baby. I saw that Miss Jepson had a pile of little blankets and so on and I think they were looking for a drawer to make a bed in, but this would be better, don't you think?' He sat back and she saw that he had cut the cask lid in half to make rockers and secured them under the box.

'Oh, how clever! How on earth do you know how to do woodworking?'

'From the estate carpenter. I used to haunt his workshop as a lad, especially when my tutor was planning a Latin lesson. Not that this is anything very complicated.' He set it rocking. 'No joints to dovetail. If you've got something like an old blanket to cut up we can line it. I found some round-headed tacks out there which would fix it safely. How do you come to have so many tools?'

'Dorothy's brother is a carpenter and he stores some of his things up here. I'll find a blanket, there's sure to be one in the scrap box.'

They cut and pleated the blanket, which was a soft cream wool one, banged their fingers hammering in the tacks, created a thicker pad for the base and finally leaned against each other with a sigh of pleasure at the result.

'That is surprisingly satisfying,' Giles said. 'Master William should be snug in that.'

'Such a good idea of yours,' Julia murmured,

finding that it was also surprisingly satisfying to lean against Giles's shoulder and share their small triumph.

He reached out and set the cradle rocking on the worn rag rug. 'I will feel like one of the kings, bearing gifts,' he said with a chuckle.

'Which reminds me, I have some presents to wrap. Only handkerchiefs and lavender bags, but if the ladies are entertaining us to dinner, I thought I should take a token. There should be a jar of sweets in the larder. I'll wrap those up for Molly, I'm sure she'll prefer them to sensible handkerchiefs.'

She began to get up, but Giles was on his feet first and offered his hands to help her. It was difficult to let go once she was standing, hard to move away from him. It was just his warmth in a room that was chilly despite the banked fire, she told herself. That and a reluctance to break away from the emotional warmth that working on the cradle together had generated.

They were quite still, only touching where their hands clasped, yet she felt as though she was naked, skin to skin with him, her every nerve, her every thought, bared.

If he kisses me now I will not let him stop. If I just take one step forward...

Chapter Seven

Giles drew a deep breath and Julia released his hands before he could move or speak.

'I've some silver paper in the dresser somewhere.' She talked as she searched, covering the sudden awkwardness. 'And some ribbon in my sewing basket. I can make these trifles look quite festive, I think.'

Presents. Focus on gifts, not on that moment just now when all I wanted to do was to melt into the arms of the man behind me. I still do.

With an effort she made herself think about the fact that it was Christmas, that they were expected back at Bluebell Cottage in a few minutes.

Presents.

But she had nothing for Giles, unless…

She looked thoughtfully at the larder door and mentally reviewed the contents. Yes, the very thing. And exceedingly warming for a man who ended up in snowdrifts with remarkable regularity. If she could just get him out of the house for a while.

'Giles, could you go into the front garden and cut some holly? Ours has got much better berries than the bush in Bluebell Cottage garden.' As soon as he was gone with a pair of small shears she went to the larder and searched the racks under the stone slab. Yes, one last bottle of ginger wine remained, although *wine* was perhaps too mild a description for its fiery potency. The curate had become quite tipsy on two glasses last Christmas, even breaking into a most inappropriate popular song when he had called with the carol singers, involving a bishop, an ass and a passing milkmaid.

She swathed it in brown paper, added some very masculine dark brown and orange ribbons, wrapped the bonbons for Molly along with a length of hair ribbon and put them in the bottom of her basket under the silver-paper-wrapped parcels. She was just in time before Giles came in with an armful of holly, thick with blood-red berries.

'That is perfect, thank you. If you put it into this sack, we can carry it without getting pricked.'

'There is something in the front garden I want to show you,' Giles said, as he wrestled the holly into the sack.

Julia followed him down the hall and out of the

front door and stood looking out over the view from the top step. 'It is becoming cloudy over the Vale. Perhaps rain is coming from the west.' The clouds were massing, heavy and grey, but without the tint to them that spoke of snow, and the wind held rather less chill than it had first thing. 'Yes, I think a thaw is coming. And then you can escape,' she added as she followed him down towards the gate, crunching through his footprints.

Giles came to a halt under the bare branches of the old apple tree that, in the spring, showered anyone entering the gate with pink and white blossom. 'Yes, I could,' he agreed, his voice expressionless. 'A fine old apple, this.'

Julia nodded, wondering why he wanted her to look at her own tree. 'It still bears a small crop, despite its age, and the thrush sings from the very top of it. I think he likes the view.'

'Look up high, on this side. I don't expect you can see it from the house.'

Julia moved round to his side of the trunk and tipped her head back, squinting through the tangle of branches. 'It really needs pruning. Oh! Mistletoe.'

They were standing very close and she clutched at his arm to steady herself, dizzy from looking upwards, but Giles did not move. When she lowered her gaze to meet his eyes he was watching her, his gaze dark and intense. 'Mistletoe is always a good excuse to snatch a kiss at Christmas, but I do not want to snatch, Julia. Nor do I want to beg or to present you with a decision that will cause you worry. We are skating on thin ice, I think, and I can hear it crack every time we touch.'

He shook his head, as though exasperated with himself. 'Now we are standing here I regret bringing you out to see the mistletoe. I should have had more self-control because something is happening and I do not know whether it is simple proximity or Christmas magic or something more, but—'

Julia went up on tiptoe, hands on his shoulders, and pressed her lips to his, sealing in the words. Giles kissed her, his mouth moving over hers, gentle yet intense, their breath clouding the chill air between them. She did not want to think, did not want to hope or wish for more than this. Dare not, because this was surely founded only on starlight and snowflakes.

And ice cracking beneath us.

'Julia.' He stood looking down at her and she wanted to cry, or to run away or to reach up and pull his head down again.

'Julia, dear! Mr Darrowby! Yoo-hoo!'

The front door opened and there was Miss Margaret, bundled up like a multicoloured snow-woman, Miss Jepson peering over her shoulder. 'Oh, do forgive us for coming through the house like this, but we became anxious when you did not return. The snow is so treacherous and there are so many ditches and hollows.'

Her sister came past her and down the steps into the front garden. 'We came armed with our shovel and broom in case you needed help.'

They stood together, beaming at the pair under the tree, and Julia conjured up a bright smile from somewhere. 'I am sorry you were anxious. I had some domestic matters to arrange and we were just gathering some holly, the tree has such good berries. I thought you might like some cut for decorations at dinner. But we are ready to come back now.'

They all trooped back into the house. Julia checked Fred's water and took the basket of presents, Giles threw the remains of the blanket over the crib and picked it up under one arm with the sack of holly in his free hand and set off towards Bluebell Cottage, Miss Margaret at his heels.

Her elder sister held back a little and good manners compelled Julia to slow her pace. 'Such a considerate and pleasant young man, the Viscount,' Miss Jepson remarked quietly.

'Yes,' Julia agreed, then stopped dead. 'You know who he is?'

'I recognised him—he is the image of his father, whom I knew years ago in London, and of course I know that the family name of the Viscounts Missenden is Darrowby.'

'Er…' Julia racked her brains for something to say.

'And it was a godsend that he was here last night, although how he came to have midwifery knowledge I cannot imagine. Or is he simply a very good actor?'

'He helped the wife of one of his gamekeepers in an emergency. He thought that a little knowledge and a calm manner might help matters.'

'It most certainly did. And you know him well?'

'Not at all. We had never met before. He took refuge with me when he was trapped by the heavy snow.'

They stopped and watched as Giles helped Miss Margaret over the wall and the two walked on, apparently talking about the woods, from the gestures Miss Margaret was making.

'What a strange collection of clothing—I could swear that is a livery coat and breeches with the buttons changed.'

'Yes, it is.' Julia made herself smile and wondered if the Spanish Inquisition was any easier to deal with. 'What he was wearing when he arrived was completely wet and he was very cold.'

'Quite. You will forgive me, my dear, but you have no mama to advise you—young gentlemen of the aristocracy, however pleasant, do have a somewhat cavalier attitude to female virtue on occasion.'

'I assure you, Lord Missenden has done nothing to alarm me,' Julia said, praying the cold was keeping the blushes from her cheeks.

'You may not have been alarmed, but, forgive me, only one bed was slept in last night,' Miss Jepson said drily.

Oh, Lord, I should have thought to make the beds...

'Yes. Lord Missenden fell asleep fully clothed, exhausted. I looked in, went to pull off his boots, which did not wake him, sat down to adjust the covers and I must have dropped off, too. It was all perfectly, um, proper.'

They had reached the wall and Julia lifted her basket over, then turned to help the older woman. Miss Jepson stayed where she was, mittened hands clasped together, a look of determination on her face. 'That is as may be, but he had already spent one night under your roof, had he not? My dear, the Darrowbys are high in the instep, as the saying goes. There is no doubt of what is the right thing for him to be doing now, but one cannot rely on the nobility to always take that attitude with ladies who are not quite their equal in rank, particularly if those ladies are unprotected, as you must appear to him to be.'

Julia stopped, well short of the gate to Bluebell Cottage, and waited for Giles and Miss Margaret to disappear into the back yard before she spoke, schooling her tone into a calm reasonableness with an effort. 'I do appreciate your advice and warning, Miss Jepson. But as nothing at all untoward occurred and as no one but you and Miss Margaret know of the circumstances, I cannot feel that there is anything more to be said. Lord Missenden will be on his way as soon as it thaws sufficiently for him to reach the village.'

The older woman sighed, then climbed over the wall. 'It would be a very fine match, my dear,' she said as they entered the yard.

'I cannot contemplate life with a man on whom a marriage has been forced by duty and obligation.' Julia found she was losing her temper. 'And I do not care even if he should be a duke!'

'Who is a duke?' Giles opened the back door for them, then closed it on the cold as they hurried inside.

'Oh, simply a figure of speech.' Julia set down the basket and began to unravel her scarves and coat. 'Where are Annie and the baby?'

'Asleep in the parlour. Miss Margaret is making up the cot with the little blankets and coverlet that she and Miss Jepson have been making.'

'It is delightful,' Miss Margaret announced, standing back with a flourish to display the crib.

She set it rocking. 'See what clever Mr Darrowby has contrived, Caroline.'

'Most ingenious. And what a good idea to bring holly, Julia. We have been so much distracted by anxiety about Annie that we have neglected to decorate the house this Christmas. Why do you and Margaret not create some arrangements in the dining room and light the fire in there? I think we should all take our Christmas dinner in style this year and if Mr Darrowby would be so good as to move the sofa in there once Annie is awake, then she can join in as well.'

'Of course.' Giles picked up the log basket and the small hatchet for splitting kindling. 'I'll bring in wood before it gets dark, shall I?'

'Most kind, Mr Darrowby,' Miss Jepson murmured. She hesitated and he glanced at her, arrested by a look of indecision on her face that seemed out of character. 'Mr Darrowby, you will not hurt her, will you?'

He almost said, *Who?* But there was no need, really, they both knew whom she was talking about. 'I have no intention of doing so,' he said stiffly. 'Miss Chancellor will come to no harm through me.'

'I do not mean physical harm,' Miss Jepson said, blushing slightly. 'I mean her feelings.'

The hatchet slipped through Giles's fingers, landing with a thud and just missing his toes.

He set the log basket down and straightened up to his full height. 'I can assure you, ma'am, I do not trifle with a lady's feelings.'

'I am sure not. Not intentionally. But she watches you when she thinks you are otherwise occupied. And you watch her and I do not think it is simply because you are a man and she is an uncommonly attractive young woman. But of course, she is doubtless beneath your touch—I do know who you are, my lord, although I think it would be best if the other members of the household are in ignorance of the fact. Things slip out, however careful one is about gossip.'

She means well. She wants to protect Julia, Giles told himself as he fought the desire to administer a sharp set-down. *But... I watch Julia? I look at her in such a way that an observer thinks I might be more than simply attracted? And she looks at me?*

'I am sure you are mistaken, ma'am, but I thank you for your concern for Miss Chancellor.'

He picked up the hatchet, tossed it on to the log basket and made as dignified an exit as a viscount who has just been lectured on his duty by a spinster could, his mind in as much of a stir as his emotions.

There was something to be said for the chill of a log store in the depths of winter—it was certainly calming. Giles leaned against a sawhorse and tried to sort out his feelings. He was attracted to Julia, but any man would be—she was attractive, intelligent, good company and she made him laugh. She was kind to her friends and independent in her attitudes. And when they touched he could feel that ice cracking—or perhaps hear a fuse fizzing.

He had certainly felt he should make the offer of marriage, even though he had no wish to be leg-shackled, and he had felt something that was more than piqued pride when she refused him so flatly.

Thwarted desire, he told himself.

But did that add up to what Miss Jepson had been implying? He made himself think the word. *Love.* Surely not. No one fell in love in two days and after a few kisses. That kind of thing was for folk tales and romances.

Giles was still brooding on Miss Jepson's words and their implications as he moved the couch for Annie into the dining room and set a low table beside it so she could eat her dinner. Master William—fed, changed and blowing bubbles in his sleep—was snug in his cradle beside the hearth.

He tried to study Julia without not only her noticing but also without Miss Jepson's eagle eye on them. She seemed natural enough, he thought, wondering how one told if a woman was in love with you. Or if you were in love with her, come to that.

But, he argued with himself as he took in the tray laden with cutlery to set the table, *if Julia loves me she would have agreed to marry me.*

She distracted him by coming in with a large copper jug brimming with holly and trails of ivy which she set down on the sideboard. 'I do admire your skills as a footman. Perhaps it comes with wearing the livery,' she suggested, teasing as she rubbed at a smudge on the belly of the jug with her sleeve. 'I am certain that you have never laid a table in your life before.'

'I am quite capable of observing how it is done,' Giles said, refusing to rise to the bait.

She laughed and leaned across him to tweak a table napkin into perfect order and he caught a hint of her scent, something herbal and citrusy, and his body stirred.

'Oh, Giles.' She straightened up on a sigh and smiled at him.

'Yes?' It was curiously hard to breathe.

'This is nice, isn't it? No formality, kind people, the baby.' She looked across at the crib and her smile softened into something tender. 'So perfect for Christmas.'

'Yes, perfect,' he agreed as Miss Margaret bustled in with a stack of plates, singing a carol, very slightly out of tune, under her breath.

And it *was* perfect, he realised. Perfect despite the ache in his chest and the turmoil in his mind and the lack of privacy to talk to Julia. Or perhaps to kiss her and make love to her until she admitted that she loved him and he would know whether he loved her because, just at that moment, he had no idea and to make a mistake over this would be cruel indeed.

The goose was perfect, thanks to Dorothy's skill with the unfamiliar range. There were potatoes, roasted golden brown, and carrots drenched in butter and an interesting dish made of dried peas and a cabbage that was made very palatable with the addition of an excellent gravy.

Giles insisted on pouring some of Miss Jepson's brandy over the plum pudding and setting it alight, despite her protests that it was for medicinal use only. The resulting blaze made Molly shriek with delight, waking William and reducing Julia to helpless giggles as Giles almost set the tablecloth on fire.

Julia looked at Giles, fighting both blazing pudding and his own laughter, and wondered if her heart would break when he left. It felt as though it might. There was a dull, miserable ache beneath the happiness and joy of the present moment. She told herself to live in that moment, hold it tight for the memories, and managed not to let the tears of laughter turn into anything else.

They ate the pudding and then sat nibbling on cheese and nuts despite everyone protesting that they were quite full. Julia helped Dorothy carry out the dirty dishes and brought in her basket of presents and shared them round.

'I've nothing for you,' Giles said. He poured out two small glasses of the ginger wine and they sipped as they sat back and enjoyed watching the others opening their gifts and exclaiming with pleasure.

Julia looked at him and wondered at how serious he looked. Almost sad, she thought, puzzled. 'You made the crib and you cut the holly and you dug the path so we could all be together at Christmas,' she said. 'And we shared the stars. That is more than enough.'

Giles looked down and she saw she had, quite unconsciously, put her hand over his on the table. He tightened his fingers around hers for a moment, then, with a glance at Miss Jepson, released her.

'Is that rain I can hear?' He stood up and went to the window, drew back the curtain and they all heard it, the sound of heavy rain battering against the panes. 'The thaw has broken with a vengeance.'

'That's a blessing,' Miss Margaret said comfortably. 'It will make the most terrible mess, of course, and the snow looks so pretty, but the wild birds and animals will find it easier to feed with the soft ground and the roads will be open, after a fashion.'

'If they aren't waist-deep in mud,' her sister retorted. 'And the streams will overtop their banks, I've no doubt.'

The intensity of the rain increased as they cleared the table and went to the kitchen to all join in with the washing up, leaving Annie and the baby dozing in front of the fire.

'Have you an umbrella I might borrow, Miss Jepson?' Giles reached up to set the last platter on the dresser.

'Why, yes, there's that big one the Vicar left here last Tuesday.' She pointed to the object leaning against the doorframe like a large and tattered crow. 'But why should you need one?'

'Because I think it would be best if I went back to Beech View and looked after the cat and the fires tonight. Then I will set out in the morning as soon as I can assess the state of the path down to the village.'

'But Fred can perfectly well look after himself for the night, we left him plenty of food and water,' Julia protested. Behind her a door closed and she looked round to find that, unaccountably, they were alone in the kitchen.

'I need to go, Julia,' he said and something in his voice, the gentleness, stiffened her spine and her pride.

He thinks I am going to beg him to stay, she thought.

'Yes, of course. Your friends must be anxious and you will want to find out how successful your rescue plans were. It would be dreadful if, after all, the poor man was trapped into an unwanted marriage.' She said it firmly, with a smile on her lips, and was pleased at how steady her voice was. 'Don't forget your hat and scarf, and your gloves are on that chair over there.'

Giles pulled them on, threw the gaudy knitted scarf around his neck and picked up the flapping umbrella. He should have looked ridiculous. The breath caught in her throat.

'Julia—' He had one hand on the door latch, but still he looked at her.

'There are no stars tonight,' she said. 'The magic is quite gone.'

I have to let him go.

'So it seems. Goodnight, Julia, and thank you for rescuing a sad rake from his folly. I doubt I will see you in the morning.'

'Perhaps we will meet at a Royal Academy

view some time in the future if my plans come to fruition,' she said.

For a moment she thought he was going to step back towards her, take her hand perhaps or drop a kiss on her cheek, but Giles nodded and opened the door. Then he was gone, leaving just the darker mark of the rain on the stone of the threshold to show he had been there.

Julia took off her apron and folded it with great care, then went to find Annie to borrow the baby for a cuddle.

Chapter Eight

'*Meow.*'

Giles looked down to where Fred had hooked his claws into the cloth of his breeches. 'I have fed you. I have given you a fresh sawdust box. You are warm and your mistress will be home soon. I even put up with you sleeping on the end of the bed and snoring all night. What more do you want?'

The cat gave him a disgusted look, removed his claws and stalked off down the hall. Giles shrugged, let himself out and surveyed the depressing view in front of him. The heavy rain had been replaced by a steady drizzle from low cloud that shrouded the Vale like a sodden blanket. The snow had dissolved into muddy slush wherever it was not protected and the trees and bushes were bedraggled and dripping.

The prospect of the walk in front of him was not pleasant. Giles told himself to show a bit of backbone and set off down the path, using the stout stick he had found in the woodshed. The ice remained in treacherous patches and he had no intention of breaking a leg on the way down.

The damp air was still cold and that at least was welcome after the almost sleepless night he had passed. It was all due to that damned cat snoring, of course. He was doing the right thing and Julia's cool, smiling reaction as he left confirmed it.

There are no stars tonight.

And Miss Jepson, well meaning, interfering, wanted a good match for her young neighbour, that was all her words to him had been about.

He opened the gate without a glance at the apple tree and its hidden mistletoe and made his way along the lane. There was smoke rising from the chimneys of the other large cottages that he passed and at the end of the row, where the dwelling was more a house than a cottage, two men were clearing the front path. Giles hailed them and they came down to the gate. He glimpsed livery beneath their topcoats and scarves.

'Good morning. What is the best way down to the village, would you say?'

'Good morning, sir.' The taller one doffed his hat. 'Just along the way you are going and there's a bend and you'll meet the road. It's steep, sir, you'd best watch your footing, but it's a sunken lane and protected by the woods, and the snow doesn't usually lie deep.'

Giles instinctively reached for a coin to tip them, remembered he had none and trudged on. By the time he reached the first cottages at the foot of the hill he was wet, cold, bruised from falling, and feeling he had gone several rounds at one of the more stringent boxing saloons.

There were enough people around to direct him past the pond and stocks on the green to Beech House. He pounded on the door knocker and found himself face-to-face with an unfamiliar butler, presumably hired with the establishment.

'I'll thank you to go round to the service entrance, my man. I assume you've come for work clearing the snow.'

Giles decided he was tired of scratchy livery and carpentry, footman's duties and snow. He drew himself up and looked the man in the eye. 'I am Lord Missenden. Sir Felix is expecting me. I assume there is a room prepared and my luggage unpacked. I require a hot bath as soon as I have spoken to Sir Felix.'

Just over an hour later—bathed, warm, comfortable—Giles lounged in a deep armchair, surrounded by his four friends. From a room at the back of the house came the sound of feminine laughter and someone playing the pianoforte.

'So what happened?' he demanded.

Felix waved the others into silence. 'These idiots got down to the village as the roads became impassable, realised once they asked where they were that they had made a mistake and were sent along here. We had to assume you were safe enough, even if causing an uproar—the cottages up there all had lights in the windows, apparently. Anyway, to cut things short, Mrs Fanshawe was routed in no short order—rumours of my massive debts were more than enough to make sure of that. It seems she'd have put up with almost any kind of bad behaviour if I had money.'

'So where are they now?'

'Gone, first thing this morning as soon as the word came that the turnpike was clear to the next town at least.'

'So your sacrifice was in vain, old fellow,' Hal Woodley said with a grin. 'Did you cause a scandal? How's the frostbite? I do hope we haven't ruined your marriage prospects.' He stared at Giles. 'Now what have I said?'

'Nothing.' Giles forced a smile. 'I was taken in by kindly cottagers, warmed, clothed and fed.'

'It sounds as though you had the best of the bargain,' Woodley said. 'Felix is a wonderful host, no doubt about it, but dodging scheming females under the mistletoe is confoundedly wearing, you have to admit.' He gave an exaggerated shudder. 'We can all look forward to the New Year free of parson's mousetrap.'

'Yes,' Giles agreed. 'That's a welcome prospect.'

Five days had passed since Giles had left Beech View and walked down to the village. There had been no word, of course, but Peter and John, the footmen from Falconer's, the end house, reported seeing him on his way past and then added the news that Sir Felix Wheaton's party was still in full swing at Beech House and they were rumoured to be seeing in the New Year in style.

Miss Jepson and Miss Margaret dropped by to see her daily, so kind and concerned, without quite saying why, that Julia wanted to scream. They had hired help from the village while Annie was regaining her strength and so Dorothy returned to Beech View, bringing with her more news of Beech House, gleaned from a shopping trip down to Lower Bourne.

'They are doing themselves ever so well. Mr Poulton, the butler, says they brought crates of wine and brandy with them and he's had to place orders with all the local farmers because they've been eating so well. And Sir Felix brought a fancy French cook and there's some really pretty young ladies with lovely gowns, so I hear from Jen Potter, who helps in the kitchen. I wonder if they'll have dancing tonight, seeing as it's New Year's Eve.'

'I am sure they will,' Julia said, stabbing herself painfully in the thumb as she darned a pair of stockings. 'How pleasant for them.'

She insisted that Dorothy go down to the village in the afternoon before the light went to see in the New Year with her family. 'I have been invited to Bluebell Cottage,' she reminded her.

When the clock struck eight she dressed in her blue-velvet evening gown and did her hair, feeling that she was putting on armour against the kindness of her friends. She was certain they had guessed she had fallen in love with Giles and they sincerely pitied her for it, even as they made careful remarks about wild young aristocrats, their habit of toying with helpless females and the importance of preserving one's reputation at all costs.

I am not a helpless female, she thought rebelliously as she fastened her best pearl necklace around her neck and put on her pearl earrings. *And I love him. And if I had thought he loved me... But he did not or he would have said so and he would not have gone.*

'Wouldn't he, Fred?'

Fred, his eyes fixed on a promising hole in the skirting board, ignored her, although he did condescend to come downstairs and join her by the fireside as she waited for the clock to strike eight, the time when Julia would make her way along to Bluebell Cottage.

The rattle of the front-door knocker took her by surprise. Her heart was beating uncomfortably fast, she realised as she stood and picked up a candlestick. The last time the knocker had sounded Giles was on her front step in a state of nature, poised to set her comfortable little world on its head.

But, of course, this would be a message from one of the other cottages—good wishes, no doubt, or a small seasonal token. She opened the door wide, a smile on her lips, and froze.

The man standing in front of her was the same, but this was undoubtedly Lord Missenden the Viscount, hat in immaculately gloved hands, his broad shoulders supporting a fashionable caped coat open to give a glimpse of a crisp neckcloth and silk waistcoat.

There ought to be words, some kind of polite social remark or perhaps a lightly turned joke about history repeating itself, but she could only stare at him until she finally managed to croak, 'What?'

'I have come, Miss Chancellor, to invite you to see in the New Year at Beech House.'

'But… I am promised to Bluebell Cottage.'

'Sir Felix's carriage is already there. I explained to him that I owed the ladies hospitality, so they, and Annie and the baby, will be conveyed down in comfort. The staff at the house are eager to meet young William.' As he spoke a carriage drove past, heading back towards the lane to the village.

'But…' It seemed the only word she could manage.

'I can only offer you a curricle, which seems a rather chilly choice for the last night in December, but I have come to tell you, Julia, that the stars are out again. I think we can see them better in the open.'

'The stars?' She put out a hand and drew him into the warmth, closing the door on the cold night.

'The stars and the magic. There is something I very much want to say to you, Julia, and I want to say it in the starlight. Will you wrap up warmly and come with me? I had to leave you before I could understand what I was feeling, you see, and I am hoping you will forgive me for that.'

Suddenly she could move, could speak, could feel. 'Yes, I will come and, no, there is nothing to forgive because I needed time to think as well.'

He waited patiently while she ran to find her cloak with the fur hood and her muff and gloves, set the guard around the fire and told Fred to be good, then he took her arm as they walked down the path, a little slippery with frost. But there was no need, she thought, her feet were floating above the ice.

The curricle was at the gate, already turned, two horses patient in the shafts. Giles helped her up, then drove in silence to the lane and turned uphill. 'I found this viewpoint, right over your chimney tops,' he said as he reined in.

'Oh.' The view was breathtaking, as clear as it had been that night they had looked out from the window. But they were higher now and the sky was a bowl of black velvet above them, spangled with light.

'The stars are back, Julia, and I do not think the magic ever went away.' Giles dropped the reins, but the horses stood still. 'I did not understand how I felt, only that it was an ache in my heart and, when I left you, that the ache became torment. My friends were joking about wild plans and adventures, about avoiding parson's mousetrap, and I realised that all I wanted was to be with you, to start building something wonderful for the rest of our lives. I love you, Julia. Will you marry me?'

There was no need to think, no room for doubts when the sincerity was warm and true in his voice.

'Oh, yes, Giles. I love you so much and I thought it would be so wrong to marry you.'

Then his arms were around her and he was kissing her, holding her so close that she could feel the beat of his heart. How long they kissed, she had no idea, but then the curricle moved and Giles released her as he found the reins. 'I should not keep them standing in this cold. Or keep you out in it either.'

'No. Let us go down and let them go to their stable. The magic will come with us, I think.'

'Now that we've found it,' Giles agreed, 'I do not think it will ever leave us.' He linked his left hand with her right and drove downhill towards the lights and the laughter and a new year filled with love and magic.

* * * * *

CHRISTMAS WITH THE MAJOR

Laura Martin

For Jack and George,
there's nothing better than your smiles
on Christmas morning.

Chapter One

Cecilia pulled the collar of her riding habit up further around her neck and shivered. It had been snowing when she'd left Whiteburn Hall, but instead of the blizzard-like conditions that were raging now it had been more of a gentle flurry. Something she'd been convinced she could ride twenty miles in easily.

Cursing loudly, in language her guardian would most certainly not approve of, Cecilia squinted through the snow. It was still at least five miles to the Crawleys' home, her planned destination, and there was no way either she or her horse would make it in this weather. Images of her frozen body being found when the snow thawed popped into her head and quietly Cecilia grimaced—that fate would still be better than the one her guardian had planned for her.

She shivered, looked back over her shoulder and deliberated. It was fifteen miles back to Whiteburn Hall and no doubt if she ever arrived there safely she would spend the entirety of Christmas locked in her room as punishment for trying to flee. Or five miles to the Crawley house, where her oldest friend would have a warm welcome and a few days of happiness before Cecilia had to return to reality.

Her decision made, she pushed on, but her horse, Lady Bea, had only taken a couple of steps when she stumbled, slipping on an icy patch.

Immediately Cecilia jumped down, soothing the horse and checking her over as best she could in the poor light. There didn't seem to be any obvious injury, but she knew it was reckless to push on with her journey, in either direction. The only sensible thing to do would be to look for shelter until the morning.

Taking as much care as possible, she remounted and pressed Lady Bea to continue, picking the safest route through the thick snow. Every minute that passed the visibility worsened and the wetness seeped through her clothes just a little more.

She almost cried out in relief when she saw the outline of a building ahead of her. Whatever it was, whoever owned it, surely they wouldn't begrudge her a safe haven for the duration of the snowstorm?

The little cottage came into focus as she moved closer and Cecilia was surprised to find it was strangely familiar. Only when she was almost at the gate did she realise it was Rose Cottage, one of the many properties that made up the Crawley estate. When she'd been young and had spent a few summers with the Crawleys, exploring every corner of the estate with her dearest friend, Elizabeth, they'd visited the cottage. It had been empty then, used as an occasional place to house guests when they had a large number visiting. It still looked empty now, but Cecilia didn't mind. As long as it was warm and dry she could cope with not having a roaring fire to sit in front of.

Quickly she dismounted, leading Lady Bea to the shelter at the back of the cottage. It only had space for two horses, but Cecilia was pleasantly surprised to see fresh hay and a clean stable. Her fingers numb, she saw to Lady Bea as swiftly as she could before turning towards the cottage.

'Please, please, please,' she begged as she tried the front door. It was locked, as was the back door. And all the windows. With her spirits sinking she felt around the doorframes for easy spots to hide a spare key with no success.

Later she would tell the Crawleys that she spent a long time deliberating, but that wasn't quite the truth. It took her only thirty seconds to decide to pick up the hefty, palm-sized rock and bring it

down on the glass of a windowpane next to the
back door. The glass shattered and Cecilia nearly
cried with relief as she reached in through the
hole and unlatched the door. She'd pay for the re-
pairs, of course, and the Crawleys would never
begrudge her shelter on a night like this.

Although the house was empty, as soon as she'd
shut the door behind her Cecilia felt the warmth
begin to suffuse through her body. It might have
been purely psychological, coming from the relief
of knowing she didn't have to spend any longer
in the snowstorm, but she wondered if the cottage had retained a little heat from whenever it
had last been occupied as well.

Cecilia moved into the little cottage, stepping
into the comfortable downstairs room furnished
with armchairs and looking longingly at the fireplace. She knew it was a dream, thinking she
might be able to light one herself. Her whole life
she'd been sheltered from having to do anything
even remotely practical by her status as England's
wealthiest heiress. Even in recent years, when her
existence had become a little less comfortable at
the hands of her ever-more-desperate guardian,
Mr Archibald Turner, she'd never been forced to
do anything remotely resembling work.

She sighed and moved on. A fire would be
heaven indeed, but there was no point in dwelling on what she couldn't have.

Upstairs there were two bedrooms, one furnished with a comfortable-looking double bed with thick covers. The second looked less inviting with a narrow single bed covered only by a couple of sheets.

'Time to get warm,' she murmured to herself. Grimacing, she peeled the wet layers of clothes from her body, shivering as her skin was slowly exposed to the air. Even her chemise was wet and after only a moment's hesitation she pulled that off over her head as well, hugging her body with her arms to try to conserve some warmth. Quickly she wrapped herself in a sheet, then slipped under the thick covers, revelling in the softness of the bed. With a sigh of contentment she wriggled down even further, wondering what it said about her life when she was happier here in this little abandoned cottage than she had been in the past year.

Not far now, Joe told himself, pushing himself to continue even though the muscles in his injured leg were screaming in pain.

It had been foolhardy to set off from his parents' house in this weather, but Joe had been eager to get away. Tomorrow the first of the guests would start arriving for the annual Crawley Christmas Eve ball at the end of the week and he had been so desperate not to be there. He didn't want to see the pitying looks or hear the whispered comments of sympathy behind raised hands. Even worse were the enquiries about his health—all the while their eyes would flicker to his injured leg as if trying to see through the fabric of his trousers.

No, an hour spent in a blizzard was better than that.

It couldn't be far to the cottage now, just a few hundred more feet, but in this weather it was hard to be sure. All the normal landmarks were covered in a thick layer of snow and it was only his good sense of direction that kept him on the right path.

With his head down Joe battled on, letting out a sigh of relief when he saw the neat little form of Rose Cottage in front of him. In a couple of minutes he would be stripped down, out of his soaking wet clothes and tucked into the luxurious bed in the upstairs bedroom.

'Home,' he said with a grin as he unlocked the front door and stumbled inside, quickly closing the freezing night out behind him.

In the year since his return from the war he had probably spent more time in this little cottage than anywhere else. At first there had been the three weeks he'd spent delirious in the military hospital, then the two months back at his parents' house as he worked on learning to walk again.

By that time he'd felt stifled and in need of some space and he'd chosen Rose Cottage to be his haven. There were many finer properties on the Crawley estate and much further afield, but Joe had always liked the little cottage set back from the road and secluded in its own garden. Another benefit was its size, perfect for a man who just wanted his own company. Here he could survive without any servants, without a cook or a maid, just the woman from the local village who came to clean twice a week. It was his own little slice of solitude.

Now he thought of this as his home and he was pleased to be back here after spending the week with his loud and cheerful family.

Quickly he shrugged off his wet coat and pulled off his gloves, hanging them up to dry. He was soaked to the skin, but knew it would take too much effort to light a fire tonight. He was tired and his leg ached and all he wanted to do was fall into bed and sleep for at least twelve hours. In the morning no doubt he would wake up to a cold cottage, but he would deal with that then.

Joe ascended the stairs, slipped into his bedroom and felt his way to the bed. It was completely dark in here, the thick curtains shutting out any natural light from the moon or the stars even on a clear night, but Joe knew his way around the small room by touch alone so didn't bother to light a candle. He peeled his wet clothes from his body, throwing them over the chair in the corner of the room, and once he was naked he slipped into bed.

As soon as his body touched the sheets Joe knew something was wrong. The fabric should have been cool against his skin but instead it had a wonderful warmth to it. His arm brushed against something soft and immediately he stiffened. There was someone in his bed. Someone warm and soft and, if he wasn't very much mistaken, someone completely naked just like him. Squinting in the darkness, he saw the petite form and on the pillow a long mass of hair. Definitely a woman.

Joe hesitated, not knowing what to do. It wasn't every day you found your bed occupied by someone else. He didn't know whether to shout, to gently wake the woman up or to light a candle. Slowly he eased himself backwards, planning on standing up and moving away, but as he shifted he heard the subtle change in the woman's breathing and knew she had awoken.

Cecilia's eyes sprang open, but she couldn't see anything in the dark. Despite her blindness she knew instantly that she wasn't alone. The rhythmic breathing of another human being was just to her right, somewhere on the other side of the bed.

Her heart was hammering in her chest and her hands shaking as she groped for something to defend herself with on the little table beside her. She didn't know who else would be out on a night like tonight, but they must have seen the smashed glass and followed her in. Whether to rob her or something worse she didn't know, but she wasn't going to lie around to find out.

Cecilia's hand closed around something metal and heavy. From the feel of the grooves beneath her fingers she thought it was probably a candlestick and before she could lose her nerve she swung it through the air and heard it connect with a dull thud. The force of the impact jarred her arm and for a moment she stayed completely still as the person on the other side of the bed collapsed without a sound.

She was shaking as she scrambled out of bed, quickly pulling one of the bedsheets around her naked body, dashing over to the window to open the thick curtain in an attempt to let in a little more light. The thick clouds covered the moon and the stars, but still the room brightened a fraction as the thick material was pulled back.

Quietly she crept back over to the bed. The man was undressed, completely so, but had fallen in such a way that his lower half was covered by the bedsheets she'd thrown off. Her eyes raked over the sculpted muscles of his chest, the narrow waist and downwards, to where the sheets covered his manhood. She chastised herself—it wasn't as though she'd never seen the naked male form before. She'd studied numerous paintings and sculptures in her quest to become more proficient in her sketches, but this was very different. The man in front of her wasn't made of stone or paint. He was pure flesh, muscle and skin, and she was so tempted just to reach out a hand and...

Cecilia caught herself and pulled back, focusing instead on the man's face. He had a strong jaw, blond hair and symmetrical features. He was a handsome man. A handsome man who looked just a little familiar.

Joseph Crawley, Cecilia realised. She'd only gone and bludgeoned the brother of her best friend. A man who had much more right to be in his family's cottage than she did. Again her eyes danced over his body. He was still breathing, at least, and every so often he would shift slightly as if he were about to come round.

She bit her lip, wondering how angry he would be when he awoke with a dreadful headache.

'Major Crawley,' she said quietly, not knowing if she wanted him to awaken yet or not. 'Major Crawley, I'm ever so sorry.'

There was no answer. He'd stopped shifting and gone dreadfully still. With a tentative hand Cecilia reached out and laid her fingers on his chest. It was rising and falling rhythmically and the skin was warm. She felt relief mixed in with remorse.

She should withdraw her hand from his chest now she'd reassured herself he was still breathing, but she felt unable to move. His skin was soft beneath her fingertips and the hair on his chest a coarse contrast to his skin.

'Major Crawley,' Cecilia whispered again. Now her eyes had adjusted to the darkness she could make out a jug of water on the little table next to the bed. Thinking a sprinkling of cold water on his brow might revive the man in front of her, she dipped her fingers in. Just as she was drawing her hand out Major Crawley jolted in the bed and Cecilia lost her grip on the jug. She could only groan with despair as the whole contents emptied over the man she'd knocked unconscious. Now he was dead to the world and dripping wet to boot.

Quickly she grabbed at the sheets, meaning to mop up the worst of the water, but as she tugged she realised her action would only have one inevitable consequence: to expose Major Crawley's naked lower half.

Cecilia shrieked as a hand reached up and grabbed her wrist.

'I would thank you to leave my dignity intact.' His low, sonorous voice rang clearly through the room. As she watched, wide-eyed, he raised his other hand to his head and touched a spot on his scalp. 'What the devil have you done to me?'

Finding her voice, Cecilia was horrified to find she didn't sound in the least bit apologetic as she spoke. 'I hit you.'

'I can feel that. What with?'

She picked up the hefty candlestick from where she'd dropped it on the bed.

'Good Lord, woman, put it down. My head hurts enough already.'

Cecilia placed the candlestick back on the bed, only then realising that Major Crawley still had her by the wrist and was studying her face in the darkness of the room.

'Lady Cecilia,' he murmured. The man had a good memory. They couldn't have set eyes on each other for a decade. The last time she'd seen him she and Elizabeth had been peeking out of Elizabeth's window at the Crawleys' town house, watching him ride off in his regimental uniform. He'd looked dashing and debonair. She'd been eleven years old and she was surprised he'd even noticed his sister's little friend, let alone recognised her ten years later.

'Major Crawley.'

'I would ask what you were doing in my bed,' he said, his eyes all the time flitting over her face as if taking in every last detail. 'But I'm cold and wet with an awful headache, so I think your explanation can wait.'

'I thought you were going to assault me,' she blurted out, even though the information hadn't been solicited.

He looked at her for a long moment, his gaze assessing her. 'I wasn't.'

'I know that now…'

How could she explain her fears to an honourable man? He wouldn't understand how she'd spent the last six years dodging the advances of her guardian and more recently the attempts to thrust his reluctant son upon her. How finding a man sliding into bed next to her made an overwhelming panic rise up inside her.

Gently he let go of her wrist and she let go of the sheet she'd been gripping on to. He stood, wrapping the sopping sheet around him, and they faced each other. It was only then that Cecilia remembered she was standing basically naked in front of this man. When she'd jumped up she'd pulled one of the covers around her body, but her shoulders were bare, as was one of her legs as it poked out of the split in between the embroidered blanket.

'I shall let you get dressed,' Major Crawley said, not attempting to hide how his eyes took in the pale skin of her shoulders. He walked slowly over to the chair where Cecilia could see he'd thrown his clothes and picked up the discarded garments, before limping to the door.

She'd heard he'd been injured, listened to all

the gruesome details as Elizabeth had retold them, knew about the festering wound that had nearly claimed Major Crawley's life. She also knew how he'd become a recluse since returning to health. How he only ever visited his very close friends or family and spent much of his time secluded away, not wanting to engage with society. Cecilia could understand that. Society was draining even for the most dull and un-noteworthy. A decorated major with a war wound would have been mobbed by the ladies wanting to hear about his heroic deeds. All made worse by the fact he was an attractive man, of course.

Once the door had closed Cecilia sank back down on the sodden bed and closed her eyes. Her heart was still thumping in her chest from the shock of finding a man climbing into her bed. His bed, she corrected herself. His bed. His cottage. His sheets she'd poured water over. His naked chest she'd spent far too long looking at.

With a sigh she stood. Tonight had been one poor decision after another and now she was snowed in inside the little cottage with a man she'd assaulted with a candlestick. Major Crawley might be a reasonable man, but already she could tell she'd pushed him to the limit of his tolerance and she felt apprehensive of what the rest of the night would bring.

Chapter Two

Joe poked at the fire, watching with satisfaction as the logs crackled and spat, sending plumes of smoke up the chimney. During his youth he'd been pampered and indulged like all sons of the nobility, even second sons. He'd never had to make his own bed, chop wood for a fire or make even the simplest of meals. Everything had been done for him. He'd even had a man to help him dress for dinner.

The army had knocked most of that out of him. Sometimes one of his men would make him a cup of bitter tea or bring him a plate of the evening meal when he was busy working at his desk, but unlike many of the senior-ranking officers Joe hadn't bothered with a manservant or singling out one of the soldiers to take on his domestic tasks. He'd needed his men to see they were in everything together.

War was a great equaliser and, for his men to

follow him into battle, to believe he would bring them back out again, he couldn't afford a great chasm between them. So he'd washed his own clothes. Made his own bed. Brewed his own tea.

And now he was home...well, he couldn't imagine relying on someone else to do these basic and personal tasks so he continued to do them himself, despite his mother telling him, *'You'll never find a wife'* or *'You'll never be accepted into society'*. One day she would realise that he didn't want a wife, didn't want a place in society. He just wanted the solitude of his little cottage and his own company.

There was a hesitant knock on the door and Joe grumbled for her to come in. Lady Cecilia Bronwen, who had no right to be in his little cottage. No right to disturb his peace. Yet she'd been in his bed, assaulted him, thrown water over him and almost entirely exposed his naked body to her gaze and he'd only been home twenty minutes.

'Warm yourself up,' he said without looking up.

'Thank you.' Her voice was soft and melodic. Joe wasn't interested in society gossip, but his sister still insisted on telling him snippets whenever he visited the family home. If Elizabeth was to be believed, this young woman standing in front of him was the richest and therefore most sought-after heiress in England. You could tell she was high-born by the refined accent and the way she glided into a room rather than walked, although Joe was a little perplexed as to how she was so handy with a candlestick.

She paused before him and waited until he looked up.

'I'm sorry, I had to borrow some of your clothes,' she said. His eyes raked over her, taking in the too-large trousers she was holding bunched around her petite waist and the shirt that was just a little bit see-through in the flickering light of the fire. He swallowed, reminding himself who it was standing in front of him. Lady Cecilia would only want one thing from a man—marriage—and that was something he couldn't give. He tried to pull his eyes away from the silhouette of her body. 'My clothes were still completely sodden,' she said in explanation.

'Sit,' he said, motioning to one of the arm-chairs. He didn't much care if she was comfortable or not, but he needed her to move so he would stop staring. His eyes didn't seem capable of looking away by themselves.

She daintily wrestled with the trousers, took two steps and promptly fell over the excess material that pooled around her feet. With a squeal of surprise she catapulted forward, letting go of the waistband of the trousers and falling towards Joe. Instinctively he held out his arms, catching her before she went head first into the fireplace, and carefully set her back on her feet.

He tried not to look, tried not to allow his eyes to travel up the length of her now bare legs, but it was impossible. She was standing right in front of him and he was only human.

'Thank you,' she said, her voice trembling a little, and for the first time Joe realised that he wasn't the only one who'd had a shock. Lady Cecilia might not have been whacked over the head with a candlestick, but she hadn't had the night she'd planned.

'Sit,' he said again, trying to sound a little less gruff. He watched as she looked down at the trousers pooled around her ankles and deliberated. Carefully she stepped out of them before retreating to the chair. The shirt she was wearing reached almost down to her knees, but as she sat she quickly tucked her bare legs up and under her body before she raised her head to meet his eyes.

Turning back to the fire, Joe chastised himself. For an entire year, ever since his injury, he'd barely thought of women. Now was not the time to suddenly start fantasising about one. And certainly not Lady Cecilia.

'I must apologise,' Lady Cecilia said after a minute.

'What for?'

'Breaking into your cottage. And hitting you

over the head. And throwing cold water over you.'
She coughed in embarrassment.

'Why are you here, Lady Cecilia?'

She sighed and Joe could hear the mountain of
pain behind the sigh. He watched as she played
with a strand of damp hair, twirling the blond
ringlet round and round her finger—it was hard
not to be mesmerised.

'I was travelling to your parents' Christmas
Eve party.'

'On a night like tonight?'

'You must have set out in the snow, too,' she
shot back.

He grimaced, remembering the long walk in
the thick snow, and found he was unconsciously
rubbing his injured leg. The muscles felt tight and
sore and no doubt his limp would be more pronounced for days.

'I am not always free to come and go as I
please,' she said slowly, as if selecting her words
carefully. 'I saw an opportunity to slip away this
evening and took it, despite the poor weather conditions.'

Joe frowned. *Not always free to come and go
as I please.* It was a strange thing to say. He knew
young ladies had more restrictions on their activities than men, but surely no one would keep
her from a friend's ball.

'But you found you couldn't make it to Hawthorn House?'

'The snow was too thick. I saw the cottage and I thought your parents would not mind if I sought shelter...' She paused, waiting for him to look at her. 'I had no idea you would be staying here.'

He believed her. Not many people knew what he did with his life nowadays.

'I'm sorry,' she said again. 'I was desperate so I broke the window in the kitchen, the one by the back door.'

'A drink,' he declared, deciding he would worry about the broken window in the morning. 'I need a drink. Would you like one?'

He'd warmed up sufficiently now and the fire was roaring fiercely in the grate. What he needed now was something to distract him from the half-naked woman sitting only a few feet away.

Inappropriate, he told himself. She was Lady Cecilia, his little sister's friend. The last time he'd seen her she couldn't have been much more than nine or ten, still a child. He'd noticed her, of course he had, he noticed everything, but he hadn't paid her any attention.

She wasn't a child now, though, far from it. She was an attractive young woman. An attractive young woman he couldn't stop looking at.

'Pull yourself together,' he murmured. He'd been too long without a woman, that was all.

In the past year he had barely thought about his baser needs, but he was only human, it was natural for him to want a woman's touch every now and then. Just not this woman. And certainly not right now.

'Pardon?' Lady Cecilia said, swivelling her neck round to follow his progress across the room. He felt large and lumbering under her gaze.

'Whisky?'

'Yes, please.'

He poured two glasses, looking on with surprise as Lady Cecilia drank hers in two large gulps without spluttering. She closed her eyes and Joe could imagine the warmth the liquid had given her deep in her belly. He took a mouthful of whisky himself and lowered his body into the other armchair.

'Why were you out in the snow?' she asked, hugging her arms around her body and unconsciously pulling the shirt a little tighter against her skin. Joe tried to avert his eyes, but found he just couldn't get them to obey the command.

'My parents' Christmas Eve ball,' he said.

'You were travelling to it, too?'

He laughed and heard the note of bitterness in his voice. 'Away from it.'

'Oh.'

'I don't dance,' he said, motioning to his injured leg.

'A ball is so much more than dancing,' Lady Cecilia said with a shrewd look in her eye.

'I don't socialise,' he corrected himself.

She would know about his injury. Everyone knew about his injury. He'd been lauded a hero, awarded a medal for bravery and his friends had told him he'd been the talk of the town for weeks. What people didn't know about was the rest of the pain, the hidden damage. The men he'd lost whose faces he still saw in his dreams every night, the irrational panic he felt when there was a loud noise. The injury to his leg was easy to understand, easy to explain, it was the rest of the damage that made him shut himself away.

'You were fleeing before any of the guests arrived.'

'I prefer to think of it as making a timely exit.'

Lady Cecilia smiled then, the first true smile he'd seen, and it lit up her entire face. She shifted, allowing one delicate little foot to poke out from under the shirt, and leaned forward.

'I'm sorry I've invaded your sanctuary,' she said perceptively.

He *did* think of this cottage as his sanctuary. No one else ever came here, only Mrs Green from the village who cleaned twice a week, but his family never came or his friends. This was where he retreated when he needed space and time on his own.

'It's only for one night,' he said gruffly. 'I'm sure even I can cope with company for one night.'

They sat in silence for a moment and Joe watched as Lady Cecilia closed her eyes and turned her face to the fire. She looked tired, not just physically but emotionally. He'd become good at spotting the signs after seeing it in the mirror every day this past year. Wondering what could be bothering the richest heiress in England quite so deeply, he tried to push the thought from his mind. It was none of his concern. Tomorrow Lady Cecilia would be out of his cottage and on her way. He might never set eyes on her again. And tonight he refused to get drawn in by those deep, dark eyes.

'I'm sure you're tired,' he said stiffly. 'You should take the second bedroom, the bed in the main bedroom is soaked.'

'What about you?'

'I'll sleep here.'

'I couldn't allow you to do that,' Lady Cecilia said. 'Not when it's my fault your bed is ruined for the night.'

'What do you suggest, Lady Cecilia?' he asked, his voice low and his eyes fixed on hers. 'That we both squeeze into the single bed in the second bedroom?'

He saw her swallow, saw the flash of something that looked very much like desire in her eyes, then she stood and smiled at him.

'Very well,' she said with the composure of a queen. 'I hope your night is not too uncomfortable.'

He handed her a lighted candle to guide her way and couldn't help but watch as she walked away. The outline of her body was visible through the thin material of the shirt she wore and never had Joe been so tempted to do something so foolish. Silently he chastised himself, but still watched her retreating form, exhaling loudly as Lady Cecilia closed the door behind her before she ascended the stairs.

Chapter Three

Cecilia woke to the sunlight streaming in through the window. It had been so dark when she'd slipped into bed the night before she hadn't noticed the curtains were not closed, but this morning the watery winter light had woken her from sleep. She stretched, feeling the soft cotton of Major Crawley's shirt, and felt a moment of guilt. No doubt he had spent the night uncomfortable in an armchair, all because she'd doused his bed in cold water.

Trying to forget the memory of how he'd looked at her the night before when she'd risen to go up to bed, she closed her eyes, but all she could see was his face. The unruly blond hair, the first shadow of stubble across his jaw, the pale blue eyes that seemed to take everything in and the pain in his expression he tried to hide so carefully.

'Don't be a fool,' she told herself primly. She'd lost her parents at the age of fifteen and not long after had experienced her first fortune hunter. He had pursued her relentlessly, as had the many men who'd followed and over the years Cecilia had learned it was best never to even dream of a happy ending. Not that she thought Major Crawley was a fortune hunter, just a man who had made it clear to the world he had no interest in marriage.

Quickly she rose and donned the dress she'd been wearing the day before. It was now only slightly damp and, once her skin got used to the coolness of the material, only a little uncomfortable.

Quietly she descended the stairs, unsure if Major Crawley would still be sleeping and reluctant to disturb him after her antics of the night before. She listened at the door for a few moments, her hand raised to knock, but waiting for some signs of life.

'I don't know what you expect to hear,' Major Crawley's voice came from behind her. He'd just exited the other downstairs room, which Cecilia had entered the cottage through the night before, a small but functional kitchen.

She straightened up, the blush burning on her cheeks.

'Unless you were peeking through the keyhole.'

'I would never...' she began to protest before

glancing at the door and realising it didn't have a keyhole. As she turned back to Major Crawley he had a small smile on his lips.

'Breakfast?' he asked, stepping back and allowing her to go into the kitchen ahead of him.

There was a small table in the room, made of smooth wood with notches and scratches all over its surface. Along one side was a bench and on the other a couple of chairs. The rest of the kitchen was unremarkable—a fire, worktops, and an assortment of knives and ladles stacked at one end. The window she'd smashed on her quest for an entry point the night before had been boarded over neatly and the door was firmly closed against the snow. What hit Cecilia as she walked in was the delicious smell coming from one of the pans hanging above the fire.

She looked around for a maid, someone who would be cooking the bacon that was sizzling in the pan. There was no one and nowhere else anyone could be hiding.

'Are you cooking?' she asked, surprised.

'Of course. There's only the two of us here.' Cecilia shifted uncomfortably—she didn't need the reminder of how inappropriate her being here was.

'It smells good,' she said, taking a step forward and inhaling the scent.

'Nothing like toast and bacon to start the day.

Sit. Have some tea.' He seemed a little more jovial this morning, less like a bear ready to pounce. Still, she could hardly begrudge him his gruffness the night before after everything she'd put him through.

Cecilia watched as he flipped the bacon, served up toast and added the meat to the plate before setting it in front of her. A man had never cooked for her before. She was quite certain her guardian, the old man so interested in her fortune, had never even set foot in the kitchen of Whiteburn Hall. It wasn't usual, but she was fast learning not much about Major Crawley conformed to expectation.

He sat down opposite her and raised his cup in mock salute. 'To your health, Lady Cecilia.'

'Thank you,' she said, her manners stopping her from diving into the breakfast head first, but her stomach grumbling loudly at the delay. She took a delicate bite and had to stop herself from sighing with pleasure. A young lady wasn't meant to enjoy food quite as much as she did. She was lucky her guardian was so miserly when it came to mealtimes—otherwise she had no doubt she would have bloomed into a woman double her current size. Cecilia knew when she was a wealthy spinster, living a quiet life away from society, she would have to invest in a good cook and ensure she went on plenty of long walks to compensate.

'I hope you slept well,' she said, feeling a little guilty again for taking the only usable bed.

'No,' Major Crawley said. Most men would lie, they would spare a lady's conscience, but Major Crawley just gave her that grim smile she was beginning to recognise.

She took a bite of the bacon and let it melt on her tongue. It really was good.

'I shall get out of your way today,' she said, glancing out the window. The glass was frosty and didn't afford much of a view of the conditions outside.

'Unlikely,' he said with a shake of his head.

'Excuse me?'

'It is unlikely you'll be able to go anywhere today,' Major Crawley elaborated. 'The snow is two feet thick and by the clouds to the east I wouldn't be surprised if we had more fall before the afternoon is out.'

'You're an expert on the weather now,' Cecilia couldn't help but grumble. She had hoped to make it to Hawthorn House by this evening and try to forget this little episode with Major Crawley had ever happened. Soon her guardian would start searching for her, no doubt making a great fuss about her disappearance in the hope the ensuing scandal might force her to marry his son.

Major Crawley regarded her with his pale blue eyes and gave a little shrug. 'You don't need to be an expert to see there will be more snow falling from clouds as dark as those.'

They ate in silence for a while, all the time Cecilia trying not to show how much she was enjoying her breakfast. Her mother had told her years and years ago that a proper young lady did not show her delight in the simple pleasures in life. She should never be seen enjoying her food or drink, never be seen to shriek in delight at the wind whipping in her hair while riding horseback, never be seen to sigh in pleasure when a dashing gentleman kissed her hand. Her mother had been the belle of the Season when she'd met Cecilia's father, she'd had the pick of suitors, and it had surprised no one when she'd chosen to become a countess.

Cecilia had always tried to emulate her mother, but just enjoyed everything far too much. Well, she'd enjoyed everything until her parents had died suddenly six years ago from a winter fever within a couple of weeks of each other. Now there was always a solemnity to her actions that hadn't been present before.

'Where did you learn to cook?' she asked, leaning back from the table and cradling her teacup in her hands. It was odd Major Crawley living out here all alone without any servants. He would have been raised in the same way as she, with maids and footmen and cooks ready to see to his every need. But somehow, somewhere, he'd shaken all of that off and decided the life of privilege wasn't for him.

'The army,' he said. Cecilia waited for him to elaborate, but was fast realising Major Crawley was a man of few words.

'You had to cook your own food in the army?'

'No.'

She took a sip of tea, looked at him and raised an eyebrow in question. Eventually he sighed and let just a little more information about himself slip out.

'They had cooks. Big tents where you went to have your meals in the morning and evening when you were in camp. But army life taught me to be more self-sufficient, not to rely on anyone else for anything.'

It was a different world. One that Cecilia knew she would never experience. There were women who followed the army around, some of them even respectable—the wives of the Colonels and the Majors and the Lieutenants. But she never planned to marry and the only other women who followed in the wake of the thousands of men who made up the army were prostitutes and women with something to sell.

'But things are different now you're home, surely?' she pressed.

He shrugged. 'I find I cannot tolerate having

another person do the things that I can easily do myself. It's not as though I'm terribly busy otherwise.' There was a hint of bitterness in his voice and Cecilia wondered if he had lost his way since returning home. She knew it happened to a lot of soldiers, they no longer felt as though they fit into the civilian world, but Major Crawley was one of the privileged few. He didn't have to look for work, he had property, money, a family to love him.

Abruptly he stood, as if signalling that was the end of their conversation. Quickly he gathered together the plates and took them over to the sink. He'd already filled it with warm water, boiled over the fire and cooled while they had their breakfast, and without looking back at Cecilia he began to wash the plates.

'Let me do that,' Cecilia said.

He turned and stared at her, then went back to scrubbing a plate.

'I'd like to help,' she said, a little louder this time.

'Have you ever washed a plate before in your life?'

'No.' There was no point lying about it.

He turned back to the sink again.

'How hard can it be?' Cecilia asked, pushing up the sleeves of her dress so the material at the wrists wouldn't get wet.

Still Major Crawley didn't step aside so Cecilia inserted her petite frame in between him and one of the work surfaces to his left and slowly began to nudge her way in closer to the sink.

After a few seconds, when he must have judged that she wasn't going to be put off by his stubborn refusal not to move, he stepped aside and allowed her to dip her hands into the water. Cecilia picked up a plate, watching out of the corner of her eye as he dried his hands on a cloth. They were strong hands, he was a strong man. She could imagine him dressed in his military uniform on the battlefield, leading his men. He cut a dashing figure, despite the scowl she couldn't imagine him without.

Trying to think back to when she'd known him in childhood, she wondered if he'd always been this way. The man she remembered before he headed off to war had smiled more, laughed and joked, fooled around with his older brother and teased his little sister.

Side by side they washed the plates and cutlery, Major Crawley putting everything away in its place once it was dried.

After she'd finished the last item Cecilia reached out for the cloth resting on the side, her hand gripping on to it just as Major Crawley touched it, too. Their fingers only brushed one another, but Major Crawley jumped back as if he'd been burned.

Feeling her heart pounding in her chest, Cecilia looked up slowly, but Major Crawley had already turned away and was pulling on his coat. Without another word he opened the back door, letting in a cold gust of wind, and then walked out into the snow.

Joe pulled some more hay from the sack and arranged it so the horse could reach easily, all the time stroking the beautiful mare's nose and murmuring softly.

'You'd think I was a lad of twelve the way I jumped,' he murmured, shaking his head ruefully. Lady Cecilia hadn't even meant to brush his hand with her own and he could just imagine her confusion now at his reaction. No doubt the pretty young heiress was used to men *wanting* to touch her, not fleeing from the faintest contact.

He did want to touch her, that was half the problem. All night, the entire six hours he'd spent folded up uncomfortably in the armchair, he hadn't been able to stop thinking of her. The image of her body silhouetted under the thin material of his cotton shirt was seared into his mind and had tormented him as he tried to sleep. All night he had listened for the faint noises of her moving around upstairs, just a few feet above him, and all night he had imagined a thousand things that were certainly not appropriate for a man to imagine about his sister's closest friend.

'Too long without a woman,' he grumbled, patting the mare's neck as he threw one of the old blankets he kept in the tiny stable over her back.

He hadn't been with a woman since his return from the Peninsula. At first he had been too ill, delirious with fever and the festering wound in his leg. Then he had to work for months to get his strength back, to learn how to walk again, how to move, how to do everything again. If he was honest, that wasn't the only reason, though. For months now he had been at peak physical fitness despite his injury. He could walk for ten miles without taking a rest, could ride, chop wood, do any number of physical tasks, but still he hadn't pursued even the briefest of relationships with a woman.

Rebecca—she was why. 'Not the woman I thought she was,' he murmured to the horse, straightening out the blanket and checking the mare had everything she needed.

The woman he had been betrothed to. The woman he had thought he would spend the rest of his life with. The woman who had promised to wait for him.

She had waited. They'd met three years ago when he'd been home on leave and for two years she'd written him letters and promised one day they would build a life together. She'd waited the entire time, only to turn him away when he returned, with disgust in her eyes.

That was why he hadn't pursued any sort of relationship with a woman since. That look of disgust meant he wouldn't any time soon either.

'One more day, girl,' he said, peering out of the stable and up at the sky. Surely by tomorrow the snow would have cleared and he could send Lady Cecilia on her way. He had survived the war, he could survive one more day of sharing his cottage with the pretty young heiress.

'One more day until what?' A voice came from somewhere to his left.

He cursed under his breath. She was going to catch a chill and then what would he do with her?

'What the devil are you doing out here?' he barked, knowing his tone was far too harsh for a lady, but unable to temper down his frustration.

'Seeing to my horse,' she said as if it were the most natural thing in the world.

'I'm doing that.'

'Well, I didn't know that, did I?'

'What did you think I was doing?'

'How should I know? Going for a stroll, doing a spot of fishing, watching the birds.' He heard the sarcasm in her voice and, instead of responding, just glared at her. Lady Cecilia gave him a sunny smile and squeezed past him into the stable. As she leaned forward to greet her horse, her hip grazed against his thigh and Joe had to tense to stop himself from jumping back.

'Good morning, my beauty,' she said, stroking the horse's neck and allowing the animal to nuzzle into her.

'You'll catch a chill,' Joe said stubbornly, grimacing as he realised he sounded like a stuffy old man.

'So might you.'

He looked down at his coat and boots and then across to hers. It was difficult to deny she was better dressed for the weather, with gloves protecting her hands and the collar of her coat done up to just below her chin. Still, she hadn't fled the cottage quite as quickly as he had.

'You don't like to be touched,' she said, not turning around to face him as she spoke.

He almost spluttered. Most people weren't so direct.

The seconds ticked by in silence as he wondered how to answer that statement.

'Is it because of your injury? Elizabeth told me a little about it. I can't imagine I would be keen on having anyone touching me after having doctors prod and poke me for months on end.'

He mumbled something incomprehensible.

Better for her to think that than to suspect the real reason.

'Was it really awful?' she asked.

'Yes,' he said, surprising himself with his honesty. He rarely talked about that time in his life despite it taking up much of his thoughts.

'Do you remember it all?'

'No.' He paused and then slowly continued, 'That's the worst part.'

'Not remembering?'

'The half-memories. Patches of time where I'm not sure if something happened or if was just a dream.'

'You were delirious?'

'For three weeks.'

'Yet you survived.'

He grimaced. He had survived. He never regretted that, despite the injury he had to live with, despite the cold sweats when the memories of the battles crept up on him. So many hadn't come home, he could never be so ungrateful as not to appreciate the life he'd been given.

'I survived.' Even though he'd been told time and time again his odds were poor if he insisted on keeping his leg.

'Is your injury why you hide out here?' Lady Cecilia asked.

'What?' he spluttered before he could help himself.

'Not in the stable,' she said, turning to face him with that impish smile he was beginning to recognise. 'Out here at the cottage.'

'Why do you think I'm hiding?'

'You chose to walk five miles in the snow rather than be comfortably ensconced in your parents' home when their guests begin to arrive for Christmas.'

It was pretty damning evidence.

'No.'

'No, you're not hiding or, no, it's not because of your injury.'

'No to both.'

'Hmmm,' she murmured, pulling a face as if she didn't believe him.

'I needed some space to decide what to do with my life,' he said, surprising himself with his candour. It was true one of the reasons he'd chosen to live out here by himself was to avoid the curious questions about his injury, about the army and to stop raking up all the painful memories, just as he knew he was also out here so he avoided ever having to accidentally bump into Rebecca again, but he also liked the quietness, the opportunity to take time to consider what his life held next for him.

'And what have you decided?'

'I haven't.'

She nodded, as if she finally believed him.

'Shall we go back inside?' he asked. Although she was well wrapped up, Lady Cecilia's cheeks had turned rosy in the cold and the tip of her nose was pink. She nodded and they both moved for the door at once, their bodies colliding. Joe felt a stab of pain shoot through his leg, but managed to keep his balance, his arms instinctively coming up to encircle Lady Cecilia to stop her from toppling.

With her body pressed against his she fit under his chin and there she stayed for a couple of seconds as he felt her breathing steady as she composed herself. After a moment she took a step back and looked up at him, their eyes meeting, and Joe felt an intense wave of desire flood through his body. She looked so perfect standing there in his arms, so kissable. He wanted to run his hands through her hair, to touch the soft skin of her cheeks and kiss her until they both forgot who they were.

He saw the flicker of desire in her eyes, saw the unconscious sway of her body towards him, and for a moment he was tempted to give in. They both wanted it, both felt the inexplicable attraction, even though he'd been far from the perfect gentleman towards her.

With great effort he stepped back, ensuring she was steady on her feet before moving. He would not seduce his sister's dearest friend. He wouldn't take away her future, her chance to make a great match, not for a few hours of pleasure, however much he wanted her.

Chapter Four

In front of them the fire crackled and spat, causing Cecilia to look up from the book she was reading and stare into the flames. She was ever conscious of Major Crawley sitting just a few feet from her, aware every time he shifted or moved, aware of every breath he took.

Foolish girl, she told herself. She'd nearly kissed him that morning out in the stable. After everything she'd promised herself, after all her years of self-restraint and careful behaviour. One smouldering look from a man she wasn't sure even liked her and she was ready to throw it all away.

Forcing her eyes back to her book, a rather dry factual book on the Great Fire of London a couple of centuries ago which seemed to be blaming the whole episode on one poor baker, it was only a few seconds before she heard Major Crawley shift. He rose, slipped off his jacket and began rolling up the sleeves of his shirt. Cecilia tried to look away, but the rhythmic motion of his fingers mesmerised her and she couldn't help but watch as he revealed his tanned forearms.

His eyes came up and met hers and she thought she detected a hint of amusement on his face before he turned to face the fire. She watched as he prodded at the logs with the poker before settling back into his chair.

'Good book?' he asked, his eyes raking over her, but his expression giving nothing away.

'A little persecutory,' she said. In response to his raised eyebrow she elaborated. 'They are blaming the Great Fire of London on one man.'

'When in reality it was down to poor town planning and a sense of invincibility,' Major Crawley said.

'Well, yes.'

'But it is much more sensational to go on a witch-hunt.'

She nodded, knowing she should return to her book, but unable to look away from the man in front of her.

'How about a game?' Major Crawley said.

'A game?' He didn't seem to be the sort of man who liked to play games. Far too serious.

'A game of morals.'

'You have one of those?' she asked.

The games made of linen squares stuck to

pieces of wood were fast becoming popular among the *ton* to play after dinner parties or between friends. You had a little carved figure, some counters to signify coins to pay any fines and a dice to roll. The winner was the first one to the last square and you were disqualified once you'd lost all your counters.

'I do.'

'Who do you play with?' she asked.

He shrugged. 'My many companions, of course.' He gestured around the little room and she couldn't help but giggle.

'I can just imagine you sitting here by yourself and playing.'

'I'm not *that* much of a lost cause.'

Together they unpacked the box and Cecilia wondered if it had ever been opened before. The lid was stiff and the pieces lined up perfectly inside. As Major Crawley rose to get drinks—an essential part of any game of morals, he told her—she peered at the squares. You could advance more quickly if you landed on the virtues: honesty, prudence, sobriety, charity, sincerity and humanity. Then there were squares with sins: idleness, passion, folly, lies, blasphemy, cheating and perjury. And squares with punishments for those sins: the whipping post, the pillory, the stocks and Newgate.

'Your counter, Lady Cecilia,' Major Crawley

said, passing her a carved lady with a flamboy-
ant dress and a hairstyle modelled on the fashions
from the last century.

'We are the only two here,' Cecilia said softly.
'For today, at least, why don't you call me Cecilia?'

He looked at her and for a moment she saw the
fire flare in his eyes and she felt a heat begin to
rise up from somewhere deep in her body. Then
he inclined his head and murmured, 'Cecilia.'

It took her a minute to recover from the deep,
low voice saying her name as if she were the only
woman on earth.

'Joe,' he offered. It suited him. She knew his
parents called him Joseph, his sister, too, but she
suspected he preferred the shortened version of
his name.

'Shall we play, Joe?' she asked, testing out his
name. It seemed awfully familiar. There were no
other gentlemen she'd ever called by their first
names, not even her guardian's son, who she'd
been residing with for the past four years. Peter
Turner—to his face she called him Turner, and in
her mind she called him The Wet Rag, or sometimes just Rag for short.

'Ladies first,' he said, handing her the dice.
She rolled and moved her counter, leaning over
the board and reading the square she landed on.

'Passion,' she said. 'Proceed to the ducking stool to cool that fire and pay a fine of one.'

Joe raised an eyebrow and watched as she pushed her counter to the ducking stool.

'It's a bit excessive,' Cecilia murmured. 'Ducking a girl just because of a little passion.'

'Compared to what society does to a woman who shows passion, I think your little lady has got away lightly.'

'True.' Many a woman of Cecilia's acquaintance had been ruined by just one kiss, one inappropriate touch. She glanced up at Joe sitting across from her. If anyone ever found out she'd spent two nights here unchaperoned with an unmarried man she would be ruined. Not that she had anything to be ruined from, it wasn't as though she was ever planning to marry, but her reputation would be destroyed and the gossips would tear her apart.

'No one will ever know,' Joe said, as if reading her thoughts. 'You can tell my family you only just set out and you can tell your guardian you've been with my family the whole time.'

'I wouldn't put it past him to already be hammering on the door at Hawthorn House,' Cecilia said. She could picture the rotund old man wheezing through the snow and demanding his ward back from the Crawleys.

'He cares that much about you?' Joe asked,

rolling the dice and moving a couple of spaces. 'Sobriety,' he said, raising the glass of whisky in the air in salute.

Cecilia snorted. 'He cares about my money.'

Joe raised an eyebrow in question and she sighed. For so long she'd dealt with her guardian alone, it would be good to have a moan to someone about the impossible situation.

'I am rather wealthy,' she said, feeling her cheeks redden as they did whenever she spoke about money. It wasn't boastful, just a fact. She'd been touted the wealthiest heiress in England. Cecilia didn't know if it were true, but she suspected she was in the top three at the very least.

'What has that got to do with your guardian?'

'His fortunes have been declining in recent years and he wishes to prop his up with mine.'

Six years he'd been working on Cecilia. At first it had been flattery and compliments, gently ushering her and his son, The Wet Rag, together at every opportunity. Encouraging her to turn down other suitors. As she'd neared her twenty-first birthday he'd become more desperate, less subtle. There had been the comments about what she owed him for taking her in, an insistence that she pay him back by marrying his son. When Cecilia had stood strong against this pressure he'd become less and less pleasant and more recently Cecilia had spent her evenings dodging his wandering hands and trying to ignore his spiteful comments. He was the reason that in recent months she'd learned to lock her doors *and* put a chairback beneath the handle. Her guardian, in his desperation, had turned to drink and when he was inebriated he got a certain look in his eyes that Cecilia did not trust. More than once he'd brushed past her too closely or let a hand rest where it shouldn't.

'He would like me to marry his son, Peter Turner.'

'Peter Turner...' Joe mused. 'Not that insipid-looking chap who couldn't find his own boots even with the help of a map?'

'That sounds like him,' Cecilia said, smiling at the look of horror on Joe's face. It was a relief she wasn't the only one who disliked the man.

'Tell me you're not even considering it.'

'I'm offended, Major Crawley, that you even have to ask.'

'Joe,' he said softly.

'Joe,' she repeated. 'Anyway, my birthday is on Christmas Day and then I'll be twenty-one. I shall be in charge of my own inheritance and no longer obliged to live with the Turners and their scheming.'

'What do you plan to do?'

She shrugged. 'Go away. Far away.'

He nodded as if he could understand that desire.

'I'll buy a little house somewhere, set myself up as a spinster. Perhaps become involved in some charitable organisations.'

Joe laughed. 'A spinster. You're far too young and pretty to be a spinster.'

'You think I'm pretty?'

'Of course. A man would be foolish to deny it.'

Cecilia felt a peculiar warmth somewhere deep inside her and smiled.

'Do you know how many marriage proposals I've had in the past four years since my debut?' she asked.

'Apart from Turner the younger?' He shook his head.

'Twenty-four. That's six a year.' Cecilia shook her head slowly and took a moment to roll the dice, counting the squares. 'Greed,' she read. 'Go to Newgate and miss a turn.' She looked up and saw Joe's expression. 'I'm not boasting about the proposals—none of them was worth anything. None of them cared for me, none of them really knew me. They just all saw the inheritance, the money they could be in possession of if they were smart enough to fool me.'

'It must have been very difficult to tell who your friends were. Charity, move three spaces forward.'

Cecilia laughed, hearing the note of bitterness in her voice.

'I was fooled a couple of times before I worked out why I was quite so popular.' She tried not to think of the mistake she'd very nearly made. Her naïve seventeen-year-old self had been flattered by the attention from the rakish Lord Melbry. He'd danced with her, kissed her, led her off into darkened rooms to whisper his messages of love into her ear. She had been all ready to elope with him, completely besotted. It had only been luck that meant she'd overheard his conversation with one of his friends, declaring it the easiest seduction he'd ever performed and the one with the biggest rewards.

Cecilia had been devastated, with the loss of a man she thought she had loved and had loved her in return, but more lastingly with the loss of her innocence. She suddenly began to see the new friends and suitors for what they really were—just interested in her wealth.

'I understand not wanting to get hurt,' Joe said slowly, his eyes focused down on the table in front of him. 'But do you really want to commit yourself to a lifetime of being alone?'

'I could ask you the same question,' she said, trying not to make it sound as though she was lashing out in retaliation to his words. 'Surely it is better to be out there in the world than hiding yourself away here in this cottage?'

Joe looked up and grinned, one of the first true

smiles she'd seen on his face. 'We're a pair, aren't we? The spinster heiress and the lame Major.'

Cecilia giggled, wondering how he would react if she moved her fingers forward a little across the table to touch her fingertips to his. It was an urge she was finding hard to suppress, but she knew that even though she was seeing a softer side to Major Crawley right now, he probably would not like the invasion of his personal space.

'Humility,' Joe said, moving his piece a few places forward. 'Take another turn.'

Cecilia watched as he rolled the dice again, taking in the soft curve of his lips and the smooth skin of his jaw as her eyes danced across his face. Still she was waiting for him to answer her about his plans for the future, but it looked as though he was not going to elaborate any time soon.

'Don't you get lonely here?' she asked quietly.

'No,' he said with a conviction that told Cecilia he'd been asked the question before. Probably by his mother. 'I've learned to enjoy my own company.'

'Good. So in the months you've been here what have you decided about your future?' she pressed.

'You're relentless,' he murmured. 'Did my mother send you to find out what I'm doing with my life?'

'You've found me out,' Cecilia said with a smile. 'I'm nothing but a spy for Mrs Crawley.'

Joe took the dice between his fingers and twisted it backwards and forward for a few moments, looking down at it intently. 'Do you know, I still haven't been able to decide.'

She wondered if he was stuck in the past, stuck in the war, mourning for lost friends and unable to move past the grim reality of battle. Over and over again she'd heard of men returning from the war changed, finding it difficult to slot back into everyday life, not able to understand the petty grievances of their loved ones now they'd seen larger things to worry about.

'Do you think living here has actually stopped you from moving forward?' Cecilia asked, knowing she was going too far, probing into too personal a matter, but not being able to stop herself.

Joe rolled the dice, the clattering the only noise as his face set into a neutral, unreadable expression. 'Six,' he said, moving his piece along the board to the very last square, which had a picture of a church steeple on it. 'It would seem I'm the winner.'

Without another word he got up and poked at the fire.

'We need more wood,' he said, glaring at the almost-empty basket.

'Do you always run away when someone's questions get a little bit close to the truth?' she asked quietly. It was far too presumptive to say to a man she barely knew, but although they had only just become reacquainted she wanted to help him. As much as someone with such little experience of real life could help.

'Nine years I was in the army. Nine years. That's almost a third of my life,' he said, looking into the flames. 'I don't want to go back, but I'm finding it a little harder to move forward than I had anticipated.'

'So it's not about your injury?'

'Not entirely,' he said, then sighed, and Cecilia wondered if the man in front of her knew what was holding him back from participating in life again. He fell silent, then gave a shrug, picked up the basket that normally contained the firewood and headed for the door.

Chapter Five

Pulling on his thick coat, Joe threw open the door and ventured out into the snow. It was even thicker than earlier, with soft flurries still falling from the dark cloud above, making him doubt whether Cecilia would be on her way tomorrow. The idea of having her company for one more day was more appealing than he liked to admit, despite her probing questions and knowing eyes.

'Gosh, it's cold,' her cheerful voice rang out from somewhere behind him.

'Go back inside,' he growled. He was only out here because of necessity. There was no way he would let the fire die down and they needed more wood, but there was no need for Cecilia to accompany him.

'I thought I'd lend you a hand,' she said, taking the other handle of the wicker wood basket and lifting it.

'I'm perfectly capable of fetching the wood

myself,' Joe said, feeling the familiar irritation he always did when someone doubted his physical prowess.

'I never said you weren't,' she said carefully. 'I just thought I would help.'

'Do you often take on tasks around the house?' he asked, hearing the sarcastic tone to his voice, but unable to stop it.

'No,' she said. 'Never. But then again my guardian has a houseful of servants paid to do this sort of thing. You have no one. So I should help.'

'Go back inside,' he grumbled, 'or you'll catch a chill and be stuck here even longer.' The image of Cecilia lying in his bed popped into his mind and he found it very hard to shift it.

He started pulling the cold logs from the pile and throwing them into the basket, making quick work of the task. Throughout his rehabilitation he'd been eager to become fitter, stronger than he had ever been before. Physically he was in peak condition, the rational part of his brain knew that, but still it felt as though some part of him was lacking.

Once the basket was full he hefted it up, ignoring Cecilia's outstretched arm offering to help. He strode back towards the house and deposited the basket inside the door, waiting for Cecilia to enter before he did.

'You are a very stubborn man,' she said as she put her booted foot on to the step.

Joe was just about to answer when he saw Cecilia start to slip. Her boots were no match for the thick ice that was hidden under a layer of white snow and her foot began to slide forward at an alarming rate. He lunged to catch her, gathering her to his chest, but the movement meant he, too, lost his footing and they both tumbled into the house together. Cecilia landed on top of him, her petite body still managing to wind him as an elbow connected with his solar plexus.

They lay there for a few seconds, both stunned and unsure if the other was injured. Joe scrambled to his feet, cursing loudly when his leg gave way, tumbling him back to the floor. On the second attempt he was more successful, levering himself up using the doorframe.

'Are you hurt?' he asked, reaching out his hand to help Cecilia. She grimaced as she sat, moving her ankle from side to side with a wince of pain.

'I think I've just pulled something,' she said. 'Nothing that won't heal.'

'Can you get up?'

Carefully she stood, letting out a low groan of pain as she put her weight on her ankle.

'I seem to be fine if I stay still,' she said. 'It just hurts a little when I move. I don't think it's even properly twisted.'

Joe hesitated. Chivalry was inbuilt into him, he couldn't ever sit before a woman, fail to open a door or assist a woman in need, but right now he was hesitating. What he *wanted* to do was sweep her up into his arms and carry her to one of the armchairs. It was only a few paces away and he wasn't doubting his physical ability. His leg might trouble him still, but he was perfectly capable of carrying someone as petite as Cecilia. The reason he was hesitating was the woman in front of him, or, more precisely, the feelings she elicited inside him.

He knew that if he gathered her close to his body, however briefly, he would feel her skin against his, learn the curves of her body as she rested in his arms. Already he was finding it hard to banish the inappropriate thoughts whenever he brushed against her in the small cottage, it wouldn't take much for him to be tipped into doing something completely inadvisable. Something like kissing her.

Unable to resist, he glanced at her lips. They were rosy and full and looked perfect for kissing.

'Come here,' he said, knowing it was a mistake, but still sweeping her up into his arms all the same.

He carried her the few paces to the armchair and gently deposited her there, trying to keep hold of his desire as her body brushed against his.

'Thank you, I'm sure I could have hobbled,' Cecilia said, probing her ankle through the material of her dress. As he watched her he felt an unfamiliar sense of affection. Cecilia had come crashing into his life only very recently, but he realised he felt as though he'd known her for so much longer. He was comfortable around her and he struggled to be comfortable around anyone.

'I'll get you something for it,' he said, turning quickly. Opening the front door, he deftly avoided the doorstep with the hidden ice and walked around to the side of the cottage. Under the windowsill were a few perfectly formed icicles and he broke them off, returning inside to find something to wrap them in. 'Let me see,' he said, motioning to her ankle.

Joe ignored Cecilia's blushing cheeks as she lifted the hem of her dress. All he wanted to do was check she wasn't badly injured. The skin of her calf was smooth and creamy and he found his pulse quickening as his fingers came to rest on her ankle. He heard her inhale sharply, but a quick glance at her face told him it wasn't in pain as she studiously avoided his eyes.

'Hold this against it,' Joe instructed when he had satisfied himself there was no great injury. 'It'll help with any swelling.'

'Another skill you picked up from your time in

the army?' Cecilia asked as she took the icicles wrapped in a piece of fabric from him.

'There were never enough doctors,' he said grimly, trying to forget the dozens of times he had watched his men die when medical intervention might have saved them.

'Do you still think about it?' she asked. 'The battles, the men, your time away?'

'Yes. All the time.' It felt strange to be admitting it. Normally he gave a terse reply to any questions about his time on the Peninsula—it discouraged any follow-up questions and allowed him to wallow in his memories alone.

'If it wasn't for your injury, do you think you'd still be in the army?' she asked quietly.

'Yes.' He hated it, had hated war and fighting and death, but the army had been his life for nine years and it was hard to imagine anything else.

'Perhaps…' she said thoughtfully, grimacing as she shifted the icicle fabric to another spot, 'you need to find some way to contribute that doesn't involve actually fighting, of course.'

Joe glanced over to the small pile of papers in the corner of the room. On the top was an envelope, thick with documents and as yet unopened. His time in the army had been spent commanding men, making decisions and fighting on the front line. That was how he'd wanted it. There had been numerous offers to secure him a different post, something safer where he would work on an advisory level, but he had always turned it down. Somehow it hadn't seemed fair, the thought of leaving his men without their commander. Still, the higher-ranking officers had always grumbled about what a shame it was to put someone like Joe at risk over and over again. Someone who could speak four languages and solve problems even the sharpest of mathematicians had trouble with.

Since his return to health he'd had a couple of offers from a friend in the Foreign Office, mainly translation work. *To help keep the peace even if you're a lame horse nowadays*, Theodore Long had written.

Always he'd sent the packages back unopened, but perhaps it was time to stop wallowing in self-pity and find himself something else to focus on.

'Let me see,' he said softly, guiding her hand away and placing his fingers back on her leg. There was no bruising, no obvious swelling.

'Will I live?' Cecilia asked, her smile breaking through her mock-serious visage.

'Don't fret, you'll live to see your spinster house yet.'

She grinned up at him and it struck him he'd never known anyone so happy at the thought of living out their life as a spinster. Women of Cecilia's birth and upbringing were expected to marry, and before they did they were expected to obsess about their choice of suitors, about proposals and eligible bachelors. They weren't meant to *want* to be ridiculed by society and spend their lives alone.

Suddenly Joe felt uneasy. The pieces were all beginning to fall into place: the reaction she'd had when he'd climbed into bed beside her, the handiness with a candlestick, her insistence that she would not marry, that she would stay a spinster.

'Cecilia…' he said, unsure how to put into words the question that was burning in his mind, 'has that Turner boy tried to force you? Is that why you're so adamant you won't marry?'

She laughed, but there was little humour in it and Joe felt sick to his stomach. The idea of anyone touching her…forcing her…made him feel angry beyond belief.

'Turner wouldn't know where to start,' she said grimly.

'Someone else, then?'

He saw he'd come to the correct conclusion by the flare of desperation in her eyes and wondered at the world that left an innocent young woman open to this sort of abuse.

'No one has ever laid a hand on me,' she said. Joe believed her, but wondered at what cost.

'Your guardian?' he growled.

Silently she nodded. 'Among others. Life

changes a little when you have no one to look out for you.'

'Surely you have someone?' he asked, thinking of his large family, the group of friends who still maintained frequent contact despite his foul mood this past year, the men who'd served under him who would have given up their life for his.

'No. No family whatsoever since my parents died. I have a few true friends—your sister, of course, and one or two others—but no one who can protect me from the man who is meant to put my welfare above anything else.'

'What has he done?' Joe asked, forcing his voice to remain calm.

'Nothing, not really. Nothing that I could report him to a magistrate for, but I've learned that doesn't mean anything.' She paused, closing her eyes for a few seconds as if trying to block out the memories, then laughed bitterly. 'What does it say about your life when your staunchest protector is Peter Turner, a man who couldn't stand up to the friendliest of beetles?'

'He tried to protect you?'

Cecilia shrugged. 'In his own way. He'd distract his father if he was getting too insistent I sit on his lap, or pour his father another drink if he wouldn't let me leave the dinner table and make my escape.'

'Your parents left you in his care?' Joe asked, incredulous.

'No, not knowingly. The relative who was supposed to be my guardian died a few weeks after my father. Mr Turner was the last resort after him.'

'And this is why you want to be a spinster? Not all men are like the Turners, Cecilia.'

She caught his eye and he felt something squeeze inside his chest. There was such sadness in her gaze and a sense that she was wise beyond her years.

'Are you offering, Major Crawley?' she asked and Joe was quick enough to school his face into a neutral expression. Of course she was joking, but it wouldn't do to look like a petrified rabbit at the idea of marrying her.

'You wouldn't want to tie yourself to a lame dog like me,' he said.

'A lame dog is better than a lecherous one,' she said quietly. 'But don't fear, I will not press you into marriage. And, no, it is not just because of the Turners I've decided to become a spinster. In three days' time I turn twenty-one. Then I inherit my father's fortune. I'm told it is quite considerable and, over the past few years, I've realised that people will do almost anything to get their hands on that money. Even pretend to be in love with me.'

Joe grimaced. He could just imagine the fortune hunters rubbing their hands together in glee when Cecilia made her debut. A pretty young girl with no parents or family to guide her, soon to be in possession of one of the biggest fortunes in England.

'What's your excuse?' she asked, her eyes seeming to look beneath his skin and into his soul.

Joe almost laughed at the directness of her question. His mother could learn a lot from Lady Cecilia. For months his mother had tried to convince him that one near miss on the marriage front shouldn't put him off for life, but had never been able to come out and ask directly what had happened with Rebecca.

'I don't have a fortune women are eager to possess, I'm not a perfect physical specimen and I'm a grumpy old cripple, too, not exactly the sort of man women are clamouring for.'

'Any woman would be lucky to have you, Joe,' Cecilia said softly, all traces of humour gone from her voice. He looked up at her then, saw the kindness and affection in her eyes and realised that there wasn't any pity there. He hated pity, had grown used to it, but Cecilia didn't look at him that way.

His hand rested on her leg and he felt the warmth and softness drawing him in. It would be so easy to kiss her, so good, so satisfying. Already he could imagine their lips meeting and was filled with a desire so intense it shocked him. He wanted to kiss her until they were both senseless and then make love to her for hours in front of the flickering fire.

Ever so gently his fingers moved on the bare skin of her leg. He heard her sharp intake of breath, saw the flush on her cheeks and the sparkle of desire in her eyes. For a moment he was about to go through with it, and then quickly he pulled away. As much as he might want this he couldn't do this to her. She'd just told him about being pursued by men who shouldn't have an interest in her—her guardian, the fortune hunters. While he was neither of those he wasn't offering her what she deserved: a future. If he ruined her now, he would take away any chance of her being happily married one day soon and, although she might protest she didn't want that, he'd seen the wistfulness in her eyes.

'And any man who just sees your fortune is a fool,' he said quietly, standing to put some distance between them.

Chapter Six

'Don't stick the bread right in the flames, it'll get charred to a crisp,' Joe said, laughing as she pulled the toasting fork back a few inches and inspected the burnt patch on her bread. 'Here, have mine.' He handed her a perfectly toasted piece of bread and popped another piece on his fork, lowering it closer to the flames.

They were running low on food, Joe had informed her apologetically, but to Cecilia freshly toasted bread and a generous spread of butter was her idea of heaven. They'd pulled their armchairs up to the fire and were using up the last of the bread. Tomorrow, no matter the conditions, they would have to venture out at least as far as the village to buy some food.

Glancing sideways, Cecilia felt a pang of sadness. No more snow had fallen this evening and the skies were looking clearer. It was still bitterly cold outside, but tomorrow the snow would probably thaw enough for their little secluded interlude to be over. Cecilia would have to return to the real world and Joe would disappear from her life.

She thought back to the moment when he'd nearly kissed her, earlier that afternoon. For a heady few seconds she'd been swept away in the fantasy and she had hoped he would take her in his arms. Of course it was foolish, to want a man who had no intention of ever marrying to seduce her, but she'd wanted it all the same.

As Joe handed her the second slice of toast she busied herself spreading the butter, handing one back to him once it was done.

'Delicious,' he said, relaxing back in his armchair as he ate. Cecilia couldn't help but smile— never again would she get to see a gentleman so relaxed, so at home. All the constraints of society meant that unless you were married then everything had to be done properly, all the time. It was unheard of to sit in an armchair by the fire with an unmarried man and no chaperon, just enjoying the crackle of the flames and a simple piece of buttery toast.

'That was heavenly,' she said, licking the butter off her fingers.

She saw Joe watching her and wondered for an instant if she'd disgusted him with her behaviour, but it wasn't disgust in his eyes. He gripped hold of the arms of the chair and mumbled something under his breath.

'Pardon?'

'Women,' he said, even though the first thing he'd muttered had been considerably longer than one word.

'What about us? Are you extolling our superiority? Our grace and wisdom, our composure and dignity?'

'Something like that.'

'Tell me,' Cecilia said, feeling bold and licking the last of the butter from her fingers. 'Which women were you referring to?'

'All of you.'

'All of us? I wasn't aware you were acquainted with *every* woman in the world.'

'Just the troublesome ones, it would appear,' he said, watching her intently as her finger popped out of her mouth for the final time. There was desire in his eyes and it should have scared her, but instead she felt a shiver of excitement. She knew hardly anything about him, other than little pieces of news passed on from Elizabeth and what she'd learned these past couple of days. Still, it was enough. Enough to know he was an honourable man, one who would not try to seduce her. Even if a small part of her *wanted* to be seduced.

Behave, she told herself. Although who would ever know? If they were lucky no one would ever realise she'd spent any time here, so no one would know of a kiss. Just one kiss. Something to take into her spinsterhood.

'Elizabeth told me of your engagement.' The words were out of her mouth before she had time to stop them. The engagement hadn't been a success, he was still a bachelor, after all, but it wasn't a topic he would want to discuss. And it was sure to dampen down any feelings of desire towards her. Silently she cursed, that wasn't what she'd hoped to do, although perhaps it was for the best.

'Did she?' Joe said, raising an eyebrow in a gesture that spoke of indifference, even though Cecilia could see it was feigned.

'Miss Rebecca Farnham, wasn't it?' She didn't know why she was pressing the subject.

'Let's not talk about Rebecca,' he said quietly.

'Did she hurt you?'

'*That* is talking about her. And I wish to think of more cheerful things.' He sat forward in his chair. 'The present, not the past.'

'I'm sorry if she hurt you. You don't deserve that.'

Joe smiled then and Cecilia felt the full force of his masculinity hit her squarely in the chest. She was almost out of her chair and on the way to his lap before she caught herself.

'And what do I deserve, Cecilia?' He said her name as if it were silk, rolling it softly over his

tongue and making the heat rise up from somewhere deep inside her.

'Something…nice,' she ventured, hardly able
to think let alone speak. Her eyes were fixed on
his, unable to pull away, and she could feel the
colour rushing to her cheeks, betraying her as it
always did whenever she was embarrassed.

'Something nice,' he mused. 'You'll have to
be a little more specific. There are lots of *nice*
things in this world.'

Joe leaned forward in his chair, his knees
brushing hers, and even through the fabric of her
dress she fancied she could feel his warmth. Closing her eyes, Cecilia tried to compose herself. It
was just Joe, her friend's brother, the man who
had given her shelter. Joe whose strong arms she
kept picturing wrapped around her, whose lips
she wanted to kiss and whose body she wanted
to feel against hers.

'I need to…' she said, standing abruptly, but
stopped as he caught her hand.

For the past four years she'd been dodging the
advances of her guardian and the droves of fortune hunters. Always she'd avoided any close contact, anything that could be misconstrued as a
sign of affection, never wanting to give a man
the chance to claim she was encouraging him.
But right now she wanted to encourage the man
in front of her and that scared her more than her

deepest fear—getting caught in a compromising position with a suitor who only wanted her fortune.

'What nice things do I deserve, Cecilia?' he asked, his voice low and seductive, and she felt the last of her resolve crumbling.

Sinking back down into the armchair, she felt the warmth of the fire on her face and the heat of Joe's body as he manoeuvred himself closer to her. In the flickering firelight he looked dashing, the shadows playing across his face and accentuating the glint of his eyes and the fullness of his lips.

'There's only one thing I want,' he murmured, reaching forward and tucking a stray strand of hair from her face. Cecilia felt the tickle of his fingers as he lingered longer than he should and looked up into his eyes, knowing that with that one look she would be lost.

Instinctively she felt her body move towards his as his hands tangled in her hair. He kissed her, softly at first, teasing her lips with his own until Cecilia felt as though every inch of her body was on fire. Then he whispered her name and deepened the kiss until Cecilia was lost in a whirlwind of desire and heat.

She shuddered as he ran his fingers down the back of her neck, caressing the skin no one else had ever touched, and urged him to continue as he traced a trail over her collarbones. Somehow Joe had looped his other arm around her waist and pulled her into his lap, their bodies pressed together as they kissed and Cecilia knew if he undressed her now she wouldn't find the will-power to resist.

'What are you doing to me?' Joe murmured, his words tickling her ear.

Before she could answer he was kissing her again, his lips soft against hers.

It seemed to last both an eternity and no time at all and Cecilia found herself willing the seconds to stop ticking by so Joe would never have to pull away.

'We need to stop now,' Joe said, his voice unusually gruff.

Cecilia nodded, seeing the desire in his eyes, feeling the evidence of his arousal even through the thick layers of her skirts.

'But I just can't seem to resist,' he murmured, kissing her just below her earlobe.

Part of her wanted to urge him on, to tell him she didn't care, that she wanted this more than she wanted her virtue, but years of being told it was her most important asset won out. Still she didn't move, just shifted subtly so she could see Joe's face properly.

'Will you just hold me for a moment?' she asked.

He wrapped his arms around her even tighter, pulling her back to rest against his chest, and Cecilia felt her body relaxing. There was something so comforting, so right, about the touch of another person. Not since her mother had died six years ago had anyone taken her in their arms and held her. Even among friends there had to be a certain level of formality and, after losing her family, no one had ever been close enough to hold her again.

And if you become a spinster no one will ever hold you again, the little voice in her head whispered.

It was a sobering thought, the idea that she was resigning herself to a life with no physical intimacy and probably no emotional intimacy either.

'Do you really want to go and live as a spinster?' Joe asked, his voice slightly muffled as his breath tickled her neck.

'Why do you ask?' It was disconcerting, this way he seemed to read her mind.

'You're not built for a life of solitude,' he said after a moment, his fingers tracing a lazy pattern over the back of her neck that made her want to sink deeper into his embrace.

'I always thought I would marry,' Cecilia said softly, voicing the thoughts that she'd kept inside for so long. 'I wanted love and children and a home full of people...'

'Not all men are like your guardian.'

'I know.' The truth was they might not all be like her guardian, but a good many she'd encountered in the past few years were more interested in her money than her. The worse thing was how adept so many were at hiding it. She'd been deceived more than once, sure someone was a true friend, only to find out they didn't have any real interest in her beyond her fortune.

'You say you're worried about fortune hunters?'

'Of course.'

'Then just marry someone rich,' Joe said with a shrug, as if it were as easy as that.

'I was engaged once,' Cecilia said. 'Secretly. We planned to elope, to marry without anyone knowing. By the time we returned I would be Lady Melbry.' She saw Joe's eyes widen in surprise.

'Melbry lost all his money, didn't he?' Joe asked quietly.

'Gambling. Turns out he had a compulsion. And he wasn't very good at it.'

'But you didn't know this when you became engaged to the man,' Joe said, realisation dawning in his eyes.

'He was still lauded as one of the wealthiest men in England. I thought he *must* love me as he said he did because he didn't need my money.' Cecilia heard the bitterness in her voice and knew that even after twenty years had passed she would still be hurting from what he'd done to her. He'd stolen the last of her innocence, her trust in people, and now there was no getting that back. 'So you see I can't just marry someone rich, I would still doubt their intentions.'

'Most matches are made for reasons of money or status or property,' Joe said slowly, but Cecilia could see he understood her reasoning a little more.

'I know, but on Christmas Day, I turn twenty-one and I inherit my father's fortune. I will have the freedom to make my own decisions, to go where I please, to live as I please. Why would I give that up, give my autonomy, my freedom and my fortune up, for marriage? If I married, my husband would own everything, including me.'

Joe was silent and suddenly Cecilia felt a little awkward sitting in his arms. It was entirely inappropriate, even though there wasn't anyone there to witness it. She shifted forward, thinking she would get up and break the connection between them, but Joe's hand caught her arm and held her back gently.

'I understand,' he said, waiting until her eyes came up to meet his to continue, 'but promise me something.'

Cecilia found herself nodding before he continued.

'Don't rule out a different life yet.'

For one heady moment she thought he was offering her something and Cecilia felt the rush of excitement and happiness, followed by the cold realisation that he was speaking in general terms. It made her feel out of control, this sudden awareness that this was what she wanted. Not freedom, not autonomy to make her own decisions. *This.* Joe. She wanted him to enfold her in his arms and kiss her until she forgot everything but him.

'I won't,' she said, trying to keep the sadness from her voice. She knew he wasn't offering her anything more than a kiss and that made her heart tear inside her chest.

'I just can't see you happy as a spinster, living your life alone.'

She shrugged. It wasn't the future she'd imagined for herself either. What young girl dreams of a life of solitude instead of charming princes come to sweep them off their feet?

'I won't be alone,' she said. 'It's not as though I'm going to a convent. I can still socialise, have friends, it's just a husband I'm deciding not to have.'

'And children.'

She felt the pang of sadness, but pushed it away.

Gently he cupped her cheek. 'As long as you're happy,' he said and, before Cecilia knew what was happening, he kissed her again. 'Sorry, I couldn't help myself.'

Wriggling off his lap, she returned to her own armchair, trying to push away all the entirely un-realistic hopes and dreams she was having about the man sitting a few feet away. He was kind, that was all, that was his only reason for all the questions about her future.

Chapter Seven

Joe pulled the thick curtains back and looked out grimly at the snow. It was still thick, but there were telltale signs of melting: the top of plants visible as dark specks in the blanket of white, little puddles under the icicles and the sound of dripping of melting snow.

Today they would have to return to reality. Cecilia would have to leave his little cottage and make her way to Hawthorn House and he would go back to being alone.

Restlessly he paced backwards and forward across the small chamber. He had insisted Cecilia take the main bedroom now the sheets were dry and had spent an uncomfortable night tossing and turning on the narrow bed of the second bedroom. If he was honest, it wasn't the hardness of the bed or the inadequacy of the blankets that had kept him awake, but thoughts of the woman in the next room. He shouldn't have kissed her, it hadn't been gentlemanly to take advantage of an innocent young woman like that, however much she might have wanted it. Yet he knew if he re-lived that moment a hundred times he would always make the same decision.

Could you...? He shook his head, banishing the thought before it even formed. He wasn't what Cecilia wanted or needed, even if he was in a fit state to share his life with someone. No, this little interlude had woken him up, given him a shake and shown him he couldn't continue how he was, but that didn't mean he was ready for a relationship. Especially with a woman as vibrant and alive as Cecilia. She needed a man to whisk her through society, to escort her to balls and show her the world wasn't the awful place her guardian and those fortune hunters had made it out to be.

But maybe... It was tempting, the idea of sweeping Cecilia into his arms and planning a future with her. If he examined his feelings he knew it was what he wanted, but it wouldn't be what was best for her.

With a grumble he pulled the curtains closed again and got dressed, avoiding looking at the puckered and shiny skin that covered the lower half of his left leg.

It wasn't even the physical injury that was holding him back. Months of rehabilitation and work meant that he was now as strong as he had always been, even if he did walk with a limp. He knew Cecilia would never hold his injury against him, but that wasn't all that had been taken away a year ago. He'd lost his purpose, his sense of self-belief, and he knew he needed to find that before he even considered drawing anyone else into the mess he called his life.

Downstairs he stacked the wood on the fire, set the kettle on the hook above it and sat back on one of the hard chairs to await Cecilia. There was still no sound of movement above him and as he sipped the hot cup of tea his mind began wandering to the envelope he'd been studiously ignoring for well over a week. Another request for him to work, no doubt, but this one he hadn't sent back without looking like he had the rest. It was still sitting there, as yet unopened, but for the first time in a very long time he felt a flicker of curiosity.

Rising, he walked out of the kitchen and headed for the pile of papers, lifting the envelope and taking it back to the warm kitchen before setting it down on the table. Ten long seconds passed before he opened it, then, his mind made up, he tore a strip off the top and pulled out the thick stack of papers.

On the very top was a handwritten note, signed by Theodore Long, with noticeably no official heading or seal, just the familiar looping hand-writing he recognised from his university days.

Crawley,
Take a look—see if you can figure it out.
I've got five men working on it, no luck yet.
Would be good to exercise that brain of yours again, wouldn't it?
Best wishes,
T. Long

He smiled at the note, imagining his friend's clipped aristocratic voice with the always-present hint of humour. Putting aside the top sheet, he looked at the papers beneath, frowning at first as he tried to decipher what language it was written in. Joe was fluent in French, Spanish and Portuguese with a basic understanding of Russian as well. It only took him a moment to realise this wasn't any recognisable language—the letters were strung together in an order that wouldn't make sense, even in the most bizarre of languages. This was code.

It was just like Theodore Long to not even give him a clue as to the base language, who they had intercepted it from. Probably his old friend would think it would hinder any leaps in deduction on

Joe's part, preferring for him to look at it with a completely clear mind, no assumptions made.

Feeling a soft buzz of exhilaration, he soon became engrossed in the code, only pausing to fetch paper and a pencil to make his own scribblings on to avoid corrupting the original document. He was concentrating so hard he didn't hear Cecilia rise and begin to move around upstairs and when she appeared at the kitchen door it was a full thirty seconds before he registered her presence.

'Good morning,' she said softly.

He looked up and instantly all thoughts of deciphering Long's coded message flew from his mind.

'Good morning,' he said, taking in her tousled hair and flushed cheeks and wondering why seeing her in such a natural state should be so arousing.

'The snow is beginning to melt,' Cecilia said and he was pleased to hear the touch of sadness in her voice. It had been a pleasant interlude, these past few days, and he was glad he wasn't the only one to find it so.

'I shall escort you to Hawthorn House later this morning,' he said.

'There's no need, I'm sure I can remember the way.'

'There's every need. The road will be treacherous in the ice and if you fell from your horse you may lay undiscovered for hours because there will be so few people venturing out.' He said it brusquely to try to hide the true concern he felt at the idea of Cecilia travelling alone.

'We shouldn't arrive together,' Cecilia said. 'I know I'm not looking to marry, but I'd still like to preserve my reputation if at all possible.'

She would marry. Of course she would. A vibrant, attractive young woman like Cecilia couldn't stay a spinster for ever. Once out of her guardian's clutches she would slowly start to trust in people again, to see the good in the world. Then it would only be a matter of time before some young gentleman caught her eye. Perhaps it might take a little longer for her to trust her suitors, but eventually she would, he was sure of it. The idea of Cecilia sinking into someone else's arms made him feel unsettled—it wasn't an image he wanted to have.

As Cecilia placed her booted foot into Joe's hand she pushed upwards and settled herself in the saddle. The pull in her ankle ached as she exerted herself, but as soon as she was settled the discomfort died away.

'I never know how you ride that way,' Joe murmured as he looked up at her.

Cecilia shrugged. Side-saddle was the only way she'd ever been allowed to ride. To sit astride, like a man, would be to invite gossip and the women of the *ton* loved to gossip, especially about someone as wealthy as she. Whenever she socialised her every move was scrutinised, pulled apart and appraised, and always Cecilia had felt as though she'd been found wanting.

She'd almost offered Joe her horse, but had caught herself at the last moment. There would be nothing he hated more than the perception that he was so invalided that he would take a mount from a woman. Reminding herself he'd walked the five miles here from Hawthorn House without any difficulty in the thick snow, she dismissed any thoughts that he might struggle physically and settled herself deeper into the saddle. Joe was not an invalid, he'd proved as much the previous evening when he'd wrapped those strong arms around her as she toppled into his lap. Cecilia's next thought was of their kiss—that wonderful moment when his lips had met hers. The moment everything had seemed to change for her.

Sparing a sideways glance, she felt the disappointment bloom in her chest. Joe was now just as he'd always been with her. There was no hint he was torturing himself over their kiss. No hint that he wanted anything more than the pleasant interlude these last few days had been.

'Shall we?' he asked, motioning for her to lead the way.

For a few minutes she rode in silence, glancing back over her shoulder before they rounded the bend in the road for one last look at Rose Cottage. Despite the calamities of the first night her stay had been lovely and Cecilia couldn't admit it out loud, but it was the happiest couple of days she'd had for a long time.

'Do you know who will be at your parents'?' she asked once the cottage had disappeared from view.

'My mother was eager to point out all the *fun young people* she was inviting,' Joe said with a grimace. 'I think she hopes one day I might just give in and marry one of the debutantes she keeps trying to thrust at me.' He paused and Cecilia wondered what exactly had happened with the woman he'd been engaged to. Rumour had it that she'd called the wedding off when confronted with the idea of an invalid for a husband, but Cecilia couldn't see anyone being that heartless. And it wasn't as though Joe was any less able to do anything physical now he'd recovered fully, even if he did have a little bit of a limp. 'The usual crowd will be there, I'm sure. The Rutledges, the Growbers, the Freemantles, probably a few eligible young gentlemen in the hope someone will catch Elizabeth's eye.'

'I haven't danced for so long,' Cecilia said, feeling the first flush of excitement. Her guardian had kept her at Whiteburn Hall these past couple of months. As her twenty-first birthday approached he had become more desperate to somehow get his hands on her fortune and as such had given up all pretence of goodwill and kindness and had forbidden her to leave the house. With only him and The Wet Rag for company Cecilia had felt she was losing her mind sometimes, although even the promise of freedom wasn't anywhere near enough incentive to get her to agree to marry Peter Turner.

She glanced down, wondering how it would feel to be swept around the ballroom in the arms of the man by her side. He had told her he didn't dance, not after his injury, but she had seen him move around and wondered if his reluctance was more to do with his not wanting to socialise than with his physical prowess.

'I love to dance, to feel the music taking hold of my body, to surrender myself to the steps.' She paused, wondering whether to ask the question that was on her lips. 'Did you dance, before your injury?'

'A little.' He was looking straight ahead as if thinking back to another time. She wondered if he was thinking about his ex-fiancée, Miss Rebecca Farnham, if he was remembering waltzing around a ballroom with her in his arms.

'And when you were home on leave from the army?' she asked.

He looked up at her with a smile on his lips, but one eyebrow raised as if in admonishment. 'If you're trying to get me to talk more about Miss Farnham, then you are going to be sorely disappointed.'

'I wasn't—' Cecilia started to say.

'I hope you aren't thinking of lying to me, Lady Cecilia.'

'You shouldn't have such a murky and interesting past,' Cecilia said, trying her best to look innocent and haughty at the same time.

'I'd hardly call one ex-fiancée murky and interesting.'

'Society would have to disagree. You were the talk of the town for weeks.' She saw Joe grimace at the thought and wondered if she had said too much.

'The things people choose to talk about,' he said with a shake of his head. 'Enough about me and my poor excuse of a foray into the world of romance. Let's talk about you.'

'Me?' Cecilia said, feeling the full force of his regard as he turned to look at her.

'You,' he repeated.

'I think in the three days we've been together you've probably found out all there is to know about me,' she said, suddenly feeling inexplicably nervous. It was the way he was looking at her, half amused, half something else, something more primal and smouldering as if he wanted to eat her up. Thankfully her voice didn't come out as the nervous squeak she'd imagined, but she heard the tremor there all the same.

'I know a little about you,' he said, pausing to brush the snow off his breeches. 'I know you like a *lot* of butter on your toast. I know you talk to yourself when you disagree with something you read in a book. I know you really love bacon, but your good manners stop you from devouring it as you wish. I know how you frown when you concentrate so that little furrow appears between your eyebrows. I know all of that...'

'You seem to mainly know about my culinary preferences,' she grumbled.

'It was an important part of your stay with me.' He looked up at her, raising his hand to pat her horse on its flank and brushing her leg with his fingers at the same time. 'I know a little more, of course. How you taste, how soft the skin on the back of your neck is, how you moan ever so quietly when you're kissed.'

'Joe,' Cecilia hissed, scandalised. She looked around to check no one was hiding in the hedgerow. His words had ignited a flush of warmth inside her, something she was sure no well-brought-up young lady was supposed to feel. The memory of their kiss was seared into her brain and Cecilia knew that no other experience would ever come close to it. Whenever she thought of the few minutes she'd spent wrapped in his arms, her whole body suffused with a happiness she'd never felt before.

'I think we're quite safe,' he said with a laugh. 'Unless anyone is spying on us from a rabbit hole or the branches of a tree.'

'My mother used to tell me gossips had ears everywhere,' Cecilia said, smiling at the memory. 'When I was young I thought they actually had ears dotted around the place, like extra body parts that didn't need to be attached.'

'I don't think even the gossips' ears can reach us out here.'

'Even so, we shouldn't talk about it.'

'About…?' Joe asked and she could tell he was enjoying himself immensely.

'About the kiss,' she ground out, unable to stop herself from looking around again.

'Still no disembodied ears, Cecilia,' he reassured her. 'If I can't talk about it, can I imagine it?' he asked and as his eyes came up to meet hers she saw the heat mixed with the humour.

'No.'

'Too late.'

Cecilia was remembering it, too, the fire she'd felt when their lips had met reigniting itself deep in her belly. If they'd been side by side she wouldn't have been able to resist leaning over and closing her eyes, inviting him to sweep her away again with the soft brush of his lips against hers. As it was she had to console herself with the memory.

'Now that warms a man up,' Joe murmured.

For a moment Cecilia found herself wishing again that things could be different, that the kiss they'd shared could be the beginning of something rather than a single interlude in her difficult life. She wanted Joe to sweep her away, to declare his undying love for her and tell her that although she was set on becoming a spinster he just wouldn't allow it, he loved her too much.

Quietly Cecilia snorted. That wasn't how the real world worked, no matter how much she might want it. The real world was fortune hunters and guardians who took too many liberties and losing your parents at the tender age of fifteen.

'Something on your mind?'

'I was just thinking how life isn't how it is in books.'

He was silent for a long moment, the only sound the crunching of his boots in the fresh snow, and Cecilia could see the emotions flitting over his face. After nearly a minute he stopped, catching her horse by the bridle and waiting for her to meet his eye.

'You're better off without me,' he said quietly.

Cecilia felt her heart squeeze inside her chest at his words. She hadn't realised until that moment how much she'd been hoping he might declare his feeling for her, that something might build from their fledgling emotional connection. In addition to her own hurt and disappointment it pained her to see that he actually meant the words, he actually thought she would be better off without him.

It hurt, this rejection, even though he was doing it in that kind way of his. He still was telling her they couldn't be together. That he wouldn't fight past his demons to be with her.

'That's not true,' she said, not wanting to sound desperate or to force his hand, but needing him to see his own worth. 'Anyone would be lucky to have you in their life.'

A shadow flickered across his face and she knew he was thinking about Miss Rebecca Farnham, the woman who'd categorically rejected him from her life. Cecilia didn't know the reason why, but she suspected it had something to do with his injury, some misplaced notion that Joe was less of a man now he walked with a limp and had a leg covered in scars.

He shook his head, reaching up to take her hand in his. 'You don't need an invalid to hold you back,' he said softly. 'You need a man to keep up with you, to whirl you around ballrooms and socialise with a smile.'

'No,' she said quietly, but could see that he wouldn't listen to reason. Until he'd kissed her the day before, she had been set on becoming a spinster. On renouncing men for the rest of her life. It probably had been a rash decision, but Cecilia knew it was one she'd made to protect herself after nearly falling for the lies of Lord Melbry. Perhaps he was right, she was young and could easily change her mind in a year or two, find some nice man to settle down with, but she *had* been resigned to leading a life alone.

Then he'd kissed her and with that one kiss awoken her to what life could be about.

And now he was snatching it away again.

'Find yourself a nice man,' he said. 'Someone good. Someone whole.'

Cecilia had to turn away so he wouldn't see the tears in her eyes. No amount of protest on her part would make Joe see himself as good enough. Even if he was exactly the man she wanted.

Chapter Eight

'Cee-cee,' Elizabeth shouted as she hurtled down the stairs and flung herself at Cecilia.

The two women embraced as if they'd been separated for a hundred years, pressing their cheeks together and clasping hands at the same time.

'My welcome is never that effusive,' Joe murmured, grinning at his sister as she rolled her eyes at him.

'I saw you three days ago,' Elizabeth said. 'I haven't seen Cecilia for *years*.'

'A slight exaggeration, little Sister,' Joe said.

'Well, it feels like years. Come in, take off your coat and warm yourself up.' Elizabeth busied herself helping Cecilia out of her coat and handing them to a waiting footman. 'What are you doing here?' she asked over her shoulder as the two women moved towards the warmth of the drawing room.

'Escorting Lady Cecilia,' he said stiffly. It wasn't the first time he'd lied to his sister. When they were growing up, despite the age gap between them, he'd tormented her tirelessly as all good brothers should torment their sisters, but he didn't often have cause to lie about anything that mattered.

'Your brother was very kind,' he heard Cecilia murmur.

'Joe?' Elizabeth laughed. 'Well, I suppose he's not the *worst* man in the world. But did you come on your own? What about Mr Turner or...' Elizabeth lowered her voice to a theatrical whisper '... The Wet Rag?'

'I did ask permission,' Cecilia said, 'but Mr Turner wasn't keen on me venturing out, so I decided to take the decision out of his hands and come anyway.'

'Cecilia Bronwen, I'm scandalised. And impressed.'

'It's only two days until my birthday,' Cecilia said with a happy sigh. 'And then I'll be free for ever.'

It was strange to see the woman he'd grown close to over the past couple of days with his sister. They were so comfortable together, so relaxed in each other's company. Joe found he was following them into the drawing room just to listen to their conversation, to hear what Cecilia might say about him.

With a shake of his head he stopped. This way danger lay. He'd escorted Cecilia back, that should be enough, now he needed to leave, to get back to his normal life.

'Joseph.' His mother sounded both concerned and delighted to see him. 'Have you changed your mind about the ball?'

'No, Mother,' he said, taking the petite woman in his arms and kissing her on the cheek, watching how she flushed with pleasure at having him home again. 'I saw Lady Cecilia struggling past Rose Cottage and came to escort her safely here.'

'Surely you won't leave straight away,' his mother said, taking him by the arm and leading him further towards the drawing room. 'It's another five miles back to the cottage in the snow.' She shook her head. 'Stay the night at least. Most of the guests will arrive tomorrow after midday, you could be gone by then if you wanted to avoid everyone.'

He looked at her hopeful face and nodded, realising how patient and understanding his family had been these past few months and wanting to do something to make his mother happy. One night at home, spending the time with his family and Cecilia, that wasn't much of a hardship.

'Wonderful, I'll tell the maids to make up your bedroom. I'm so glad you're here, Joseph.'

As he entered the drawing room he was struck by the transformation it had undergone in the past few days since he'd left for Rose Cottage. His mother and sister had been hard at work, transforming the room into a festive paradise with sprigs of holly. Mistletoe hung above the fireplace and there was a tantalising scent of oranges and spices, a smell he recalled from the Christmases of his youth.

'Where are you going to go?' Elizabeth was asking Cecilia, her eyes wide with interest.

Cecilia shrugged, trying to look nonchalant, but Joe knew she would have everything planned out, every last journey, every last eventuality. This was her big escape, the occasion she'd been waiting for the past six years.

'My solicitor, Mr Jarvis, tells me there may be a delay in obtaining sufficient funds to set myself up with a house and everything I will need, but I will be able to draw a small advance, enough to tide me over while the paperwork is being sorted.'

'So you'll leave Mr Turner's house straight away?'

'I hope only to return to pick up my belongings,' Cecilia said. Joe saw the wariness in her eyes and knew that despite the excitement she felt at the idea of finally being free she would be nervous as well. It was her first foray out into the world alone.

'Joseph, might I have a word?' his mother said, following him into the room with a concerned expression on her face. He wondered at first if there was some problem with the sleeping arrangements, but then dismissed the idea. His mother never allowed his room to be used as a guest bedroom, keeping it for her son *just in case*. She looked worried, all traces of the earlier pleasure at seeing him again gone, and was uncharacteristically wringing her hands as she approached him.

'I invited Mr and Mrs Farnham to the Christmas Eve Ball,' she said, her voice quiet as if she didn't want anyone else to overhear.

Joe nodded reasonably. The Farnhams were neighbours, a pleasant couple the same age as his parents who had moved to the area a few years ago. That was how he'd met Rebecca, at one of these Christmas Eve celebrations three years ago when he'd been home on leave from the army.

'I wasn't expecting you to be here,' his mother said. 'I thought it wouldn't do any harm—they are our neighbours after all, even after what *she* did.'

'I don't mind, Mother. I have nothing against the Farnhams.' It was the truth. Mr and Mrs Farnham had seemed perfectly pleasant people the few times he'd met them. It wasn't their fault their daughter had ripped his heart out and stamped on it, full of contempt for the man he was now.

'They're here,' his mother said, her voice hushed.

'Then I shall greet them as I would any of our neighbours. Do not worry so, Mother,' he said, patting her on the arm reassuringly.

'They've brought Rebecca.' The words came out a little too loudly so everyone else in the room turned and stared at Joe and his mother. She clamped a hand over her mouth as if wishing to claw the information back inside, but the damage was already done. Everyone was watching him warily for a reaction.

Instinctively his eyes flitted across the room, seeking Cecilia out. She was watching him with the same wariness as everyone else, but as she saw him look at her she gave him a reassuring smile.

'I didn't invite her,' his mother whispered. 'But she's recently widowed and I suppose she's back home with her parents…'

'I can't say I have much desire to make small talk with her,' Joe said softly. 'But I can be polite, Mother, you raised me well enough to do that.'

He saw the relief in his mother's eyes and leaned forward to kiss her on the cheek.

Everyone in the room was returning to their

conversations, but Joe knew all eyes would be on him when Rebecca entered.

'So I get to meet the evil ex-fiancée?' Cecilia murmured as she slipped to his side.

Despite his trepidation about seeing Rebecca again, he found himself smiling.

'If I didn't know your every last move these past three days I might suspect you of engineering this just so you could meet her.'

'Well, if you would have just answered my questions then I wouldn't have been driven to such extremes,' Cecilia teased him.

The door to the room opened and Mr and Mrs Farnham entered, followed closely by Rebecca, dressed in the customary black mourning clothes that showed her to be a recent widow.

He expected to feel *something*. Anger perhaps at the way she'd treated him, or a simmering resentment for how easily she'd broken his heart when he was at his lowest point physically and emotionally.

'Nothing,' he murmured to himself, earning a quizzical glance from Cecilia. He felt nothing. Not even a mild dislike. For the emotions he was expecting he had to care and it would appear he'd finally been able to cleanse himself of any residual feelings for his ex-fiancée. Time was a great healer. Time and distraction...

'Major Crawley,' Rebecca said, smiling tightly

as she greeted him, her eyes raking over his body and pausing on the injured leg, despite there being no outward signs of his injury.

'I trust you are well,' he said blandly. 'This is Lady Cecilia Bronwen, a close family friend.' He wasn't sure why he added the last part, but watched in satisfaction as Rebecca stiffened perceptibly and turned her attention to Cecilia.

'I don't think we've met, Lady Cecilia,' Rebecca said, the smile on her face not quite meeting her eyes. 'Although I'm sure we have friends in common.'

'I'm sorry for your loss,' Cecilia said. 'It must be a difficult time for you.'

Joe knew almost nothing about Rebecca's late husband. He hadn't wanted to know how she'd moved on so quickly, but now his interest was piqued. It could only have been a short marriage.

'So sad when you were only recently married,' Cecilia continued, putting voice to Joe's thoughts.

'Quite,' Rebecca said. 'It was a shock to everyone when my husband passed away.' She turned her attention back to Joe, a hint of regret in her eyes. 'I was very sorry how we parted after our last meeting,' she said, dropping her voice in an effort to exclude Cecilia.

'Think nothing of it,' Joe said magnanimously. 'I don't.'

'Perhaps later we could…' Rebecca started to say, but Joe had already caught Cecilia's arm.

'If you would excuse us,' he said, noting Rebecca's surprised expression. No doubt she had imagined him still in her thrall, eager for any scrap of affection she threw his way. Joe felt like shouting with joy. In truth he had thought he did still care a little for the woman who had rejected him so coldly nearly a year ago, but he didn't even feel hatred, just a desire to not be in her company for any longer than was necessary.

'Pretty,' Cecilia murmured as they strolled to the other side of the room.

'In a superficial way.'

'She thought you were still going to be in love with her,' Cecilia said in that frank way of hers. 'You could see it on her face.'

'Mmm…'

'*I* thought you were still in love with her,' Cecilia said.

Joe's eyes shot up and met Cecilia's and he saw the hint of confusion in their depths.

'I'm not,' he said, making sure his voice remained even.

'No, I see that now.' She was shaking her head as if she couldn't quite believe something. 'Would you excuse me?'

Cecilia left so abruptly he was left standing on his own in the corner of the room, staring after her. He shook his head, perplexed. There was no reason Cecilia should want him to still be in love with Rebecca and, after spending so much of the past few days together, he would have thought she would prefer it if he didn't still harbour any feelings for his ex-fiancée.

'What did you say to make Cecilia run off like that?' his sister asked, her eyes shining with interest.

'Nothing.' He'd learned long ago that the fewer words said to his sister the better if you wanted to keep your secrets.

'Did something happen between the two of you on your way here?'

'No.'

He remembered the kiss, that wonderful moment of closeness as Cecilia had sat in his lap. In that moment he'd felt content, more content than he had been for years. Part of him wanted to grasp that feeling and recreate it over and over again. Part of him wanted to sweep her into his arms and tell her they should be together.

Glancing down, he looked at his leg, the injury that had changed everything for him. He might have worked and worked until he could walk again, to recover his physical abilities, but he'd lost something along with the chunks of muscle and ligaments. He'd lost his purpose, his self-belief. He couldn't ask Cecilia to settle for a man who wasn't whole, on the inside even more than the out.

'You looked very close for two people who have only travelled somewhere together.'

'Is that so?' he said blandly, trying not to let his sister see the pain he was feeling inside.

Elizabeth glanced around the room, making sure no one was watching, then leaned in and shook her head.

'Keep your secrets,' she said ominously. 'I'm sure Cecilia will be more than happy to confide in her dearest friend.'

Chapter Nine

Cecilia sat and watched the flames flicker in the fireplace, stretching out her feet towards the warmth and giving a contented little sigh. Despite all her reservations she was glad she'd pushed on and come to spend Christmas with the Crawleys. Their home was always welcoming and comfortable and she didn't ever have to worry about anyone behaving inappropriately. Today was Christmas Eve and later that evening the rest of the guests would arrive for the annual Christmas Eve Ball. It would be an evening of merriment and laughter, and for her it would mark the start of so much more. Tomorrow, on Christmas Day, she turned twenty-one. In less than twenty-four hours she would be a free woman, in possession of her father's fortune and no longer obliged to do anything her guardian instructed. It was the best Christmas present she could hope for.

'Elizabeth said I would find you in here,' Joe

said as he entered the room, shutting the door quietly behind him. The Crawleys had about twenty guests staying in their home with the rest of the invited friends and neighbours coming just for the ball that evening. Cecilia had started the day in the drawing room, but the constant need to make small talk had exhausted her and Elizabeth had shown her to the small library, kept locked from the other guests so she might have a few moments of privacy.

'I thought you might have left,' she said. He hadn't been at breakfast with the rest of the family and Cecilia had half-expected to see him emerging from the kitchens after making his own morning meal.

'I wouldn't leave without saying goodbye.'

'Your mother hasn't persuaded you to stay for the ball?'

Joe grimaced. 'She's tried her very hardest.'

'I wish you well for your journey,' Cecilia said. She knew it sounded like a dismissal, but it felt too painful to sit and talk with him. After seeing him with Rebecca yesterday she had spent a maudlin evening feeling like a fool. A fool to think that Joe would ever care for her. In her mind she'd told herself that they couldn't be together because he still had some residual feelings for the woman he'd been engaged to. That had hurt, when she had thought that he cared for a woman who had rejected him more than he cared for the woman standing warm and willing in front of him, but at least that had been an *understandable* reason.

When she saw how little Rebecca had affected him it had been like a knife to the heart. He wasn't deciding not to pursue a future with her because of any external reason, which meant it was just because he didn't care enough.

'I could stay, if you wished,' Joe said quietly. 'If you wanted me to.'

She glanced up, but couldn't read the expression on his face. Slowly he came to sit beside her, his legs brushing against hers and their bodies far too close for propriety, but the door was closed and they were unlikely to be disturbed.

'I've enjoyed spending these last few days with you, Cecilia,' he said and for a moment she forgot all the pain she felt at not being able to have this man in front of her and basked in his words.

'And I you.'

He reached out and took her hand and Cecilia felt her heart thumping in her chest. For years she'd told herself she was quite content to be alone, to grow old a spinster without a man by her side or in her life. And she had been, until she'd met Joe. Now she wanted so much more. She wanted him.

'Perhaps our paths will meet again one day.'

She looked at him, waiting for him to say more, and then shook her head sadly as all her hopes came crashing down.

'That's it?' she asked, aware she sounded a little hysterical.

'What do you mean?'

She tried her hardest to keep everything bottled up inside, but something gave way and all the hopes and desires of the last few days came rushing out. 'You kissed me, you looked at me with fire in your eyes. You made me like you, you made me want to change my entire life plan to be with you and all you have to say is "Perhaps our paths will meet again one day".'

'Cecilia, I never promised you anything. I shouldn't have kissed you...'

'No, don't take that away as well.'

'I'm sorry,' he said, resting a finger under her chin and waiting until she looked up at him.

'Don't,' she said, feeling the hot tears fall on to her cheeks. 'Just go.'

'I'm not leaving you like this.'

'Why not? We're just strangers who were thrown together for a couple of days.'

'That's not true.' He wiped away the tears with the pad of his thumb, smiling sadly as he did so. 'I like you, Cecilia. I like you more than I have any right to.'

She shook her head. She didn't want him to like her, she wanted him to feel so much more.

'But I wouldn't be any good for you. I'm not the sort of man you need as a husband.'

'What do you know about what I want or need?'

'Trust me, Cecilia, I'm not the man for you. I'm not the man for anyone.' He glanced down for a fraction of a second as he said this and Cecilia found herself frowning.

'Because of your leg? I don't understand, Joe. You can walk, ride, do a hundred other physical activities. Yes, you limp and you aren't allowed to do the one thing you devoted the last ten years of your life to, but that doesn't make you any less of a man.'

She watched him, tried to work out if her words were having any impact. If only he could see that to her it didn't matter if he was injured or not, if he always walked with a limp. It didn't matter if he had lost his direction for a while, that was only natural after being cast out of the life you'd lived for so long. All that mattered was that she cared for this man in front of her, cared so much she suspected she might love him.

'It's not my leg,' he said slowly, as if struggling to find the right words to convey what he was feeling. 'I lost so much more than a chunk of flesh when I was injured…' He trailed off.

Ten seconds ticked past, then twenty, and Cecilia found she was holding her breath. Her whole life, her whole happiness, depended on what Joe said next, whether she'd managed to persuade him that the only person he was hurting by refusing to move on from his experiences was himself.

'Cecilia,' Elizabeth said, bursting into the room.

They'd only been sitting next to one another, but guiltily she and Joe jumped apart.

Elizabeth registered their presence, the closeness of their bodies, but didn't say anything. Cecilia frowned—either her friend had suddenly grown tactful or something she deemed more important had caused her to rush in here.

'He's here,' Elizabeth hissed, motioning out the door.

'Who?' Cecilia had images of her guardian storming Hawthorn House, righteous indignation in his eyes. There would be no point, of course, with her birthday tomorrow, but Mr Turner was the sort of man to do it anyway.

'Your suitor, The Wet Rag.'

'Peter's here?' Cecilia asked, frowning. Peter Turner wasn't the sort of man to turn up anywhere uninvited. Not on his own initiative at least.

Standing, she smoothed down her dress, refusing to look at Joe. If she did, he would see the heartbreak in her eyes, and she wanted to keep hold of the last of her dignity. She'd bared herself to him, tried to show him his reasons for thinking she would be better without him were unfounded, but still he wasn't budging.

With her head held high she walked into the hall, taking in the sodden form of Peter Turner dripping on the wooden floor. It must have started snowing again; Peter's hair was plastered to his head and his coat was heavy with water.

'Peter,' Cecilia said, noting the curious faces peering out of the open drawing-room door, 'what brings you here today?'

He grimaced, swallowing twice in a movement that made the prominence in his neck bob up and down erratically.

'I was concerned for your welfare,' he said, reaching out to take her hand, but deciding against the movement halfway through, leaving his arm dangling out in front of him as he looked around. 'I wanted to make sure you got here safely.'

Cecilia narrowed her eyes. The Wet Rag was not a bad man, not like his father. He had been kind to her over the years in his own way, protecting her from the worst of his father's schemes and the older man's wandering hands when he got drunk. The worst she could say about him was he was in his father's thrall. Peter hadn't had an original thought for a long time, or at least he hadn't voiced one, but for some reason she wondered if he had come here of his own accord. Surely old Mr Turner didn't think there was any chance of her giving in now and agreeing to marry Peter the day before she came into her inheritance.

'Father doesn't know I'm here,' he said, smiling ruefully. 'Although he probably would approve.'

'Peter…'

'Might I have a word in private?' he asked, his words coming out in a rush and his face turning the colour of a robin's breast.

Cecilia blinked, trying to find some cohesion in her thoughts, but struggling to understand what was happening. She still couldn't quite believe Peter was here, there was no reason for him to be.

Slowly she nodded, stepping back and leading the way into the library, starting as she saw Joe looming by the fireplace. His eyes narrowed as he took in Peter's wet form.

'Would you excuse us?' Cecilia asked, not able to look at the man who only a few minutes ago had crushed her hopes.

'You need a chaperon,' Joe said curtly. 'I'll stay.' He crossed to the door and closed it, turning round to face them, a stony expression on his face.

'I say, I promise not to compromise Cecilia,' Peter Turner said, looking a little nervous at saying what he had come to say in front of Joe.

'Lady Cecilia,' Joe corrected him.

'Yes. Well. Lady Cecilia.'

'Pretend I'm not here,' Joe said.

Cecilia snorted, an unladylike sound that caused both men to turn and look at her.

'You're not exactly unobtrusive,' she muttered.

'I suggest you start talking, Mr Turner. Lady Cecilia has a ball to ready herself for this evening.'

Shaking her head, Cecilia turned so she could only see Joe out of the corner of her eye, but even that was far too distracting.

'Right. Yes. Well. You see…'

'Time is ticking,' Joe said. Cecilia shot him a dark look, he was enjoying this far too much.

'Cecilia—' Turner started to say.

'Lady Cecilia,' Joe corrected again.

'Can you excuse me for a moment?' Cecilia said to Peter, not waiting for his answer and trying to ignore the lost-puppy expression on his face. She marched over to Joe, grasped him by his crossed arm and pulled him out the door into the hall.

'What are you doing?' she asked.

'Guarding your honour.'

'Don't be ridiculous.'

'I'm not. You told me you didn't want to be forced into marriage by a man ruining your reputation, I'm just making sure that doesn't happen.'

'And why do you care?'

He was silent for a few seconds and Cecilia

saw something darken in his eyes. Shaking her head, she slipped back into the room, closing the door behind her. She had to grit her teeth as she heard the door open behind her again, but resisted the temptation to turn around.

'Peter,' she said, 'please continue.'

'We've known each other a long time, Lady Cecilia,' he said, glancing nervously over her shoulder where no doubt Joe was glowering at him. 'And over the years I have grown to care for you. I know you don't love me, but I'm asking for a chance. A chance to show you what life could be like together.'

He reached out and took her hand in his and Cecilia had to fight to resist the urge to pull away. His hand was moist with perspiration and gripped hers limply.

'Would you do me the great honour of marrying me?'

'Was this your father's idea?' she asked.

'No. Well, not exactly. He's been going on for years about me marrying you, but he doesn't know I'm here today.' Turner looked at her hopefully and Cecilia wondered if he had thought there was a chance she might say yes.

'Peter, it is very kind of you to ask…'

'Please just consider it, Cecilia. I know you haven't been happy living with my father these last few years, but I'm not him. I'm my own man. We could have a very contented life together.'

'And my money?' she asked bluntly.

'Would remain yours. I could sign a document or something. This isn't about the money, Cecilia.'

Behind her she heard Joe snort and turned to scowl at him.

'If you're going to interrupt, I will have to ask you to leave,' Cecilia said primly. Part of her hoped he would—it would be easier to let Peter down gently without a hostile Joe as an audience. The other part of her, the part she was wishing wasn't so weak, was still hoping he might spring into action, declare his love for her and bundle Peter Turner out of the room.

'Give the man his answer,' Joe murmured.

Cecilia glowered at Joe, all the disappointment and sadness combining to make her feel anger at his behaviour. 'If you have ever had any respect for me, you will leave right now,' she said, her voice icy.

She turned back to Peter, her breath catching in her throat as she heard the soft click of the door behind her. He'd gone. Taking a deep breath, she composed herself.

'I'm sorry, Peter,' she said. 'It was kind of you to ride all this way in the snow, but I'm unable to accept your proposal.' She said the words softly, but still saw the flash of disappointment in his eyes.

'Of course. I knew that would be your answer, but a man has to ask.' He took her hand again and gave it a squeeze. 'Best of luck, Cecilia. I brought a small bag of your things with me, just a few bits and bobs I thought you might need.'

After a moment he dropped her hand and began to move away and Cecilia felt a surprising bubble of affection for him.

'Peter,' she said as he reached the door. He turned round with an expression of hope. 'Thank you for all you've done for me. For protecting me from your father.'

He shrugged. 'A better man would have done more.'

Then he was gone, slipping out of the door and most likely out of her life.

Chapter Ten

Joe kicked the snow with his boot and grumbled under his breath. It had been a hell of an afternoon. After he'd left Cecilia in the library with Peter Turner asking for her hand he'd retreated to his room, his head spinning with regrets and self-recriminations The first of the guests had begun to arrive and he hadn't wanted to be forced to make small talk with anyone as he left Hawthorn House. So instead he had decided to wait until the ball was in full swing, when everyone would be occupied, to make his escape.

He should be halfway back to Rose Cottage by now and instead he was only a few feet from Hawthorn House. He'd left, walked out the door, but something was pulling him back.

Not something. Someone. Cecilia. The woman he'd told a few hours earlier that he couldn't be with her. That he couldn't give her what she wanted. That he couldn't make her happy.

It was the truth. He was convinced she needed a man who could be her social equal. Who could escort her to balls and dinner parties, ride out on the hunt with her. He wasn't that man. For the past year he'd shut himself away from the world, he wasn't ready for the scrutiny of being married to the richest woman in England. She needed a man with a purpose, a man who knew what he was doing with his life, who contributed to the world.

And yet…here he was. Still standing in the freezing snow outside Hawthorn House. Unable to walk away.

'You're a fool, Crawley,' he muttered to himself. Although whether he was a fool for staying or a fool for ever letting Cecilia go in the first place he wasn't sure.

For a moment he closed his eyes. Let the memories of the last year wash over him, the loneliness, the self-imposed exile from the world. His penance for surviving when so many others hadn't. The rehabilitation from his injury, the sympathetic looks and well-meaning enquiries to his health, all that had made him feel less of a man. That had made him retreat into his own little sanctuary.

'Enough,' he murmured. It was time to take his place in the world once again. He was going to stop hiding away, stop moping for the life he'd lost. Tomorrow he would make a start on cracking the codes Theodore Long had sent him and take his old friend up on the offer of work to serve his country even though he was no longer fit for the army. And, most importantly, he was going to do all of it with the woman he loved by his side.

With his head bent against the fresh snow that was falling he made his way back to the house.

Although the ball had begun an hour ago the carriages carrying the guests who were not in residence were still pulling up, travelling slowly to stay safe in the snow on the ground and in the air. Inside he could hear laughter and merriment and, as he worked his way through the people on the threshold, he felt the warmth of the house hitting him.

Glancing around, he didn't immediately see Cecilia. He kept his head bent, trying to avoid being pulled into conversation with any of the guests, and moved from room to room, all the time his eyes searching for the woman he hoped would give him another chance.

'Major Crawley,' a voice called out and Joe stiffened. It was Rebecca, of course it was. She was weaving her way towards him and the eyes of the other guests were surreptitiously fixed on them.

'I'm sorry,' he said as she reached his side. 'I've somewhere else to be.'

He'd spotted Cecilia. She was out on the terrace, a shawl around her shoulders and her back turned to the drawing room full of people. Even though he couldn't see her face he felt the breath being sucked out of his body. She looked stunning. She was wearing a dress made of red silk that pinched in at the waist and flowed out into a vast skirt that harked back to the fashions of thirty years ago. The neckline was designed to draw the eye, plunging down further than was the norm, and the sleeves worn off the shoulders.

As if sensing him Cecilia turned and he saw the moment that she noticed him. One gloved hand came up to rest on her chest, just below the perfectly cut diamond that rested at the base of her throat.

'Cecilia,' he said, opening the doors to the terrace and slipping outside.

'What are you doing here?'

'I've been a fool.'

He saw the hope flare in her eyes at his words and felt regret at the caution that followed. She was having to guard her heart because he'd pushed her away.

'I wasn't ready for you to come into my life,' he said, moving towards her and taking her hand in his. It didn't matter to him that they were in full view of the drawing room and the dozens of guests, he didn't care who saw him bare his heart, if only Cecilia would forgive him. 'I wasn't ready to be pulled back into the real world.'

Cecilia looked up at him, pulling her shawl closer over her shoulders, whether to guard off the cold or to ward off possible disappointment he didn't know.

'I love you,' he said. 'I know it's madness, I know we've only known each other for a short time, but I love you.'

'But earlier…' she said.

'Earlier I was a coward. I was too afraid to reach out and take what I wanted, I thought you deserved more than a man who has shut himself away this past year. I thought you deserved someone whole, someone with purpose and with a perfect life to offer you.'

She shook her head, her body swaying closer to his.

'I started to walk back to Rose Cottage, but I couldn't leave you behind. I knew I'd made the worst mistake of my life. Can you forgive me?'

'You want to be with me?' she asked as if she couldn't quite believe what he was saying.

'I want to be with you. I want to be with you for the rest of our lives.'

'Do you mean…?'

'Marry me, Cecilia. I love you and I can't live without you. I know it's too soon, I know we've barely spent any time together, but I love you.'

She threw herself into his arms, oblivious to their audience on the other side of the drawing-room doors. Joe found himself smiling as her body pressed against his—it was as if they were made for one another.

Cecilia tilted her chin up and almost imperceptibly nodded her head. He kissed her, brushing his lips against hers as she melted into his arms.

'Is that a yes?' he murmured after a minute.

'It's a yes.'

Chapter Eleven

Cecilia closed her eyes and lifted her feet so they were closer to the fire. In front of her Joe was working hard to build up the logs, warming up the little cottage after their few days at Hawthorn House. They'd spent a couple of hours being congratulated by the Crawleys and all their close friends and family, but after the hundredth person had expressed their surprise at the engagement Joe had whispered in her ear, asking her if she wanted to sneak away.

It had probably been foolhardy making the trip through the snow in the dark, but they'd done it all the same and, now they were back at the little cottage, Cecilia couldn't regret it. She was alone with the man who would soon be her husband. The man she'd come to love in just a few short days.

He turned to her, the fire now blazing behind him, and pulled her to her feet.

'Have you seen the time?' he asked, motioning to the small clock on the mantelpiece. It was after midnight.

'Christmas Day,' Cecilia said.

'Happy Birthday, my love,' Joe murmured, kissing her until she forgot what he'd said. 'You are now a free woman.'

For a moment Cecilia closed her eyes. For so long she'd been waiting for this moment. Waiting to be free of her guardian, a woman of independence. Never had she imagined that she would see in her twenty-first birthday engaged. She'd been so intent of having her freedom, of living life on her own terms, that she hadn't stopped to consider what would happen when she met a man she cared for more than her plans.

'And I am engaged to the wealthiest woman in England,' he said, earning him a playful slap on the arm.

'Smart move, Major Crawley,' she said.

'I think so. And here we are all alone with no one to protect your reputation. You'll have to marry me now.'

'We are alone,' Cecilia said slowly. 'And we are engaged…'

'I'm scandalised,' Joe said, unable to keep the smile from his lips. 'But I like what you're suggesting.

Slowly he kissed her and Cecilia shivered with anticipation as his hands traced a path over her shoulders. There was a fire building deep inside her and as he pulled her body close to his it sparked and flared. He was her man and tonight she would forget the rules and enjoy every moment.

In front of the flickering flames Joe undressed her, unbuttoning the fastenings of her dress and pushing it down over her hips until it pooled about her ankles. Cecilia felt herself grow hot under his gaze as his eyes raked over her and suddenly his lips were on her skin.

'I've wanted to do this for so long,' he said, his breath tickling her neck. Cecilia closed her eyes as he pulled off her chemise and petticoats. She stood naked in front of him, her body warmed by the fire and the touch of his hands across her skin.

Consumed by a desire so strong it frightened her, Cecilia pulled Joe towards her, fumbling with his belt and the fastening of his trousers as he slipped his shirt over his head. Only when he was naked did she stop for a moment, glancing down to take in all of the man she loved.

With a growl Joe picked her up and deposited her on the rug in front of the fire, his body pressing against hers and making Cecilia let out a little moan of excitement.

Unable to wait any longer their bodies came together, Cecilia stiffening for only a moment as Joe entered her, then something primal took over and her hips began rising to meet his in perfect unison. Over and over they came together, until Cecilia felt as though something was about to burst inside her. Then with a moan of pleasure she felt her whole body tense and for a long few seconds felt as though she were floating. Above her Joe stiffened before collapsing on top of her.

After a few moments he rolled to the side, pulling her into his arms as he did so.

'Merry Christmas, my darling,' he whispered in her ear.

And as Cecilia lay there in his arms, her body warmed by the fire, she felt a wave of contentment wash over her. This wasn't how she'd imagined spending her twenty-first birthday, but it was so much better.

* * * * *

MILLS & BOON

Coming next month

CONTRACTED AS HIS COUNTESS
Louise Allen

He was dangerous, reports said, but they were hazy about who he was a danger to, other than the aforementioned blackmailers, presumably. The judgement was that he was ruthless, but honest. Stubborn, difficult and self-contained.

No one had reported on Jack Ransome's looks, on that straight nose, on that firm, rather pointed, jaw that gave him a slightly feline look. Certainly there had been no mention of a mouth that held the only hint of sensuous indulgence in that entire severe countenance. Other than those faint laughter lines...

So far, so...acceptable.

'You show no curiosity about why I have engaged your services, Lord... Mr Ransome.'

'No doubt you will inform me in your own good time. Whether you decide to employ me or not, I will present your man of business with my fee for today and for the time I will spend travelling to and from Newmarket and for my expenses incurred en route. If you wish to expend that money on chit-chat, that is your prerogative, Miss Aylmer.'

Very cool. Very professional, I suppose.

She stood, glad of the table edge to steady herself, and he rose, too, a good head taller than she, despite her height. 'Please. Sit.' The lid of the coffer creaked open until it was stopped by a retaining chain, standing as a screen between Mr Ransome and its contents. Madelyn lifted out the rolls and bundles of paper and parchment that it contained and placed them on the table in a pile at her left hand, except for one which she partly opened out. She kept her right hand on that as she sat again.

'What I require, Mr Ransome, is a husband.' She had rehearsed this and now her voice hardly shook at all. In some strange way this situation went beyond shocking and frightening into a nightmare and nightmares were not real. Father had left careful and exact instructions and she had always obeyed him, as she did now. Even so, she kept her gaze on the parchment that crackled under her palm.

'Then I fear you have approached the wrong man. I do not act as a marriage broker.' When she looked up Mr Ransome shifted on the carved wooden chair as though to stand again.

'You do not understand, of course. I have not made myself plain. I do not require you to find me a husband. I wish you to marry me. Yourself,' she added, just in case that was not clear enough.

Continue reading
CONTRACTED AS HIS COUNTESS
Louise Allen

Available next month
www.millsandboon.co.uk

COMING SOON!

We really hope you enjoyed reading this book. If you're looking for more romance, be sure to head to the shops when new books are available on

Thursday 28th November

To see which titles are coming soon, please visit

millsandboon.co.uk/nextmonth

MILLS & BOON
True Love
Romance from the Heart

Celebrate true love with tender stories of
heartfelt romance, from the rush of falling
in love to the joy a new baby can bring,
and a focus on the emotional
heart of a relationship.